THE DEPTHS

THE DEPTHS

VOL.1—KINGS VS DEMONS

M. BURKE

iUniverse®

THE DEPTHS
VOL.1—KINGS VS DEMONS

iUniverse books may be ordered through booksellers or by contacting:

iUniverse
1663 Liberty Drive
Bloomington, IN 47403
www.iuniverse.com
1-800-Authors (1-800-288-4677)

ISBN: 978-1-5320-3155-7 (sc)
ISBN: 978-1-5320-3154-0 (e)

Library of Congress Control Number: 2017913103

Print information available on the last page.

iUniverse rev. date: 08/23/2017

CHAPTER

1

MANY YEARS AGO, DOWN IN the deep, deep depths, in the bottom of Mid World's Ocean, the Tolkien Sea (thee Eighth Sea). Way down deep past the dark watery caves, where no man has ever traveled, there was a secret magical kingdom, with a very secret society of cave dwelling humanoids.. Way deep down, in the bottom of the dark abyss, lived two different species that ruled the very dark, mystical, and magical waters, the Mordainians and the OctaGods.. They were two highly intelligent, very sophisticated sea creatures. the Mordainians were led by a fierce and noble leader, King Keyiera. King Keyiera was a terrific King, who loved his people and his kingdom, very much.. The Mordainians are a cave dwelling humanoid on top, and the bottom half of a sea serpent. One day it was brought to the Kings attention, that the OctaGods were looking for the lost Trident of Tolkien. "If Cyris finds that Trident, he could crumble our entire kingdom with just one swipe"! (Said the King). He would end up with full control of the Tolkien Sea, and all its creatures. "Over my dead body! (Snarled the King).. Over my dead body"!! Cyris is the most feared Sea Wizard in the whole ocean. Cyris is the head of the OctaGods. The OctaGods are a very dark gray half cave dwelling humanoid on top, and the bottom half of an Octopi. Cyris has put together a secret army of creatures, including sea monkeys, stolen and captured sea dragons, to search all of the oceans for the Lost Trident of Tolkien. "Once I find the Trident, there's absolutely nothing that can stop me from ruling the entire sea". (Said Cyris). "I will bring that Sea God forsaken kingdom of Mordainia, to its demise"!

Back in the kingdom, the Kings son, Maximus, "Prince Maximus", was watching all of his fathers people swimming around laughing, and living what he thought were normal lives, wishing he wasn't born of royalty. "Why do I have to be all proper and boring"? (He asked). His friend Mateos.. "I just want to live a normal life and fall in love one day, and not have to make decisions for an entire kingdom". (Said the Prince). Mateos shook his head back and forth, in disagreement.. Mateos was assigned by the King to watch over Maximus and protect him, even though he was just slightly older than Maximus. "Now Max, you know if your father hears you speaking like this your going to be in big trouble, again".. (Mateos said). With a big smile upon his face.. Maximus and Mateos were the best of friends! Maximus doesn't remember a time in his life without him in it. Mateos was the fastest swimmer in all of the kingdom. He and the Prince would race around the kingdom when they were younger. Every now and then Mateos would let Maximus win, just so he would continue racing him throughout their childhood. Maximus knew it, but he never let on that he did.

One day when Mateoses parents were out on a routine perimeter sweep, they were ambushed and killed by a couple of Cyrises men, when Cyris sent them to the kingdom for an (all to familiar) assassination attempt on King Keyiras life. The two OctaGods responsible for the deaths of Mateoses parents, were captured and beheaded.. King Keyira felt responsible for Mateos, the King gave him a rank in his army, his assignment was to protect his friend the Prince. King Keyira grew to think of Mateos as another son. Not only was the Kings newest soldier the fastest member of the royal army, he was also as strong as they come. Mateos was proud and loyal to a fault.. He would without hesitation, lay down his life for Maximus and the rest of his people of the Kingdom and not think twice about it.

Mateos quickly rose through the ranks of his Kings, royal army throughout the years, but the greatest honor in Mateoses mind, was that the King trusted him with his son the Prince's life! For that, he will forever be grateful. Mateos pledged his loyalty to his King, and vowed to protect the Prince with his life, but as the two friends grew older, Mateos had fallen in love and had taken a wife. Now that Mateos was married, he had a new responsibility. Now that he was a husband and a father, he and Maximus were growing apart.. But that in no way diminished the mutual love and respect they had for one an other (not to mention for the King).. Mateos was a couple years older than Maximus, and was quickly becoming a man, and Maximus knew this, but just because he understood it, didn't mean that it wasn't hard to except. Maximus was very envious of Mateos, he wished he had found love like his friend had found. Mateos has a beautiful wife and little girl that he must look after and protect now as well. Sometimes Mateos would bring Maximus back home with him to hang out with him and his family. He was known as Uncle Maximus to Mateoses family. His daughter Kylynn adored Maximus, he and his wife Aliena thought it was the cutest thing. Every single night Mateos came home, Kylynn would race to her father shouting, "Daddy, daddy, is Maximus with you"?! Almost smashing right into her father as she charged towards him screaming, and if he wasn't with him, she was so disappointed, but if he was with him, she would light up, and with a smile across her entire face, she would swim to Maximus as fast as she could and would give him the biggest hug. She loved her uncle Maximus so much.. Mateos and his girls were such a beautiful little family and Maximus loved them dearly. Mateos was just a couple years older than Maximus, and he would always tell him.. "Patient my dear friend, love will find you in due time".. But Maximus thought he was doomed to be alone forever! "I'll never find love"! He'd reply.. But Mateos knew his friend, Prince Maximus was destine for greatness..

Meanwhile off in the darkest depths in the caves on the outskirts of the city of Mordainia, were where the OctaGods roam. Cyrises daughter Cynthia was out and about watching the Mordainians from a distance, way back from with-in the dark shadows. Dreaming that she was part of that world, and not stuck in the caves so dark and so lonely all the time! "Cynthia, Cynthia". (Cried Peretta). Cyrises slave who has been watching over Cynthia since she was a young-in. Cynthia was always breaking free from Peretta, driving her crazy! "Their you are! (Peretta said). I've been looking for you everywhere. Your father's looking for you, he wants to know why you're not doing your spells"? (She asked). "Why, what's the point"? We're never going to be like them, look, just look at them Peretta, their so happy. I wish I was born a Mordainian instead of an OctaGod!" (Cynthia replied). "Come on Cynthia it's time to go. (Peretta demanded).

Let's go"! As Cynthia turned around to leave, all of the sudden.. "Crash-Bang-Boom"! Maximus crashed right into Cynthia. He and Mateos were fooling around, racing like the old days. Cynthia and Maximus stayed staring into each others eyes. Peretta grabbed Cynthia, prying her away screaming; "Lets go now Cynthia"! (Peretta said). As she pulled Cynthia away from his gaze, Mateos started to draw his sword.. "Put that away, NOW"! (Maximus demanded). As Peretta pulled Cynthia back into the shadows, she kept looking back at Maximus who just floated there still, speechless with his eyes locked on Cynthia's, as she and Peretta disappeared into the caves. Mateos grabbed Maximus, and said.. "Lets go my friend".. Swimming off ahead of the Prince, as they raced back to the kingdom.

The following morning Cynthia awoke unlike she ever as before. She was smiling, singing, she was falling for the boy who just crashed into her the previous evening. Cynthia had a feeling that her life was bout to change forever! She just didn't know if it would change for the better or for the worse!?! Just then, Peretta came barging in.. "You are not to go back there, and see that boy Cynthia"! (She said). "You are to stay as far away from him as possible". (Peretta barked). "OK, OK"! (Cynthia replied). Soon after, Cynthia made her daily escape from Peretta and went right back to where she and Maximus had crashed into each others life. As she approached, she was shocked to find that Maximus was already there holding sea flowers, swaying back and forth speaking to himself. Cynthia slid behind a big rock, she decided to watch him for a moment. "Ummm, yah hi my name is Maximus. Gerrr"! (He grunted loudly).. And shook his head.. "Stupid, stupid". (He says). As he's smacking himself in the side of his head, right before taking a moment. (He exhaled). "Hi my name is Maximus, what's your's"? She heard him practicing to himself, trying to work up the courage to speak to her. Cynthia had started giggling.. Maximas whipped around, startled by what he see's. There she was.. "Hi, I'm Maximus". (He said). Swiftly, handing her the sea flowers he had in his hand.. "I know"! (She replied). Taking the flowers.. "I just heard you practicing a moment ago. Hi Max"! (She said bashfully).. "I'm Cynthia"!

The next few weeks, Cynthia and Maximus spent every awaking moment together. Maximus took Cynthia to all his favorite place's outside and around the kingdom, and sometime's late at night while everyone was asleep, he would sneak her into the kingdom, and sometime's even the Palace. She too would show him all of her secret place's and passage's throughout the caves. They explored so much together and of each other while dipping and dodging Peretta and Mateos. Cynthia and Maximus were falling in forbidden love. One day after Maximus was training with Mateos, he went to go meet Cynthia, but she wasn't there. He went around to all their favorite spots but she was nowhere to be found. Just as he was about to leave and go back to the kingdom, Peretta appeared. "Maximus, I'm sorry but Cynthia cant see you anymore"! Cynthia's father Cyris has found out about she and Maximus spending time together, and has forbidden her to ever see him ever again. "Maximus, I'm scared for Cynthia's safety! (Peretta said). Cyris has become obsessed with finding the lost Trident, and destroying your father's Empire"!

CHAPTER

2

A LONG TIME AGO THE Mordainians and the OctaGods lived amongst each other in harmony. Sharing their magical secret's with one an other. Until Keyira was chosen to be ruler of Mordainia instead of Cyris, and soon Cyris and the new King's feud had gotten so bad, that King Keyira had cast-out Cyris and all OctaGod's from the kingdom of Mordainia. "From this day forward, there will be no more black magic allowed to be conjured in the kingdom of Mordainia or from it's people. Let it be law.. In the name of the King"! (He proclaimed).

For year's Cyris has built a secret army of sea dragon's, vicious little sea monkey's and misguided Sea Warlock OctaGod's, with very powerful black magic power's, too one day find the Lost Trident of Tolkien, and rise up to defeat the King and his royal army. Cyris will not stop until he crumbles the kingdom, and either he or King Keyira are dead and gone!

"Why are you crying Cynthia"? (Asked her father Cyris).. "There's no room in our lives for love! Especially with the likes of one of them disgusting sea creatures. You will never be with a Mordainian, as long as I'm alive"! (He said). To his daughter with such anger.. "You will watch him die along with the rest of them"! Just then, one of Cyrises soldiers had burst in.. "I'm sorry for the intrusion, but we have located the Trident my lordship"! (He said to Master Cyris).. "Fantastic"!! (Cyris replied out loud).. "Where was it"? (He asked his General).. "It was in the bottom of the abyss, way out, deep in the Black Sea. It was incased in molted lava rock that hardened and formed the perfect hiding spot for the lost Trident for all this time"! (He answered).. "Yes, because our ancestors were to weak to find the Trident and take control of the Kingdom of Mordainia. I am not weak like they where"! (Cyris said). With such anger and disgust..

Maximus talked Peretta into taking him to where Cynthia was being held by her father. Maximus was hiding at this point, listening to everything Cyris was talking about to his General and he heard everything they discussed, he had heard it all.. "I have to go tell my father what I just heard at once Peretta! Please Peretta, tell Cynthia I'll be back for you two, and please.. (Dramatic pause).. please tell Cynthia, that I love her"!?! "I will Max, I will".. (She replied). Maximus fled through the caves like it was nothing. He whipped in and out of there without being seen or heard, thanks to Cynthia.. "Father, father, my King".. (Maximus shouted). As he entered the Palace out of breath, calling for his father, the King. "What is it my son"? (Answered the King).. "Th - th - the Lost Trident of Tolkien". (Maximus stuttered).. "He has found it father! Cyris as location of the Lost Trident and is sending his people to retrieve the Trident".. (He told him).. "But how"? (King Keyiera asked).. With such confusion and a hint of fear.. "Alert Kolten and prepare the war room, we have work to do"! (Demanded the King).. The Lost Trident of Tolkien has been hidden and buried for thousands of years. When Cyris was banished from the kingdom, he slowly started building an evil army of black magic, Sea Warlock OctaGods, sea dragons, sea serpents and vicious sea Monkey's, who have been misguided and used by Cyris for the powers that they posses! They have been misled and brainwashed by a Sadistic, Power crazed lunatic, who is motivated by revenge! Hundreds, maybe thousands of lives will end up being lost if they allow Cyris to get the Trident. He must be stopped by any means necessary and the King and his people knew it..

That night, the King held a meeting with the entire kingdom. Proudly by the King's side, stood Kolten, Maximus and Mateos. Kolten was not only the head of the King's Royal Army, he was also the King's adviser and Maximus and Mateoses Trainer, their Mentor. The King had to tell them what was about to happen, he need's them to be ready! "It has been brought to my attention that Cyris, the head Warlock of the OctaGod's has been searching for the lost trident of Tolkien". "Gasps"! From the people.. "Well it seems his army has figured out the location, and plans to unearth the Trident. If he is successful, he will gain full control of our beloved

Tolkien Sea and all it's creature's". (He said). To them all.. "So how do we stop him"? "Yeah, how do we"? Question's, after question's, came from the people.. The people of Mordainia where worried, they where on edge and the King needed them calm and focused if he was to save them and the kingdom. "Now settle down my friends, No worries, I have a plan". (Said the King). "My army is prepared for this and with all of your help we can stop this from happening and we will bring the fight to them. We will protect our people and our home, we will protect our way of life. We will survive"!! "YAAAAAAA"!! Cheers from the crowd. "Kolten (Whispered the King).. Form a search party, take all the troops you need and head off Cyrises men. I want you to cut the head off that slimy sea snake. Get him before he gets to that Trident, This is our sea"! (Demanded the King).. "Yes my Lord".. (Kolten Replied). As he turned and swam away to round up his soldiers. Kolten gathered Mateos and a couple dozen or so of his strongest soldier's and started off to the far end's of the Black Sea. Kolten and his men suited up, grabbed their sea horse's and one or two sea dragon's and road for two days until they reached Cyrises troop's.

Meanwhile back at the palace in the kingdom of Mordainia, King Keyira noticed there was something other than the Trident, bothering his son, Prince Maximus. "What's wrong my son"? (Asked the King).. (Maximus sighed). "Father, we need to talk". "What is it Maximus"? (He replied). "I'm in love, but I don't know if we can be together"! (Max cried). "Nonsense"! (Replied the King).. "Any woman in all of the kingdom would be lucky to be your wife and receive the love of a Prince my son. One day I will be gone my son, and you will be King. I know it might not seem like it right now but as long as you follow your heart, you will be a great leader my son! Go with your gut and I promise you will always make the right decision". As Maximus turned to leave, the King has one more thing to say to the Prince. "Remember Maximus.. You are the son of Keyira, the King of the greatest people in or out of the Eight Seas. You are a Posidian, you are Maximus Posidian, son of the great King Keyira Posidian, Ruler of the Mordainians and the Tolkien Sea and all its creature's"! Later on that night, Maximus thought long and hard about what his father had said to him. It was clear that the King would never give him his blessing with Cynthia. "I have to go get Cynthia away from her father and leave the kingdom for ever". He thought to himself.. So off he went as fast as he could, gathering up whatever he thought he and Cynthia would need to get away, so they can be together. Even if it meant disappointing his father, not to mention his best friend Mateos and their mentor Kolten too. Also he would be giving up his seat as rightful heir to the King's thrown.. But Maximus didn't want to be King like his father. Little did Maximus know just how wrong he would come to be!

Back in the shadowy caves where the OctaGods dwell, Cyris goes to speak to his daughter Cynthia. "Leave us at once Peretta"! (Damanded Cyris). "Yes my lordship".. (She Replied). Cynthia was sulking over her fathers very vocal disapproval of Maximus. "Cynthia my child.. (He began). He is not one of us! Don't be foolish Cynthia, he will never love you! We are savages to them.. I don't know what twisted game him and his father King Keyira are playing, but soon it wont matter anyways. Once I get the Trident dug up and take control of the Tolkien Sea and all its creatures! Well the ones that are left after we crush the kingdom of Mordainia and all its people. I will take my rightful place as ruler of the entire Ocean, and you will be by my side supporting your father when it happens". "Hahaha"! Evil laughs came bellowing out of Cyris, as his daughter Cynthia cried. "Stop your Crying at once Cynthia"! (He demanded).. "You are an OctaGod! You have your mothers black magic coursing through your veins. You are the daughter of the great and powerful Warlock of the Tolkien Sea, Cyris Octavious! You are the Great Black Magic Sea Witch Cynthia Octavious, and you will start acting like it! Do you understand me Cynthia"? (Cyris shouted). "Yes Father"! (She replied). "Good.. Now pull yourself together and meet me down at your mothers tomb. Today is the anniversary of her murder"! As Cyris exits, Peretta comes right back in, to be by Cynthia's side. She heard everything that was discussed. "Its ok Cynthia"! (She said). With the utmost sincerity.. "He'll forget all about this is a day or two Cynthia. You'll see, things will calm down". (She said). As she hugged her consolingly.. "But Peretta, (Cynthia began), I don't want to live without Maximus"! (She declared). "Crack - Bang - Boom".. A couple of small rocks slipped loose from under Maximuses hand from there he was hiding and waiting to show himself and the rocks fell to the cave floor. "What was that? Show yourself! (Cynthia Demanded). As she pulled her knife from her hair and got in front of Peretta. When all of the sudden.. "Maximus"! (Cynthia Screamed). As she swam into his arms kissing him. Maximus grabbed Cynthia in his rock hard arms and as he spun her around pulling her in closer, and as they were locked in a seductive embrace, he kissed Cynthia with such Passion, such power! As they were deep in their kiss, Peretta covered her face and looked away embarrassed. "OK you two.. (Peretta said). That's enough! Your father could be back any moment Cynthia". As their lips unlocked, Maximuses hand slowly slid down Cynthia's arm and his hand tightened around hers, and as their fingers intertwined, he looked her in her eyes and asked.. "Did you mean what you said Cynthia? I heard you say you love me, is this true"? (He asked). Very nervous of her response.. Cynthia's gaze slowly turned to Peretta and then back to Maximus, she took a deep breath and replied.. "Yes! Yes Maximus, I-I-I love you".. (Cynthia stuttered).. Maximus scooped her up in his arms and pulled her in tight, right into his warm embrace and spun her around hugging her close, but before he let go he uttered the words.. "I love you Cynthia my darling, I love you with all my heart and soul"! Once Maximus and Cynthia finally let each other go, (which seemed to have taken forever), Peretta turned and whispered.. "Ok, come on, you two need to go.. You have to stop her father Cyris Maximus! Please, take Cynthia and go, keep her safe! You need to stop him and save your kingdom and the entire Tolkein Sea, Max. If you don't, Cyris will destroy it all".. "I will Peretta, I promise"! (Maximus said confidently).. "Come Cynthia my love. We will stop your father and his men, then we will go off and find our own where we can be together. I don't want to spend waking up one more day without you by my side, my love"! (He told her).. "Oh Maximus".. Cynthia said as she threw her arms around him for one last hug before they left.

"Come on Peretta, your coming with us"! (Cynthia said). "No my deer, You need to go! I have to stay here and buy you guys as much time as I can! You two need to go and I'll keep your father distracted. (Peretta demanded). Now go on get out of here"! Cynthia hugged her goodbye. "Use everything I taught you Cynthia, and you'll be just fine my dear"! (Peretta told her).. "Take care of her Maximus, look after my Cynthia! (she pleaded). I'll make sure you get a head start".. "Thank you Peretta"! (Maximus said). As he hugged her goodbye. "We'll be back for you Peretta, I promise"! "Go on you two, you have to go"! (Peretta said). Chocking back the tears.. "I will never forget this Peretta, I will never forget what you have done for us"! (Maximus said). "I love you Peretta "! (Cynthia cried). As she and Maximus vanished out of the caves and into the shadows.

Peretta gathered her thoughts and shook off the emotions that where swirling around inside her. Peretta turned the other way and went to find Cyris but he was at his wife's tomb and she knew he would be very angry, and she was scared. "Where's my daughter Peretta"? (Cyris shouted). "She's asleep! (Peretta quickly replied).. She's very upset over you and hers fight earlier. She just needs a little time to rest up and she'll forget all about that boy and your argument, I promise you my lordship, in a day or two she wont even remember why she was mad. "Good! (Cyris shrieked). I'm going to need everyone alert and ready! We are going to war and I need full focus and concentration on the mission. This is a very important time for our people! It's time the OctaGods were at the very top of the food chain in this ratchet ocean of ours"! (Cyris said). With such anger and disgust.. "Now leave me, I'm trying to morn my wife on the anniversary of her death in piece! Go watch over Cynthia, make sure she stays put. Don't let her out of your sight Peretta"! (He demanded). "Yes my lord"! (She replied).. As Peretta turned to leave, she heard Cyris say to himself.. (Well actually, speaking to his dead wife).. "Soon my love! It's almost time, I will avenge your death my love. I have finally located the Lost Trident of Tolkien, and soon I will crush Mordainia with it, and I will kill King Keyira.. And right before I slit his throat, he will first watch his son die"!! "Hahaha"! Sinister laughs bellowed out from deep within Cyris.. When he finally stopped laughing he whispered.. "Goodbye my love, see you on the other side of this war. Soon we will be together AGAIN"! (He said). Then kissed his wife's tomb, and swam away..

Way across the Ocean from one abyss, to another abyss, in the bottom of the Black Sea, Cyrises men where busy digging trying to unearth the Trident of Tolkien.. But off in the distance, Kolten and his soldiers watched as Cyrises recon unit were removing rock, while others, used black magic and were blowing holes way deep down in the bottom of thee abyss. They had about fifteen OctaGods working removing the rock, while five of them used black magic with three sea dragons and ten of those vicious sea monkeys keeping guard. "Me and Mateos will take the Serpents and as many OctaGods as we can. The rest of you take the sea monkeys and whatever else you can, but concentrate on the Sea Monkeys first"! (Kolten

said). With authority.. "OK men, Ready!?! CHARGE"!!! (He screamed). As
he drew his sword and raised it above his head, and the royal army swam
as fast as they could, following Kolten into battle, without hesitation.

After all the sand and smoke settled and the fighting stopped, All that
were left standing was Kolten, Mateos and Three of there men. Mateos went
and rounded up the stolen sea dragon, as well as their own. While Kolten
went around to all his slain soldiers who lost their lives in this battle and
gathered their belongings for their family's. The rest of the living soldiers
piled the body's together so Kolten could use one of his magic spells that
will burn the bodies of all that died here today. It's a Mordainian tradition
of battle. Once they made sure all Cyrises equipment was destroyed, they
headed back for the Kingdom. That's when they ran into Maximus and
Cynthia fleeing from out of the caves. "Quiet"! (Kolten said). As he swam up
behind Cynthia and grabbed her, he put his sword to her throat, and said..
"Don't you move you OctaScum"! (He cursed). "No wait stop"! (Maximus
shouted). Kolten assumed she was following behind Max to hurt him, but
before he could finish his sentence, Cynthia took the knife from which she
keeps in her hair and stabbed Kolten right in his hand forcing him to let go
before he could slit her throat. As soon as his grip released, Cynthia swam
straight into Maximuses arms! "What the?? (Kolten was confused).. Seize
her"! (He commanded his men).. "STOP! (Maximus demanded).. She's not
one of them, she's with me Kolten! This is Cynthia and she will be my wife".
Mateos just stared silently at the two of them while Kolten holstered his
sword. He was shaking his head saying; "He's not going to like this! He's not
going to be happy about this one Max. She's an OctaGod, Maximus. She's
the damn daughter of Cyris, the most feared Warlock in all the Sea! Not to
mention a sworn enemy of your father, the King"! "I know! (Maximus had
replied).. "But I don't care, we're in love"! "Please Kolten?! Help Me talk to
the King, help me try and get him to understand. (Mateos pleaded with
him).. We don't want to lose Maximus forever! Max, your coming back with
Cynthia and we are talking to your father, we will make him understand!
(Mateos had demanded of his friend).. Please Kolt, he'll listen to you!
Well, maybe".. "OK then, lets go find out"! (Kolten said). With a chuckle..
"Hahaha"! Everyone laughed.. So they started off back to the kingdom of
Mordainia to talk to the King. Hoping that the win on the battlefield will
ease the blow, of his son and his secret love..

CHAPTER

3

BACK IN THE CAVES OF Tolkien, Cyris was looking everywhere for his daughter Cynthia. Cyris was getting a feeling that something was wrong. "Bring me Peretta!! (He demanded). Bring her to me at once"! His voice booming throughout the dark watery caves. "Yes my lordship"! (Said his guards).. Peretta knew this wasn't going to end well for her, as she was led off to see Cyris. "You wanted to see my, my lord"? (She asked nervously). "Leave us! (Cyris demanded his men). Where's my daughter Peretta? (He screamed). Do not lie to me either, or I'll kill you"! Cynthia shuttered with fear.. "But if you tell me the truth I'll spear your miserable life"! (He said). "Sh - Sh - She's gone"! (Cynthia stuttered). "GONE?! (Cyris furiously repeated).. What do you mean gone? You were suppose to be watching her Peretta! Where did she go"? Peretta's lower lip stopped quivering and stiffened up. She took a deep breath and said.. "She's GONE! She's far away from here, and she's far away from you! And that's all that matters". (Peretta said). With such pride.. "That's fine Peretta if you don't want to tell me. I'm sure I already know! (He said). Pulling her in close, hugging her. I already know! Goodbye Peretta"! (He said). Stroking her face one last time before snapping her neck!

Back in the Kingdom of Mordainia, Kolten and Mateos along with the others, Including Maximus and Cynthia, had just arrived. Cynthia went with Mateoses wife Aleina. "Stay with Aleina, She will make you comfortable until I send word for you my sweet Cynthia"! (Maximus said). As he kissed her cheek and swam off with the rest of the men to speak with the King. The King was waiting on Kolten and Mateos with word on the Trident of Tolkien. "Good, you have returned.. What say you Kolten? (Asked the King).. What is the situation with the Trident and how many men did we lose"? "We lost all but three soldiers my lordship"! (Kolten said). With such sorrow.. The King hung his head in light of the news.. "And, what of the Trident"? (The King asked).. But now, in a much more angrier tone.. "Well that's the good news my King! (Kolten replied). We were able to defeat Cyrises men and stop them from getting the Trident"! "That's excellent news Kolt"! (Said the King). "Yes, but".. (Kolten added).. "With all due respect, we all know that its not over sir! Cyris will not stop until he retrieves the Trident. He'll just keep sending team after team of his followers until its recovered!! We are going to have to discuss retrieving the Trident ourselves and keeping it safe now that he knows where it is your highness"!?! (Kolten argued). "Yes I know! (Said King Maximus).. But first, we are going to have to lop the head off that slimy Sea Serpent Cyris.. We are bringing the war to him! Ready the troops and get my Armor and my sea dragon"!! (Demanded the King).. "Yes my Lord! (Kolten quickly replied).. But umm.. Actually, first we need to discuss your son Maximus and I ashore you, this can not wait sir"! (He said to the King).. "I'm Listening"! (The King replied).. Completely confused.. Just then Mateos and Maximus entered, with his head held high. "Maximus, what is it my son"? (He asked). His father the King.. "Hi father. (Replied the Prince).. We need to speak"! "I'm listening Max, please tell me what it is you need to tell me"! (Said the King). Maximus took a deep breath and looked over at Mateos and Kolten and as they gave them their approval he began to tell his father everything! "Cyris is going to try and take over Mordainia and kill us all if you don't listen to everything I have to tell say! Father, you always told me to follow my heart. If I always trust my gut, my instincts will never ever stare me wrong. Well I'm in love with Cynthia"! "Cynthia"? (shouted King Keyira).. "Yes father, I am head over fins, in love with Cynthia"! (Replied the Prince).. "Cyrises daughter, Cynthia"? (He asked confused).. "Yes, but she's not with her father anymore. She can help us defeat him and his forces. She has someone on the inside who knows his plans and that will help us take down Cyris once and for all. (Maximus said). Father, when you banned Cyris, you banned all OctaGods and that was a huge mistake! All they had to turn to was Cyris!! He tricked them, he fed them all false hope. They believe if they don't follow Cyris that they will have no-one to protect them. Their scared father! We need to show them that there's another way besides destruction and devastation, that Cyris is planning to unleash. Father, if we show the people both Mordainians and OctaGods alike, that we can work together and live as one. What better way to do that, than to show them the unity of the Prince of Mordainia and Cynthia, an OctaGod!?! Then maybe, just maybe we can save them and our kingdom father! You can either except me and Cynthia and we can fight Cyris. Together we can stop him father, I just know it.. Or you can go on with your life without me. Cynthia and I will try and stop her father by ourselves and go live our life.. But just so you know.. I love u father, and I've never been more ready than I am right now at this moment in time to except my rightful place beside you at the thrown and help you my King, lead us to victory and freedom! Then down the road when its time, I will be proud to follow your legacy and rule Mordainia as King"! (Said the Prince). King Keyira looked over at Kolten then Mateos, both gave the king a nod, (Yes)! "It's the only way"! (Added Kolten). The King turned back to the Prince and said.. "Well my son, I guess I'm going to have to give this a chance! I'm not happy about it, but I will listen and see what she has to say! I'm only doing this because I believe in you my son. I know in my heart, that you will be a great leader. You will be a fantastic King just like your father Max"! (Said the King). Hugging his son the Prince. "Thank you father! (Replied the Prince).. You wont regret this"! "I already do".. (Whispered the King).. Jokingly.. Maximus exited quickly to go get Cynthia and tell her the good news. He also needs to brake it to her that she's going to have to go speak to his father sooner rather than later! "Cynthia, Cynthia.. Maximus called out. Where's Cynthia Aleina? (He asked Mateoses wife).. I need to speak with her". "She's not where I left her'? (Asked Aleina). "No"! (He replied). Maximus swam threw the kingdom checking all the shadows. All the crevices and little dark dens, but nothing, Cynthia was nowhere to be found! Maximus swam back to his father and the others. "Kolten, Mateos, She's gone, Cynthia is gone! Something's wrong"!! "What do you mean she's gone Maximus"?! (Mateos franticly asked).. "I've looked everywhere, She's gone"! Just then two of Koltens Men, Soldiers from the Royal Army came in and tossed one of Cyrises Sea Monkey Soldiers down in front of King and the others. "We found this one fleeing from the Kingdom towards the caves"! (Said one of the soldiers).. "Thank you, that will be all". (Said the King). Before the two soldiers left, they turned to Kolten for his command. Kolten nodded, and the two soldiers swam off. Maximus grabbed the prisoner by his throat with such blazing speed and strength, that he almost killed the Sea Monkey before he could tell them that Cyris had sent them for Cynthia and the other three made off with her. "Where is she"? (Maximus demanded). "She's back in the caves with her father Cyris and he's going to destroy you all.. Your all going to die"!! (Said the sea monkey).. And right before he was about to start his disgusting sinister laugh that only the sea monkey's can do. Kolten chopped his head off with one swipe of the sword! The creatures body went limp and fell as his head bounced and rolled to a stop with a surprised look still upon it's face. "Guards! (Screamed the King).. Clean this mess up and prepare for battle"! "Yes my lord"! (Replied the royal guards).. "Go my son, take Mateos and whoever you need and go get Cynthia Back"! (Said the King). Maximus nodded and he and Mateos swam off.

Back in the caves hidden away from everyone and everything, Cynthia was crying. "Why are you crying Cynthia? You need to stop this childish nonsense at once"! (Demanded her father Cyris).. "Why are you doing this father"? (Cynthia cried). "You want to know why Cynthia? Fine then, I'll tell you why.. Because Cynthia, when you where just a little girl, your new boyfriend's father murdered your mother, my wife"! (Cyris said). With disgust.. Cynthia's head slowly rose-up from her hand in mid sob. "Your lying "! (She shouted). "I wish I was my dear, I wish I was"! (He replied). "Then tell me Father, tell me what happened"!?! (She pleaded). "A long time ago, Maximuses father Keyira tried banning black magic from being used not only in the kingdom, but in the entire Tolkien Sea.. But your mother".. He paused, then laughed and shook his head, and said.. "She wasn't going to be told she couldn't practice her spells by anyone not even the King! She continued doing her black magic, your mother always said it was our birth right. One day your mother was working on a new spell, it just so happened it was the same day King Keyira and his wife Muriel were out feeding the wild sea horses, Muriel loved the sea horses and sea dragons. They ended up stumbling into the sea dragon your mother had under her new spell, when all of the sudden the sea dragon went crazy, the spell went horribly wrong! Your mother was trying to create a spell that would control the sea dragons every move with just a thought"! "So what happened"? (Cynthia asked impatiently).. "Well, everything was going according to plan until King Keyira and his wife Muriel got too close to the dragon that was under your mother Elisabeth's spell when it went haywire. Just as Keyira's wife Muriel reached up to feed the dragon, Keyira had noticed me and Elisabeth off in the distance. He left his wife's side and was swimming towards us to see what me and your mother where doing, and that's when we heard it. Keyira spun back around and raced to his wife. The scream was gut wrenching! Muriel screamed for just a split second, but it seemed like forever. Muriel was to mesmerized by the serpent, that she didn't notice when Keyira had swam off. That's when all our lives changed forever! Elisabeth lost control of her spell and the sea dragon went crazy and ripped into Muriel with his huge sharp teeth and just tore her to shreds, but instead of understanding and excepting your mothers apology, He ignored her cries and pleas for forgiveness and drew his sword from its holster and rammed it right straight into your mother Elisabeth's heart. Then when I screamed NO, he turned his sword on me. That's where these scars are from. He showed Cynthia the scars then continued.. He left us both for dead Cynthia!! He picked up his wife Muriel's body and swam off, but I survived.. And I will avenge your mothers death, if its the last thing I do! You need to choose Cynthia! Are you with your family or are you with the enemy?! Because if your not with me, then your against me"! (Cyris said). As he turned to leave.. "Where's Peretta"? (Cynthia asked). "She dead"! (He replied). Very unsympathetically.. "You killed her?! (She cried). You're not my father, your a sea monster, I hate you"!!

CHAPTER

4

MEANWHILE, MAXIMUS AND MATEOS WERE on their way to go get Cynthia from her father Cyris, when Maximus heard her cries.. "Cynthia, Cynthia! (He called out).. This way Mateos I hear her, Cynthia's through here! Oh my lord, thank the Sea Gods, you're OK, Cynthia my love"! (Maximus said). Swimming to her, scooping her up in his arms scanning her head to toe checking her for any injury's. "No, I'm not OK Max"! (Cynthia shouted). Pulling herself out of his grasp. "Did you know your father killed my mother Max"?! (Cynthia asked). "No, no I didn't! (Maximus said). I had no idea! Is this true Mateos, do you know anything about this? Did my father kill Cynthia's mother"? (Maximus Demanded the Truth).. "Yes, yes he did! but all I know is from what Kolten told me, I honestly haven't even thought about it until now! That's all in the past though. (Mateos pleaded). I know it hurts, but both your fathers lost their wives because of one another.. But only one of them lives with sorrow and regret every day, while the other lives with anger and hate fueled revenge!! I swear to you Cynthia, if Maxes father could do it all over again differently, he would! I promise you but right now we have to go! We have to get out of here, there's a mad man we need to stop and two species to save, along with a kingdom and probably the entire Tolkien Sea. I need to know right now if your coming with us or not because we need to go now"! Maximus looked at Cynthia and said.. "I'm sorry about your mother Cynthia but I'm not leaving here without you, I love you"! "Oh Max, I love you two"! (Cynthia said). Kissing Max, Cynthia then took his hand and said.. "Now lets get the hell out of here"! (She said). With a huge smile.. Cynthia took one last look back at the caves she grew up in, as she left for good! "Goodbye, goodbye forever"! She thought to herself.. Maximus turned to Cynthia and said.. "We'll send for Peretta after this is over and she can stay with us in the kingdom"! Cynthia grinned and with such sadness and sorrow in her voice, she said.. "Peretta's dead Max, he killed her"! Maximuses heart instantly broke! He had the utmost respect for Peretta and he knew how much she meant to Cynthia. As he began to tell her how sorry he was for her loss, Cynthia squeezed his hand and smiled at Maximus, letting him know she was going to be OK!

Once the three made it back to the kingdom, they would focus on stopping Cyrises Army of misguided, very powerful, black magic creatures. Cynthia pleaded with Maximus to keep what they had learned to themselves. She didn't want him to speak a word of it to his father. She figured everyone had suffered enough and she was still going to have to watch her Father Cyris die in order to save to species and her beloved Tolkien Sea. Not to mention the man she love's! If they were to survive and live peacefully in the kingdom, then they were going to have to forgive Maximuses father the King.

Now that they were back in the palace, Maximus introduced Cynthia to his father King Keyira. "Ready the troops, we move out at once"! Is what they heard the King commanding, as they entered the war room. "Father, I have someone I'd like for you to meet"! (Maximus said). With so much pride.. "Father, this is Cynthia, my love.. and Cynthia, this is my father, King Keyira"!! "Hi sir, it's nice to finally meet you"! (Cynthia said). Earnestly, and with a shy bow of respect to the King. King Keyira took her hand and said.. "No my dear, the pleasures all mine"! (He replied). "I just have one question"! (Said the King). Max rolled his eyes but Cynthia said.. "No, its ok, go ahead my King, ask me"! "Are you sure when the time comes, you will be able to go against your father in-order to save our beloved Tolkien Sea and countless lives?! (The King asked her genuinely).. I assure you, it will be the hardest thing you will ever have to do in your life my sweet child"! (He said). Cynthia stiffened up and with complete disgust in her voice, she replied.. "My father died a long time ago".. But even though she wanted too, what she didn't add was.. (He died the day you killed my mother).. But she kept that all to herself, for now.. "I understand"! (Said the King). King Keyira turned to his sun the prince and nodded. "I like this one Maximus! (He said). She's a keeper! I'll send in the men"!! Said the King before leaving them to go over any last details with Kolten and Mateos before the strike! "Oh Max"! Cynthia said throwing her arms around the prince, her firm breasts pressed against his rock hard chest, sent shivers down her spine. He gazed in her eyes, locked in his even harder arms. Cynthia's bottom lip quivered as Maximuses lips gently grazed hers, he ran his fingers threw her hair then their lips locked. Maximus kissed Cynthia with such passion, such intensity that they both completely forgot about everyone and everything going on around them. Just for that moment, that split second, it was just him and her, no one else! For the first time in her life since her mother passed, she felt completely safe!

Maximus was discussing their strategy with Kolten and Mateos. He and Cynthia told them everything they knew. Emotions were running high during the planning. There were moments when you couldn't hear anything over everyone yelling at the same time! It was turning into complete chaos until.. "May I speak?! (Cynthia asked). I have something I'd like to say"! (She said). "Quiet! (Kolten demanded). Show some respect and let the lady speak! Go ahead Cynthia".. (He said). "I just want to start by saying thank you! Thank you for excepting me into your kingdom. I promise I will do everything in my power to stop my father Cyris! I know you didn't have to trust me but you took a chance and are trying to help me stop him. I know it wont be easy, but I know what he's planning and we can do this! We can stop him before its to late"!! Cynthia turned to Kolten and Mateos, and said.. "I will be the one who kills my father! Cyris is my responsibility".. She had made that perfectly clear.. "I! Mount up".. (Kolten commanded). As he turned to his troop.. "Inform the King we ready to move out"! As the King and the royal army were riding off on their sea horses, Maximus and Cynthia were on the sea dragon Zar, while Kolten and Mateos were on sea dragons of their own. They were loaded with swords and pouches of magic spells and potions. They were all ready for this Magically Epic War between Good and Evil. Cynthia and Maximus engaged in one last kiss before they headed of to battle.. "Please be careful my love". (Maximus whispered to Cynthia).. The King at the head of the pack, as they were getting ready to go defend and protect, their way of life! "I'm proud of you my son"! (Said the King). Beaming with pride.. "I'm proud to call you my son Maximus. It's my honor to ride into battle beside you, it's an honor to ride into battle with all of you"! (Said the King). Maximus and Mateos locked arms.. "I'll see you on the other side of this my brother"! (Mateos said). Those were the last words spoken before they all fled for battle into the shadows in the deep dark depths of the abyss, in the very bottom of Mid World's Ocean, deep down in the Tolkien Sea (thee Eighth Sea).

By the time the King and his royal army arrived to the location of the lost Trident, Cyris and his men were already there! Cyrises army was huge! He had hundreds of soldiers digging and running machines. He had equipment that was used to dig up and remove the excess rocks and debris. They were blasting holes in to the bottom of the abyss. Cynthia and Maximus broke away from the rest of the king's army with Zar. They stayed hidden out of sight at first, but before they left for battle, Maximus and Cynthia formed an elaborate plan with Mateos and Kolten. They believed that this was the only way they would be able to defeat her father Cyris! Cyrises army is strong and very disciplined. She knew in-order to kill her father, she was going to have to get close to him.. They had one shot at this, and she knew it. They couldn't afford to blow this! Meanwhile The King led the attack on Cyrises army. King Keyira along with Kolten and Mateos were ready to blitz attack with the royal army. "You ready men"?! (Asked the King). "I, we are ready"! Kolten replied).. "CHARGE"!! (Screamed King Keyira).. With his sword drawn high above his head and then brought down forward. All the royal soldiers blew past the king screaming, swimming into battle. "Charge, get them, kill them, long live the king"!! Were just some of the shouts that came from the soldiers swimming into battle! "Protect Cyris"! (The general demanded).. Of his army, as the first wave of soldiers attacked. "Keep digging men! (He commanded). The rest of you, ATTACK"!!

There was such death and destruction on this day, such slaughter, such carnage! Which later came to be known as.. "The Battle of Lost Souls"! There was Mordainians fighting OctaGods and Sea Monkeys, sea dragons fighting sea dragons. There was a whole lot of black magic being used by both sides. It all combined for an Epic battle.. King Keyira hated having to kill the sea dragons that Cyris had taken control of. His beloved wife Muriel loved these majestic beasts.. But the King, he knew if they didn't kill them first, then they could quite easily kill his entire army! Cyris had them under his spell and they are programmed for destruction. As King Keyira was pulling his sword out of one of Cyrises serpents, a OctaGod swam up behind the King as his mind drifted to how his wife adored these beasts, and right before he could put his sword in the Kings back, Kolten came and cut the OctaGod right in half, ripping through his enemies head, and straight down through his body like it was nothing until he split in two and fell! The King looked back at Kolten and nodded.. "Thank you Kolt"! (Said the King). "I"! (He replied). Mateos was busy attacking Cyrises men that were still digging for the Trident, until Cyris came roaring through the soldiers battling on a mind controlled sea dragon of his own and as he approached Mateos, his sea dragon ripped into Mateoses dragon killing it instantly and knocking Mateos to the ground. Cyris then leaped from his serpent and with sword in hand, was just about to thrust his sword into Mateos when his blade met the blade of Koltens mighty sword right in front of Mateoses face. Kolten saw Mateos knocked from his dragon and rushed to his aid. Kolten got his sword up and blocked Cyrises advance on Mateos. Cyrises sword crashing into the blade of Koltens sword made such a loud and powerful impact that it through both Cyris and Kolten backwards away from each other. Kolten went flying, crashing right into a huge boulder, knocking him unconscious. Cyris was tossed backwards into the shadows. Kolten was starting to come to when Mateos rushed to his side to help. Kolten raised his arm for Mateos to help him up when all of the sudden, Mateos was grabbed from behind and thrown like a rag doll. It was Cyris! Once he tossed Mateos aside, he then raised his sword straight out and lunged forward, thrusting his sword deep into Kolten's chest, piercing his heart killing him, instantly! Cyris then grabbed a hold of an unoccupied sea dragon and road him back to the battle field. As the serpent passed over the soldiers in battle, Cyris jumped from the majestic beast and came floating down to the battle field, swinging his sword decapitating any Mordainian in arms length, even killing a couple OctaGods in the process. Cyris didn't care about any of the OctaGods fighting for him, all he cares about is revenge!!

Meanwhile, Mateos picked up Koltens dead, limp body and carried him to the King. King Keyira was in the midst of a sword fight of his own. He was in battle with a couple OctaGods when he looked over and seen

Mateos approaching, carrying Kolten's body. Mateos laid Kolts body down and shut his eyes for him. Mateos leaned down and whispered; "Goodbye my friend, I will never forget you"! (Mateos said). Swimming off back to battle. The King screamed.. "Nooooo"! Thrusting his sword forwards and backwards, side to side, (with a single tear, coming down the side of the King's face), he was ferociously cutting into his enemies. King Keyira went absolutely ballistic when he seen Kolten's dead body. The King must have killed twenty to thirty of Cyrises men, in less than a minute. King Keyira known Kolten his entire life! By the time the King snapped out of his fit of rage black out, most of Cyrises army was defeated, and his equipment destroyed. King Keyira started calling out for Cyris! "Cyris, show yourself at once! Where are yo Cyris? Come and fight Me yourself you coward"! (Demanded the King).. As he continued carving up the rest of Cyrises men that were still left fighting. "Show yourself Cyris, Now"! (He shouted). So enraged.. "Be careful what you wish for"! (Cyris said). As he approached on the last living sea dragon that was under his black magic spell. Cyris jumped from the beast and came down in front of his arch enemy, King Keyeira. Mateos shot off like a spear, chasing down Cyrises sea serpent. When he caught up with dragon, he shot up from underneath the belly of the beast and rammed his sword right threw the middle of the creature, killing it instantly. Continuing his own little fit of rage and kept attacking any remaining OctaGod, sending them retreating. The King then told Mateos to take his men and head back to the kingdom and make sure its protected, I'll handle this one! Meaning he will handle Cyris.. "I, my lord"! (He replied). Mateos and his men raced back to the kingdom under the Kings order, there were sea monkeys and a few OctaGods terrorizing the kingdoms people. "There's another one of those damn possessed sea dragons! (Mateos said). Thank the Gods that's the last one, I'm sick of these God forsaken things! OK.. (Mateos said). You two come with me, the rest of you go around the back way. We're going through the front"! (He commanded). With such anger and authority.. "Ready, 1 - 2 - 3 CHARGE!! (Mateos began screaming).. Ahhhhhhh"! Mateos and his soldiers screamed as they raced through the kingdom freeing all the hostages Cyrises men had captured. Mateos then kills the very last mind controlled sea dragon as it came crashing through the kingdom towards all the noise. Mateos lifted his sword as the beast approached, and thrusted it, right through the front of the serpents mouth, cutting through it's firing canal, and burst all the way through, right out the back of it's skull. "Arrrrrrrrrrg"! (Mateos screamed). As he continued right on ripping through any OctaGods and or sea creatures in Cyrises army, that infiltrated the kingdom. "This is fun"! (Mateos admitted). In midst of destroying his enemies.

Back in the waters of battle, the King and Cyris were face to face, just a few yards away from each other, they both stayed floating there gripping their swords, steering at each other for the first time since the day their wives died.. "You cant stop me from retrieving the Trident Keyira"! (Cyris said). "Seems to me, we already have! (Replied the King).. Looks like we already have stopped you! Just surrender now and maybe, just maybe, we spare you, your miserable life Cyris"! "HAHAHAHAHA! (Cyris laughed). NEVER"! (He screamed). Raising his sword high above his head and with all his might, he brought it down and charged forward swinging it at Keyira. The King raised his sword in defense and blocked Cyrises sword with his own! King Keyira and Cyris were locked in the ultimate battle between good and evil, right vs wrong, peace or total destruction! As the king blocked his advance with his sword, the King came around with a left hook and punched Cyris right in his face. Knocking Cyris to the ground, making him drop his sword.. King Keyira was hovering over Cyris within a flash! Just as the King raised his sword and was about to kill Cyris once and for all, he paused. He shouted.. "Long live the kingdom of Mordainia".. And just as he went to finish him off, Cyris reached back and was able to thrush both hands forward and throwing three magical fire balls directly into King Keyiras chest and stomach lifting the King and sending him flying backwards, smashing against the rocks. The Kings limp body, slid to the abyss floor. Cyris went to regain his balance, as he started forward towards the Kings body to make sure he's dead, Cynthia came out from the shadows. She had Maximus in front of her with his hands bound, and a sword to his throat, as she made her way towards her father Cyris. "We did it father.. (She cried). You killed the King! Look father, I brought you a piece offering. You were right all ah long. He was just trying to get information out of me"! It was so hard for her and Maximus keep it together with his poor father lying over there unconscious.. "He never loved me! Please father, except my apology and take the kings son and do with him what you will"! (Cynthia said). She handed over her sword to her father

Cyris, that was pointed at Maximus. As Cyris took the sword from his daughter Cynthia he said.. "Yes my child, I forgive you! We will unearth the Trident and avenge your mothers death, and Together we will rule the Tolkien Sea".. (Cyris said). With much pride.. Cyris put the sword to his side and leaned forward to embrace his daughter with a hug, as Cynthia hugged her father crying she whispered.. "I'm sorry father"! Cyris puzzled for that split moment Cyris had his guard down, Maximus came out his restraints and when Cyris turned to look back, Cynthia took her knife out her hair, (the one that Peretta had made for her years ago), and stuck it right in her father Cyrises neck. As Cynthia stabbed Cyris in his throat severing his artery, cutting through his jugular vein. Maximus, (with a knife of his own, that Cynthia had made for him, on one of their first days together), he had thrust forward, and rammed the knife right into his spine, completely incapacitating Cyris, and as his body went limp and slid down, bleeding out from his neck wound, Maximus took back the sword out of Cyrises hand, and as Cynthia covered her eyes, Maxims screamed "Ahhhhhhhh".. And he chopped Cyrises head off! Maximus and Cynthia swam to his father the King. "Father, father"! (He cried). Scooping up the King in his arms, holding his fathers head up. "Please father don't die, talk to me my King, please"!?! (He was begging).. "I'm sorry father, I'm sorry I wasn't in time to save you, I am so sorry we were too late! As Maximas lay on the ground still holding his father crying, all of the sudden King Keyira's voice spoke softly.. "Its ok my son"! He struggled to say.. "Cough - cough"! He paused for a moment and then said.. "It's not you or Cynthia's fault at all, you two saved the kingdom and thee entire Tolkien Sea. Please don't cry my son!? I am so proud of you Max! Take care of my kingdom"!?! (He pleaded).. "Cough - cough".. He did not sound good, at all.. "You and Cynthia will make such a terrific King and Queen, just look how your guys plan worked! Good bye Cynthia, look after Maximus. Good bye Maximus my boy, I love you!! Believe in each other and you will be just fine"! (Said King Keyira).. As Maximus was pleading with the king to stay with them and not die, King Keyira reached up and took his crown off his head and placed it on his sons head and said.. "This belongs to you now Maximus, its an honor to call you my son".. With the Kings dying breath, he uttered the words.. "I love you my son, King Maximus.. Long live the kingdom and it's new King". (He said). Then he died, right in his son's arms..

CHAPTER

5

THE WAR WAS OVER AND the Trident had been retrieved, and brought back to the kingdom. The next few weeks that passed, were filled with such heart brake and sorrow! Mateos and Cynthia's loved one's needed to be put to rest, buried or magically burned. Cyrises remains were to be burned with a magical spell that allowed him to be burned to ash, but his remains were gone! No one could find Cyrises body when it was time to cremate the remains, It was the strangest thing.. After that was all taken care of and the kingdom was fixed up, the new King Maximus had promoted Mateos to Kolten's position as head of the royal army. He felt it be best that his first mission be to take the Trident and hide it in the farthest, deepest, darkest crevice in the ocean where only he knew where it would be! Sworn to secrecy, until eternity.. Mateos excepted the mission with honor! Mateos knew he could never replace the great Kolten as head of the royal army, but he sure as hell was going to try to make him proud, that's for damn sure! He thought to himself with a smile..

After they were all settled in the palace, the new King and his soon to be bride hosted a victory feast for all of the kingdom. They sent word to all OctaGods in the caves, and pitch black dens throughout the Tolkien Sea, to come brake bread with Mordainians at the palace and then stay too live back in the kingdom, as long as there's peace amongst both the people! Maximus and Cynthia wish to unite their two species and they hope that their unity will do just that! As both species the Mordainians and the OctaGods ate and sang songs, with Maximus and Cynthia at the head of the table, Mateos entered with word of his secret mission. "Mission was a success my lord, the Trident is in a secure location"! (He announced proudly).. "Excellent! (Replied Maximus).. Come my friend join us, eat and celebrate, You deserve it"! Mateos joined them at the head of the table, along with his family.

Its been a little while now since the war and Maximus and Cynthia had succeeded in bringing peace and happiness to the people of the kingdom, both Mordainians and OctaGods alike. Once Maximus and Cynthia are married, it will show the unity between the two races. Each species will have one of their own in the royal palace watching over them and will have say in the laws. Which in a way, brought a calming ease over everyone. It was a symbol of peace and hope to both the people. This marriage was such a great way to put the past behind everyone and move forward into a brand new era with a bright future for both species.. Everything was coming together nicely, the royal wedding was almost among us. The OctaGods seemed to be adjusting perfectly to life in the kingdom, most even joined the royal army that Mateos is now head of. He had taken over for Kolten, which the King knew he was the right man for the job when he appointed him to the position. Its what their old mentor Kolt would have wanted, and they both knew it.. Know that Mateos was Commander of the Royal Army, he would do everything in his power to bring safety to his King and their people! He would protect them all, Mordainians and OctaGods alike as if they were his own family!! He will give his soul for the kingdom.

Cynthia was living with Maximus in the palace. They were sleeping in separate quarters until they wed. Cynthia couldn't help but think back to how she use to dream of this life one day and how it never seemed possible, but now that her dream has become a reality, it just don't feel right without Peretta! She even began to miss her father Cyris a little bit. Even Maximus was having a hard time handling the change. He too is riddled with sadness from losing both his parents now too, plus his mentor/friend. Maximous and Cynthia both, were once so filled with life and optimism for the future! But now they both had that little spark in their souls, ripped out their chests and killed along with their loved ones..

The Royal wedding day was finally here! This wedding was about to make history with uniting these two species once and for all for the rest of eternity!! After King Maximus the Mordainian, married Cynthia the

OctaGod and she was now able to have her coronation, and become Queen Cynthia. There was this eerie, uneasy feeling, Cynthia got in the pit of her stomach. "What's wrong my love? (King Maximus asked).. What's seems to be troubling you my love"? "Something's wrong Max, I can feel it in my gut"! (Cynthia replied). Cynthia was use to chaos and despair, so Maximus just chocked it up to his new bride is just having a hard time adjusting to her new life! Everything just changed dramatically and she just needs a little more time to get comfortable He thought to himself.. "She'll be just fine"!

Maximus seemed to be adjusting to being King just fine! The people loved him, he kept his word about opening up the gates to the kingdom for all the OctaGods. He and Cynthia, his new wife, had expanded the sea horses and the sea dragons stables, and built a training facility that they both not only were teaching in, they were also studying at the training and learning center in the middle of the kingdom is where they taught magic courses and survival classes. Both Mordainians and OctaGods both taught and or learned at the new center, together. Cynthia herself passed the time by teaching a hunting and survival class. She taught all the young-ins, of both species, to hunt from the shadows without being seen or heard. She taught them to be invisible lethal hunters.. It was giving Cynthia a sense of purpose again. It was actually starting to make Cynthia happy again. It was also giving King Maximus a little piece of mind also. The center kept his wife busy and happy, while he and Mateos were busy training the soldiers of the royal army to protect the kingdom and all its people. The royal army has almost doubled in size since the war. The Mordainians and OctaGods were training, fighting and conjuring up magic together now, instead of against each other.. "You are doing a tremendous job with the soldiers Mateos! (Said his friend Kind Maximus).. Kolten would be proud"! "I! (Mateos replied). So when are you going to make me an uncle, brother Max"? (Mateos asked jokingly).. Punching his friend playfully, in the arm, with a big smile on his face. "You will refer to me as My King or My Lordship"! (Replied Maximus). Punching his friend back in his arm! "Hahaha".. They both laughed.. "It's good to finally laugh again Mateos my friend, but I honestly do not know Mateos! Things are a little awkward right now with how our fathers had just died and now that she's head of her people because she married me. As much as I want a son, I don't think it's the time to bring it up! (he said sadly).. Cynthia's been having a hard time adjusting to life with out Peretta, she's been her only companion throughout her entire life Mateaos! Besides, she's committed her time to the center, teaching her course. So not yet I just can't add any more stress on her right now, I don't want to push her away by rushing things with springing any baby talk on her right now, she doesn't need any of that added pressure. I'm afraid I'd lose her if I did that! (Maximus admitted). I don't know Mateos, I guess I just need to wait for the right time"! "Hahahaha"! (Mateos laughed). "Oh Maximus, my dear, poor, naïve friend Maximus.. There's never going to be, the right time Max! (He told his friend).. I don't know if there will ever be that quote, unquote, (right time), but what I do know is that Cynthia loves you Max, and you love her! You will make a wonderful parents my brother, I can guarantee it.. Besides, you guys will always have me and my wife and daughter to help you"! (He said). Mateos was very happy for his friend Maximus that he found his true love. He knew Maximus was going to be a terrific King and he knew if he had a child, that it would bring back that spark that his friend Maximus once had! Cynthia as well, lost some of that fire inside and a child would fix that for both of them and bring them closer together than ever! The love of a child is priceless, Mateos knew that Maximus and Cynthia deserved that more than anyone, they both deserved that happiness! Just like their hope and love gave them that spark, a child would do the same and more..

Back in the Palace later that evening, Maximus and Cynthia were discussing how much their lives had changed and how lucky they are. Cynthia has been feeling a lot better now. Cynthia not only been teaching the children in her course at the center, she's also been looking after the sea horses and the sea dragons at the stables they had rebuilt. Cynthia loves to feed them, and has been working with them, gaining their trust! This has been making Cynthia very happy, feeling needed.. "It's all thanks to you my love"! (Cynthia said). Throwing her arms around her husband Maximus. "I love you Max"! (She whispered). "I love you too my sweet Cynthia"! (He replied). Kissing the back of his wife's neck. Cynthia closed her eyes and bit her bottom lip moaning softly. Cynthia my love, I been watching you with the children at the center and with the animals at the stables.. Maximus felt like it was never going to be a better time then now to bring it up, thinking about what his friend Mateos had said. Maximus took a deep breath and decided to take a leap of faith and said.. "I love you Cynthia, I love you more than life itself.. You're my wife, my soon to be queen! I would love for us to add to our family, I want you to have my child Cynthia!?! Mateos so nervous, speaking so fast that he was dizzy.. Cynthia looked up at her husband and couldn't help but smile. She was remembering why it was she wanted to marry Maximus in the first place, she knew how much he adored her! "Oh Maximus, I love you so much my dear"! (She said). With such joy.. "Yes Max, yes I'll have your baby my love"! (She said). Placing both her hands upon his face. "I love you Max, I love you with all my soul. I would love to bring a child in the world with you, nothing would make me happier"! (She told him).. "You made me so happy Cynthia! (He whispered). Kissing her.. "I love you more than I could possibly describe"!

The following morning Cynthia was happier than usual, she was singing and dancing and twirling around all over the place, thinking of how blessed she is, and how she's going to try and forget all about the bad stuff that has happened in the past and just start enjoying her new life! Cynthia was over in the stables feeding the sea horses and sea dragons. She was talking to Zar, the oldest sea dragon of the royal kingdom. Zar loved Cynthia just like he loved King Keyira's wife, Muriel. As Cynthia patted Zar, she went into deep thought and he swam away to his trough. As he was busy eating and Cynthia was thinking about how foolish she has been acting, not enjoying her beautiful new life and was mad that she was feeling sorry for herself, and that's when all of the sudden.. Cynthia was grabbed from behind. Cynthia was snatched by this creature had bound and gagged her so fast that he was there and gone with her in a flash.. It all happened so fast, that Zar never even looked up from his feeding. This creature was huge, he was wearing a dark hooded robe like cloak. He was no Mordainian nor an OctaGod, he was to big! He had removed her blindfold when they where alone in the caves outside the kingdom. Cynthia had that eerie feeling in her gut again. She knew this feeling, she had felt it before.. She had thought to herself.. Cynthia was terrified, but she decided to not show him any fear! The creature was breathing very heavily, but in a very low, deep, spine chilling voice, he creature leaned forward and said.. "I'm the one who has taken your father Cyrises body, I have it! (He taunted her).. He's not dead, he will be stronger than ever and he's coming to finish the job, he will be back to kill your husband and destroy your new kingdom along with all Mordainians, along with all OctaGods who have betrayed him and pledged their loyalty to Keyira! (He promised)!! "Excepting a Mordainian as King, They will all DIE"!! But the beast wasn't there to kill Cynthia, he was there to deliver her a message. "You need to leave the kingdom at once! (Said the creature). Its not safe here, we will bring the gates of hell to your kingdoms doorstep, soon"! (He said). "Who are you and why are you telling me this"? (She asked him).. "I am Kavizious, and your father has something he needs you to see"! (He replied). "My father?! (She asked surprised).. But, he - he's dead, I watched him die"! Kavizious pulled out a knife and as he horrified Cynthia with it by dragging it across her lips and down her neck he spoke.. "I told your father I'd just kill you now, but he wants to speak with you. So maybe, just maybe, if you leave the kingdom and go see what it is he wants you to see, then maybe, he might spare your life! Tomorrow night, leave the kingdom and ride for one full nights length and we'll find you"! (He said). Right as he was just about to cut Cynthia's hands free from her restraints he added.. "Tell Mateos I want the location for the Trident or I'll kill his family in front of him"! Then swam off disappearing into the shadows without a trace, like he was never there.. Cynthia made her way back to the kingdom and collapsed crying hysterically. "help me Maximus"! She cried out for her husband.. Some of the kingdoms people were out in the garden enjoying their day when they heard her cries. As they swam to her aid, one of them told the others to get help; "Alert the King! (he said). Are you ok my lady lordship"?! (The kind stranger asked her).. Helping Cynthia try and catch her balance and calm down some. "Yes, thank you kind sir! (she replied). I am now"!

Back at the palace, Maximus was furious! He sent a platoon of soldiers, his finest warriors to hunt down his wife's attacker. Cynthia knew they would never find him, the only way they would see the creature is right before it took their lives! "Your not going to find him Max"! (She said). "Who was this creature Cynthia, what in the Gods names did he want from you"! (The King asked frantically).. "I do not know Max, all I know is he said his name was Kavisious! (She replied).. And what else I do know is this.. We are all in danger! We are not safe Maximus! (She cried). He will be back, and he's bringing Hell with him he promised, and I believe him"!

Cynthia's fear then turned to rage.. "I don't know how, and I don't know when, but somehow my fathers behind this"! (She said). With disgust.. "Cyris sent that beast, he had said Max. He also said.. He's the one who took his body"! "Why would he do that"? (Maximus wondered). "I don't know my love, but its going to be bad, I can feel it! I don't deserve this life Maximus!! I've been waiting for everything to blow up in my face, and as soon as I started feeling happy again and put my guard down, look what happens! Maybe if I leave the kingdom, the beast Kavizious will leave our people alone so they can live in peace! Maybe if".. "Stop that, just stop that talk right now Cynthia! (Maximus demanded). Your not going anywhere! You deserve everything you have accomplished Cynthia my love. You absolutely deserve it, you deserve it more than anyone I have ever met"! Max assured his wife, as he consoled her. H was embracing Cynthia, hugging her, making her feel like everything would be just fine, like only her husband King Maximus could. "You're my wife Cynthia, I married you for a reason. You were put in my life for a reason, the thrown chose you Cynthia! This was your destiny my love! once you married me, you became Queen of Mordainia and I honestly couldn't think of anyone more deserving than you. Besides, your forgetting one thing my Queen".. "Oh, (She replied). What may that be my King"?! "The royal army has doubled in size now, No-one can harm us"! Cynthia couldn't help but feel safe again.

Meanwhile Mateos was notified of his friend Queen Cynthia's attack. Mateos was extremely angry that he wasn't there to protect her. He put the whole kingdom on lockdown and had his men searching high and low for this creature, They searched the entire Tolkien Sea, but he was nowhere to be found. The soldiers were on high alert, awaiting for Mateoses next Command. The royal army was ready for war at a moments notice! King Maximus begged his friend Mateos to bring his family to the palace where they would be completely safe. The King was worried about his friends daughter and wife, he didn't take Kaviziouses threat to wife Cynthia about Mateos lightly. Mateos agreed it would be best for his family to stay at the guarded palace until this creature is captured and they locate Cyrises missing remains. They need to be certain he is truly deceased.

Elsewhere, deep, deep down, at the bottom of the black abyss, in the dark, dark, volcanic waters, across the triangle of no return, is where

Kavizious had brought Cyrises body, and is awaiting for his full recovery. Soon, Cyris will come to realize that he and his black magic have become very powerful, Too powerful.. Cyris is stronger now than he ever was! Before Cyrises wife Elisabeth died some years back, she and Cyris had created a spell that on the day the last one of the two dies, they would both meet in the after world and both cross back from the after life back to the waters of the living. When Cyris was killed that day in battle, he awoke in another dimension, he was in Hell.. But so wasn't his beloved wife Elisabeth who was there awaiting for him to die and awake in this realm, the hell realm.. When they cross back over to the realm of Mid World's Ocean, the Tolkien Sea, and once they are brought back, she will have the most powerful black magic in all of the Eight Seas. She will be so powerful that she could bring an entire army of sea hell demon soldiers with her through the realms gate! So now Elisabeth and Cyris will finally be able to get their revenge on their enemies. Cyris, now with his wife by his side once again, will not stop until they destroy the kingdom of Mordainia.

The day Cyris took his last breath out on the battle field and died, he arose in this sea hell realm. In this dimension, there was fire as far as he could see. There were these very large, very mean looking creatures. One of the creatures came to Cyris and led him to his wife Elisabeth (who had died a few years back, and has been waiting ever since).. "Elisabeth"! (Cyris shouted). Racing to her.. She was even more beautiful than he remembered. He thought to himself.. "Where are we Elisabeth"? (Cyris asked). "Why this is non-other than Sea Hell my dear husband"! (Elisabeth replied). With such darkness in voice.. "And we will bringing Hell with us back to Mordainia and unleashing it upon the entire Tolkien Sea, and anyone else who stands in our way".. Cynthia through her arms around her husband Cyris. "It's good to see you my dear husband.. When you awake, you will have an ally. His name is Kavizious and he is a worrier, like no other! He is a hell demon, times ten!! He will protect you and obey your every command my love! He will watch over you back in the Tolkien Sea, until your body and mind are nursed back to health. He will also retrieve my remains that have been magically preserved until I could conclude my spell, and reconnect my mind back in and be back in our realm of the Tolkien Sea. Heal up and realize your strength and power and how enhanced it is! I will be back with you soon my love. Our spell worked Cyris! We will be able to get our revenge and unleash hell upon the kingdom of Mordainia as well as the entire Tolkien Sea, this will be a war like no other that Mid World, above or below the Salt Water, has ever seen! Before Elisabeth died, she concocted a very powerful black magic spell that would only work if she died and went to Hell, which she did. Within precisely two weeks time, a portal in the triangle of death would open and she could send through one hell demon of her choice to help set up the rest of the spell back in the realm of the living, back in Mid World's Ocean, the Tolkien Sea (thee Eighth Sea). She of course sent back Kavizious who would need too get her and Cyrises remains to the triangle of death and placed in specific places so at the time of Cyrises death, the both could be brought through the portal and back into their bodies, but with unbelievable powers! Kavizious did all this just to be back at war doing what he does best, and that is Death and Destruction.. Kavizious has carried out his mission perfectly.. He is now about to show Cyris just how strong he has become! Kavizious could make it through the realm fine because he has already died, and crossed through before, Kaviziouses first time was as painful as possible. This was Cyrises and Elisabeth's first time crossing through, it was going to be rough, but it's only the first time that hurts!

Cyris awoke in the deep dark depths of the abyss, feeling like he was engulfed in flames. "Ahhhhhhh"!! (Cyris had screamed).. But nothing had came out, Cyris couldn't move, he felt like he was burning alive from the insides out. He had no sight, no hearing, no speech, he couldn't even move. It seemed like forever now that Cyris has been stuck in this state of living sea hell. "Take it easy my lord"! (Kavizious said). Cyris has been having the same nightmares every single day and night since he has crossed back over. The cold sweats, shivering, moaning in pain. "Wait, I just herd him speak"! Cyris thought to himself.. For the first time Cyris has heard Kaviziouses voice and had his own thoughts that he could process and understand. Cyris uttered the words.. "Who are you? Are you the one she called Kavizious?? Where is my wife Elisabeth, is she here?! "Yes! (The creature replied).. It is I, your loyal servant Kavizious. Come Cyris my lord, you need your rest".. "Please Kavizious (Cyris pleaded). Where is my wife"? "Recoup my lord, and I promise when your feeling better, you will wake up and see your wife Elisabeth, I promise! (Kavizious said). Trust me, for now you need your rest".. But right before Cyris slipped back into a state of unconsciousness, right back into his nightmares that ended up becoming way to often since his return from the dead, Kavizious told Cyris about his encounter with his daughter Cynthia. "I went and seen Cynthia! (Kavizious said). I told her I took your remains, and that your alive, and that you would like to speak with her. I didn't tell her about Miss Elisabeth though, I told her, that you had something you'd like to show her. I told her she needs to leave the kingdom before it's too late and she cant! She'll come looking to see if it's true, she wont be able to help herself"!

CHAPTER

6

BACK IN THE KINGDOM OF Mordainia, Maximus and Mateos were training side by side with the royal army, as they discussed what had happened to Maximuses wife Cynthia and the creature Kavizious who had attacked her. "If Cyris really is alive, then we have got a big problem! We are going to have to defend the kingdom, and our people against his advances. He's going to want payback against his people who have joined us in the kingdom! We must devise a plan to stop him from any army he brings forth to destroy us"! (Maximus said to Mateos).. "Yeah, not to mention his arch nemesis' kid, had married his daughter and turned her against him.. Then they killed him, together"! (Mateos added sarcastically).. "Yes, I know my dear friend Mateos, thanks for the update"! (Said the King). With a smile.. "No but in all seriousness, I cant fail the people Mateos, I just cant"! (He said getting serious again). "We will not be defeated my lord! (Mateos replied). We will kill Cyris, (Again), if we have too, We will protect our kingdom and it's people, always, no matter what it is! With the help of me, of course"! (Mateos added). He was joking again, (of course), trying to lighten the mood..

Over in the stables of the sea horses and sea dragons, Cynthia was feeding them and visiting Zar. Cynthia kept looking over her shoulder, but it wasn't in fear. She was looking over her shoulder, hoping Kavizious would return. Cynthia head was running a million miles a minute, she had so many unanswered questions. She couldn't help but wonder if her father really was alive or dead, and if he was dead, then where is his body and what did this creature want with it. She couldn't help but wonder.. Was this all a set up!?! Cynthia had no idea, but she decided that she needed to find out!

Cynthia decided she was going to go ahead and leave the kingdom and go find out what the creature Kavizious is up to. She decided she was going to wait until the middle of the night and ride out the kingdom and find the creature! She was going to go find out if her father Cyris really was alive and if he was, she was going to go kill him, Again!! Before anyone else gets hurt.. (She thought). "I miss you so much Peretta! Please Peretta, help me, I don't know what to do.. Please show me the right path and help me over come this"!?! She prayed to her fallen friend..

Later that night while Maximus was asleep, Cynthia snuck out of the palace and out to the stables. She grabbed Zar, her favorite sea dragon and she took off out of the kingdom! "I have to keep the people of the kingdom safe! "I have to kill my father once and for all".. She thought.. As she raced through the watery caves and out into the deep dark depths of the abyss, in Mid World's Ocean, the Tolkien Sea (thee Eighth Sea). To find Kavizious, and kill her father Cyris if she needs too.

Back in bottom of thee abyss, in the volcanic ruins of the Triangle of Death, Cyris was just awakening from one of those all to familiar nightmares of his, when he realized just how good he felt! His hearing was back, along with his voice and his mobility. He was feeling way better than a hundred percent, he was feeling a hundred, thousand percent!! "Oh this is going to be fun"! (He said). Raising his hands, and firing magical fireballs from them. Cyrises black magic powers were exceptionally enhanced. He was going to be able to inflict some serious pain and misery with his new found powers. Just then Kavizious returned, but this time he wasn't alone.. "Elisabeth, my love"! (Cyris said). With a big smile, rushing straight into her arms. "Kavizious, go find us the Lost Trident, while me and Cyris work on our spells and get prepared for war"! (Elisabeth demanded).. "Yes my Lords"! (Kavizious replied). As he exited the cave. "Now come my love! (Elisabeth said). We have a demon army to summon.. We will rule both realms my dear, we will bring hell upon them my darling husband. (She assured Cyris).. With me by your side, you will take your rightful place at the thrown with full control of the Tolkien Sea and all it's creatures, alive and also in death.. You have the most powerful black magic sorcerer by your side, there's nothing that can stop us! We will crush our enemies, and you will be crowned King!

Back at the kingdom, Maximus had sounded the alarm. "What's the problem Max"? (Mateos asked his frantic friend).. "It's Cynthia, she, she's gone! (The King replied).. I cant find her anywhere Mateos! The sea dragon Zar is also missing from out the stable"! "Maybe she's just out for a ride with Zar Max"! "No, she would have told me she was doing that! (He said). There's something wrong Mateos, I can feel it"! (The new King said).. With fear.. "That creature that attacked her the other day told her that her father Cyris is alive and sent him for her! I'm afraid that she took Zar and went to go see if he really is alive, and try and kill him herself Mateos".. (Max just said).. "But Max, there's no-way that Cyris is alive, you killed him, remember"!? (Mateos said). To his friend the king.. "Yes, but you yourself said his body was gone! (Replied Maximus). She had to of went to go make sure, I'm sure of it, that's what I would do! Either that, or that creature Kavizious took her again, either way, I have to go find her"! (Demanded the King).. "I! (Mateos replied). I'm coming with you then"! "I don't know why, but this got Cyris written all over it Mateos, I can feel it".. (Maximus said). "Well then, looks like we are just going to have to go and kill him all over again then, now aren't we!? (Mateos said). Just this time, we make sure it gets done right! We will find the body and burn the remains right away, along with that beast, Kavizious too.. Let's go find your wife my friend, kill anyone and anything that get's in our way".. "Ready the Troops! (Demanded King Maximus).. Set a perimeter around the kingdom and lock it down! Make sure they protect the kingdom by all cost! I Want the warriors and sea dragons to be ready to move out, at once".. "I"! (Mateos replied). As he hugged his friend the King, to show him support in this difficult time. "Thank you Mateos, I couldn't do any of this without you my dear friend".. (Maximus admitted).

Mateos has the royal army troops well trained! They are strong, disciplined, loyal and they are many.. This was the biggest, the royal army has ever been. Now that the OctaGods are part of the kingdom again. There are Mordainians and OctaGods ready to stand together and fight for one another, there is sea dragons, there is witches and warlocks with very powerful magic that have trained within the army and developed their magical powers and turned it into weapon of war for the royal army, they've invented some unbelievable strategies, some very strategic offense, and defensive plans, to enable any of their enemies on site! Each member of the royal army is powerful in their own right.

CHAPTER

7

BACK IN THE ABYSS, AT the Triangle of Death, Elisabeth and Cyrises black magic has become so powerful that she could see the King and his royal army saddling up and getting ready to move out, through her magical Crystal Ball. Elisabeth was just about to go tell Cyris what she had just seen, when all of the sudden the King and his army disappeared from the Crystal Ball and She appeared, it was Cynthia.. She was on a sea dragon riding through the dark caves by herself, she was looking for something! Elisabeth's mind was going a million miles a minute. This was the first time she had even thought about her daughter Cynthia since she died a few years ago! Elisabeth's old life came flooding back into her thoughts, with an over powering force.. Elisabeth's memories stirred her black magic up inside! Her magic flowed fast and furious through her body. She was gripping the crystal ball so tight in-between her two hands, that when the magic cane rumbling out of her finger tips and "BOOM"!! The crystal ball had exploded with such force that it made a huge magical explosion, so loud, so colorful.. It shook the entire Sea floor.. Elisabeth, in such a fit of rage, let out such a scream in anger, it was frightening, it was absolutely bone chilling!

Back in the watery caves of the Tolkien, Cynthia has been searching for the creature Kavizious and her father. Cynthia had stopped to rest, just for a moment and feed Zar her faithful sea dragon, when she herd that bone chilling voice again! Cynthia got a shiver and goose bumps from her head, down to her finger tips.. "Good, you're here"! (She said). Turning around to face him. "You came"!! (Kavizious said). As he emerged from out the shadows.. Cynthia quivered at the sight of the creature.. "Who are you"?! (Cynthia demanded). What do you want with me, Beast?! If your going to kill me, just do it now and get it over with"?! "Hahaha! Kill, you?! No my dear, if I wanted you dead Cynthia, you'd be dead"! (Kavizious admitted). "Well, then who are you and what do you want"? (Cynthia demanded).. "Who am I, who am I?? I'm the reckoning my sweet child, and I have come to this world to unleash hell upon the Kingdom of Mordainia, and the Tolkien Sea.. I am the ultimate Evil Cynthia, and I am a loyal warrior of my Master, Cyris"! Cynthia's head whipped up as she thought about what he had just said.. "I'm surprised you came Cynthia, and by yourself too I see"! (He added). "Yah well, I came to slit your big ugly throat"! (She replied sarcastically).. As she lunged forward swimming right at the beast, pulling Peretta's knife out from her hair, but this time, the knife was glowing with powerful black magic raging through Cynthia's blood stream, and radiating out to the knife.. Cynthia put a spell on the blade that would release a deadly toxin once it cuts into any flesh. Anything that the blade cuts, instantly starts decaying the flesh at a very high rapid speed until there's nothing left! As she lunged forward, the creature Kavizious moved aside and pushed Cynthia head first into the cave wall. Cynthia screamed in pain. Cynthia was dazed as Kavizious reached down and grabbed her by her hair and picked her up, and said.. "If it was up to me I'd just kill you now"! (Kavizious said). Pulling his sword out from it's holster with the butt of the sword he smashed Cynthia in the forehead with it, knocking her out instantly! "But its not my call".. (Kavizious said).. Dragging her limp body off into the shadows while Zar, the sea dragon was on the ground, dragging his head back and forth on the sandy gravel, itching his eyes and groaning this weird little cry. Kavizious put a spell on him that left him incapacitated while he took Cynthia..

Back in the Depths of the Triangle, Cyris just herd from his wife Elisabeth about what she just seen in her Crystal Ball. She was just about to ask Cyris about her daughter Cynthia when all of the sudden, Kavizious came in dragging Cynthia's unconscious body. "She didn't come willingly my lords.. (Kavizious had stated).. She tried stabbing me with this".. He showed him Peretta's old knife, that she had gave to Cynthia. Cyris had recognized the knife, right away! "She pulled it from out of her hair".

(Kavizious said). "Was it glowing"? (Cyris asked him).. "Yes, yes it was"! (Kavizious replied). "It's hexed, she placed a spell upon the knife"! (Cyris said). Elisabeth was Intrigued by her daughter Cynthia. She was examining her as she lay there peacefully. She put her face right up close to Cynthia's and took a deep breath, the scent of her daughters hair and breath, brought back many more memories.. Elisabeth quickly snapped out of her little trans and swam off as fast as she could. "What's wrong, where are you going my queen"? (Cyris asked). As she fled there was a cloud of black magic following her, blowing holes into the cave walls, leaving a trail of exploding rock in her wake. As Elisabeth slowed down, so did the disaster she had created behind her. Cyris rushed to his wife's side and said.. "What's wrong my dear Elisabeth"? "I thought you would be happy my wife?! We are all together once again, our daughter's back Elisa, I thought this is what you wanted"? (He said). Still no response.. "I eliminated our enemy Keyira, and now all we need is the Trident and we will take the Kingdom, together! This was everything we ever dreamed of my evil Queen".. (Cyris pleaded). "I know my dear husband! (She finally replied).. I just keep getting these flash backs of our old life Cyris. We were a happy family once"! (She cried). "Yes! (Cyris replied). We were very happy.. But that life is over now, because of Keyira. Now his son Maximus steals our daughter Cynthia and brainwashed her. He will pay for what he has done, I promise you he will pay with his life and his kingdom"! (Cyris said). With such anger and hate..

CHAPTER

8

Meanwhile, out in the middle of the Tolkien Sea, Maximus and his men have been searching for his wife Cynthia for almost two full days now, with no trace. Maximus was starting to panic at this point now. "We are never going to find her, are we Mateos"?! (The King asked his friend).. "Don't say that Max! (Mateos replied). We will find her my friend, I just know it! She's a very strong woman Max, if anyone can survive, it's her"! (He promised him).. "We just got married Mateos, we were going to finally have a baby! (Cried the King).. I'm afraid she's already dead though"! "Nonsense! (Mateos demanded). Cynthia is as strong as they come Max, I bet she already killed the beast and is burning Cyrises remains right now before heading back to the kingdom! I Guarantee you she's alive and well, she's fine Max"! Mateos declared to his friend trying to ease his pain a little bit. "I'll take first watch, get some sleep my King"! (Mateos said). After they had set up camp to rest for a spell. "I"! (Replied the King).. Closing his eyes. "We move out at first light"! Maximus heard Mateos say, right before he fell asleep.. Kavizious lie in wait for Maximus to fall asleep before swooping in and taking Mateos. Nothing will stop them from getting their evil hands on the lost Trident! The only person alive in the entire ocean, knows where the Trident is, and that's Mateos! As soon as the king fell asleep and Mateos settled into his post, Kavizous made his move and struck his stocked pray in their camp, like a bolt of lightning darting through the dark salt water. All you seen was a quick flash of a dimly lit sphere, sharply blaze through there, and then just like that, Mateos was gone! Before anyone know what had just hit them, Kavizious was long gone with Mateos bound, gagged and tied up in a sack heading to the Triangle of death with him so Cyris and Elisabeth can extract the information on the Lost Trident of Tolkien..

When they arrived, Kavizious tossed Mateos in the corner, in one of the caves in the belly of the Triangle and swam off.. The sack opened enough for Cynthia to see who it was. "Mateos"! (She shrieked). As she rushed over to him pulling the sack off him and undoing his restraints. "Cynthia"! (He said). With much surprise.. "Thank the Gods your alive, Maximus has been going crazy looking for you my queen"! (He said). while looking around trying to catch his bearings and figure out where they are and how to get out! "Where are we Cynthia, do you know"? (Mateos asked her).. "NO! I don't, I have no idea where we are. He took me too".. (She told him).. Has anyone came and talked to you or anything"? (He asked). No, not since he took me"! (She replied). "Who took you, that same creature from before, is he the one that just brought me here too"? (He asked her).. "Yes! (She answered). His name is Kavizious! I road off out the kingdom with Zar and I road him until I couldn't ride no more! I don't even know where I was when I finally stopped to rest a moment and feed Zar, and that's when".. Cynthia stopped in mid sentence.. (Very long pause).. "That's when what Cynthia, what happened, did he hurt you"? (Mateos impatiently asked her).. Cynthia's face had such a terrified look on her, and with her voice trembling she said.. "He, he came from out of nowhere Mateos, he is the scariest thing I have ever seen! He put a spell on Zar that incapacitated him and then he was right in front of me and when I lunged forward and tried to kill him by slicing his throat wide open, he knocked me out and next thing I remember I came to in this cave, and now here you are. Although I can here Zar, I don't see him. He must have put him in a separate cave. (She told him)..

Mateos began to tell Cynthia what had happened.. "Me and your husband King Maximus, along with more than half the royal army have been searching two days and two nights looking for you and trying to find this beast, and kill him, but when we finally stopped, to set up camp and post our lookouts.. That is when he struck the camp and took just me! (He told her). Looks like he found us first, what's his name again you said.. Ka, Kaviza, what"? (He asked). "Yes, it's Kavizious"! (She replied). "Yah, that big Worm.. He took you because you're the only one who knows where the Trident is"! (She told him).. "But how, how in the Sea Gods name would he know that I'm the only one who knows where it is"?! (He asked). With such a panic in his voice.. "I don't know Mateos, but he has very powerful black magic and he said he's not from this world. He told me he was a sea hell demon, from a sea hell realm and he brought my father Cyris back from sea hell with him. That's why his remains were missing when we went to burn them in the cremation ceremony! (She told him).. He's going to torture you until you give him the location Mateos"! "NEVER!! (He screamed). He'll have to kill me first, because I'll never tell him! I took an oath that I take very seriously, and I will give my life for. I'd take my own life before I gave up the location"! "I know Mateos, (She replied), but you may have to do just that then! Unless you get the Trident first and use it against him! That might be our only chose. (She began to explain).. He has very strong, very powerful black magic and he says he has an army of hell demons with him! He will use the magic on you to try an extract the Tridents location, and then kill you! Along with everyone and everything! We have to stop them! (She pleaded). What are we going to do Mateos"? Cynthia couldn't help but wonder if her father was still alive!

Just then, Kavizious entered the cave, and fright behind him was Cyris! Cynthia didn't notice him at first. "Hello my child".. Cyris spoke to his daughter Cynthia.. "Gasp"! Cynthia froze in fear! "It's been a little while since we seen each other, hasn't it been my deer?! (He asked, rhetorically).. Cynthia was absolutely speechless, she couldn't believe it was really her father Cyris. She was so confused! Cynthia could have sworn she watched him die! Deep, deep down inside Cynthia was a little happy that her father was still alive. After all, he is still her Daddy! Cynthia thought to herself.. But Cynthia would soon come to realize how false that feeling is, you can't contain evil with love, it just wont work! Cynthia was completely petrified of what was to come next, if he was not to be stopped.. "But this cant be, your, your".. Cyris cut her off. "You thought what, let me guess, you thought I was dead"? He finished her sentence for her.. "You actually thought you and your little boyfriend would succeed in eliminating me?! "Huh". Cyris laughed at the thought.. "Well, your wrong"!! (He said). "No Father, your wrong"! (She snapped at him).. Cyrises eyes opened wide, as he glared into his daughter's eyes, and she said.. "He's not my boyfriend, he's my husband"! Mateos seen the fury growing upon Cyrises face. He felt it best, he switch the conversation, quick. "What do you want with me Cyris? (He said). Why am I here, You kept me alive for a reason Cyris, why? Answer me damn-it.. Your demon beast could have killed me at any time, so why am I here?! I'm never going to give you the location of the Trident, that's for damn sure! So you might as well just kill me know Cyris"! Cyris just looked at Mateos for a few moments, before he finally said.. "We'll just see about that Mateos, my naive friend! Shut him up for a while, I'm sick of his voice"! (Cyris ordered Kavizious).. "It would be my pleasure, my lord"! (Kavizious replied). As Cyris turned to go get Elisabeth and reunite his wife and daughter, Kavizious grabbed Mateos by his head with both hand and smashed his head right into the side wall of the cave! "NOOO! You barbarian"! (She screamed). At the sea hell beast and her father, as she hung her head low and began sobbing. "You're a monster, your not my father, I hate you"! (She said). To her father, Cyris. He looked at his daughter and smiled, turning away, and as he swam off, he said.. "Elisabeth my dear, there's someone here you should come get reacquainted with"!

Cynthia's attention was on Mateos, checking if he was ok, but quickly shifted from Mateos back to her father. She was trying to make sense of what she just heard. "Wait, what's going on"?! (She asked). With such confusion.. All of the sudden, Cynthia's mother Elisabeth, who has been dead for year's, swam right up in front of her. "Mother! (Cynthia cried). Is it really you"? Cynthia broke down crying hysterically, as she threw her arms around her mother hugging her. "I cant believe its really you"! (She cried).. Elisabeth's hug was cold and uncomfortable, she never even raised her arms, she just stayed still for a moment then she pulled away and said: "We do not show emotions like this my child, And we most certainly do not disobey our father's wishes either Cynthia! You will help us overthrow your husband and destroy the kingdom of Mordainia! You need to embrace your dark side, child. Its your birth right! You are, the dark Princess of thee UnderWorld. (She said). "Princess?! (Cynthia interrupted). I'm the Bloody Queen of Mordainia"! You will use your black magic and help your mother and father rule the dark salt waters of thee Eighth Sea! "You can't hurt your own people"! (Cynthia pleaded). "I wouldn't worry about them Traitors Cynthia, you have my grandchild to look after now"! (Elisabeth proclaimed). As she looked down and touched Cynthia's stomach. "Ah yes, just as I suspected, it's a boy! We will groom him to take over as dark ruler of the Tolkien Sea.. Well, after us any way's"! (She said). With a smile.. "Your lying"! (Cynthia shouted). "I never lie my dear, I have no need for that! (Elisabeth replied). I am a very powerful black magic, hell demon, sea witch, my dear. Trust me, you're with child Cynthia"! "I'm going to be a mother"? (Cynthia said). While holding her stomach. "I"! (Her mother replied).. "So do the right thing Cynthia! (Cyris interrupted). Join us Cynthia, join me and your mother. Your going need us to protect you and your child, our grandchild. The future King of the UnderWorld, the King of thee Under "Mid" World.

Mateos was out of sight, he heard everything! Mateos waited for Elisabeth and Cyris to leave with Kavizious until he swam in to talk to Cynthia and said; "Do you think they were telling you the truth, Cynthia"? (He asked her).. "I do not know Mateos, I do not know! (She answered honestly).. Either way, those are not my parents! I don't know who or what that thing is, but is sure isn't my mother Mateos, my mother died nine years ago, and me and Maximus killed my father back in the battle. He died when my mother died".. (She said). As she was fighting back tears. "The only way to stop them is to go get the Trident before them Mateos, you have to use it against them, before it's to late"! (She pleaded with him).. "Yes! (Mateos realized).. I have to get out of here Cynthia! I have to go get the Trident and bring it to Maximus"! (He said). "I'll stay here and be the eyes on them, please hurry Mateos"!?! (She said). Begging her friend to go as fast as he could.. "Take Zar, (She said). I know he's here somewhere, he can help you get there faster Mateos, but please be careful"! (She said). While hugging her friend goodbye. "I! (he replied). You too Cynthia"! Then swam off..

Cyris and Kavizious were discussing their strategy to extract the information about the Trident out of Mateos. "As soon as he comes too, I want the location Kavizious! (Cyris ordered). I don't care how you do it, just get it done! Just don't kill him until he reveals the location"! "I! (Kavizious replied). What of Maximus and his army my lord? (He asked Cyris).. They weren't that far away from here when I took Mateos from their camp, Master"! (Kavizious said). "Well I guess we'll just have to have Elisabeth summoned her hell demon army, now wont we!?! (Cyris said). We will wipeout Maximus and his Royal Army of Mordainia"! Cynthia was listening to what Cyris and Kavizious were discussing. "I want to help father! (She said). As she entered. I'm sorry father, I'm sorry for everything! Please forgive me father, I really want to help and show you how sorry I am, please"!?! (She begged).. "You really want to help, you really want to prove your loyalty and love for me and your mother"?! (Cyris asked her).. Not sure what to make of what Cynthia was saying. "Yes father, anything"! (She replied). "Go kill Maximus! That's how you prove your sincere my child, kill your husband and bring me his dead body"! "Fine, then, I will"!! (She replied).

Meanwhile, Mateos had found Zar and he and the sea dragon dashed through the caves and out into the open ocean, into the dark salt waters of the Tolkien Sea. It was all a ploy, Cynthia distracted her father Cyris and his enforcer, Kavizious. Mateos road faster than he ever has before in his life. Mateos and Zar just didn't stop until they reached the spot where he had hidden the Trident! Mateos dismounted Zar before he could come to a complete stop. Within seconds, Mateos had dug up the Trident and was back on Zar riding full speed out of there! They had to find the King and the men. If they cant find them they'll have to go straight to the kingdom and check there, but if not there he would have to take what men he could that were protecting their beloved kingdom and go rescue Cynthia. "Hopefully we can find Maximus and them, Zar my friend"! (Mateos said). While patting the side of the loyal sea dragon's big beefy neck. "Grrr" Zar made a noise, as he grunted in agreement!

CHAPTER

9

BACK IN THE TRIANGLE, ELISABETH was in the middle of casting a spell when all of the sudden.. "Gasp" Elisabeth gasped, she had a vision.. "He has the Trident! (She said). He's gone, he has the sea serpent and the got the Trident. We need to stop him before he get's it to the King"! (She said). "Who has the Trident"? (Asked Cyris). "Mateos"! (She replied). "WHAT"!?! (Screamed Cyris). "He's gone, he took the sea dragon and he's gone"! (She said, frantically).. Cynthia couldn't help but smile. Kavizious swam out to go check if Mateos and the dragon were gone. "YOU! (Cyris said). This is your fault Cynthia, my own flesh and blood betrayed me again! You were lying to me so he could escape, weren't you"?! (He accused his daughter).. Cynthia put on a straight face and said.. "No father, I swear to you, I had nothing to do with this"! Cyris looked to his wife to see if she had any say, but Cynthia's magic was strong and she could block Elisabeth from seeing if she's telling the truth or not. "I can not tell".. (Elisabeth admitted). Elisabeth pulled out her Crystal Ball and chanted in some language that's been dead for thousands of years. She seen Mateos unearth the Trident and ride off on Zar, with the Trident in hand! "It's true, he's gone"! (Kavizious said). Swimming right up to Cynthia, snatching her up, and said.. "This is your doing, you did this"! (He said). "YES".. And with pride, and a big smile upon her face, she said.. "You honestly think I would ever help you!?! You killed Peretta and both parents of the man I love! I would NEVER help you"! Cyris reached back and slapped Cynthia right across her face. Cyris was so outraged, that he grabbed his own daughter up by her throat and began choking her. Cynthia was struggling for her life, she thought she was about to die in the hands of her own father. Cynthia was reaching for his eyes, hoping to catch him in the eyes, forcing him to let go. She was trying whatever she could, but it was no use, Cyris was too powerful. When all of the sudden; Maximus came bursting in through the caves, leaping from his sea dragon he road in on, with sword in hand. Cyris dropped his daughter. "Cynthia"! (Screamed the King).. As Cynthia was on the sea floor struggling to catch he breath, one of her gills were damaged severely, from her father. Cyris drew his sword just as Maximuses sword came crashing down upon him. Their swords almost exploding when they slammed together, directly in front of Cyrises face. The swords contact was so powerful that the entire ocean floor in the deep dark abyss, shook from it's vicious vibrations! As Maximus and Cyris were engaged in battle, Just like his father before him! Kavizious was tearing through the royal army, taking on three, four men at a time, as they rushed in, attacking!

When all of the sudden … The whole entire ocean, lit up a bright orange-ish, red. It was in the shape of a triangle way up above them, it was the fiery Triangle of Death! Almost reaching the surface.. Elisabeth fled and began the process of bringing forth her hell demon army from the sea hell realm, over into Mid World's Ocean, the Tolkien Sea (thee Eighth Sea). They were brought there, to help her and Cyris take the Kingdom of Mordainia, and control all the Eight Sea's.. "CYNTHIA! (Maximus shouted). Find out where your mother Elisabeth has gone, and stop her! Stop that spell or whatever it is she's doing, bringing these demons through to our world Cynthia, and quick"! "I, my love"! (She replied). As she sped off, Cynthia came out of a cave and when she looked up, she could see hundreds of demons like Kavizious, coming through the Triangle of Fire. Cynthia stopped and listened for a moment, she could hear her mother, very faintly, chanting in the old language, chanting her spell. It was working, only because Mateos had unearthed the Trident and it is near. She used the power of the Trident by using her black magic to activate the Trident and she was able to open the portal. "I have to get this portal shut down so no more demons can get through"! Cynthia had thought to herself.. She kept following the chants until she had eyes on Elisabeth. Cynthia closed her eyes and swam as fast as she could, screaming.. (AHHHHH)! Until she crashed right into her mother, braking the connection, stopping the rest of the demons from being able to come through the Triangle of Fire. As hell demons were raining down upon Maximus and his army, Mateos appeared, riding in on Zar. Mateos pushed Zar to the limit, he road Zar faster and further he has ever gone before!

"Maximus! Thank the God's your alive, Catch"! (Mateos said). Throwing King Maximus the Trident! He turned to Mateos just as he tossed him the Trident of Tolkien. "You have to use it my King, it's the only way"! (Mateos told him).. Maximus swung his sword, taking off the head of a hell demon, then through his sword at another, He screamed.. "AHHHHHHH"! King Maximus, swung the Trident over his head with such force.. (Whoosh).. Maximus took the Trident in both hand and jammed it down with all his might right into the ground as hard as he could. There was a massive echo boom, that shook thee entire abyss sending everyone of those hell demons, back to their hell realm. As all the demons where disappearing, bursting into fiery clouds of magical flames, then smoke. Then they were sucked through the fiery triangle portal, just as fast as they came through it, they were gone. The shock waves sent everyone else flying backwards. "NOOOOO"! (Elisabeth screamed).. Mateos tossed Cynthia her knife that she keeps in her hair from Peretta, He stole it off of Kavizious when Kavizious picked him up and slammed him into the cave wall knocking him out. "Do it Maximus, do it now"! (Cynthia screamed). At her husband.. With Cynthia's approval, Maximus took the Trident, and jammed it down into Elisabeth's crystal ball, that Cynthia stole from her, and had rolled it close enough for Maximus to crash the Trident right into it, busting the crystal ball, into a million pieces.. Cynthia had figured out the Crystal Ball was the power source to her parents hellish, black magic. As the crystal ball shattered, you could hear the shrieks and cries from Cynthia's parents as they and Kavizious burst into flames, Cynthia swam aver to her father, and with Peretta's knife, she jammed the knife right into his throat, and with as much hate and disgust that she could muster up, she said.. "Rot in Sea Hell"! Taking the knife back out his throat and swimming away, right into her husbands awaiting arms. Elisabeth, Cyris and Kavizious got sucked back through the portal of the fiery triangle and poof, they disappeared and so did the Triangle of Fire! Just like that, they were gone! There was no trace left behind. There was no Cyris, no Elisabeth or her hell demons, and there was no Kavizious. The only sign of them even being here, the only thing left behind was a few sea dragons wondering around aimlessly, under that evil control spell, and Kaviziouses burnt, black cloak, slowly floating down to the floor, of the abyss.

Maximus picked up Cynthia in his arms, spinning her around, and as they kissed, Mateos and the other's were in the background celebrating their victory. "We did it my love"! (Maximus said). To his wife Cynthia.. "No my dear, (She whispered). Kissing him patiently, you did it! I love you my sweet Maximus, I love you with every ounce of my being"! Cynthia was very emotional, tears were flowing as she thanked her husband. "Thank you Max, thank you for saving me. More than once! I don't know what I would have done if you didn't crash into me that day. I am so lucky you found me"! (She proclaimed).. Maximus smiled and said; "Oh no my dear, you got it all wrong. You're the one that saved me"! (Maximus told her).. Cynthia cried tears of joy.. "By the way Max, (Cynthia said). Your going to be a father"! Placing her hand on her stomach, with a big smile ear to ear.. Maximus was overwhelmed with joy! "You, you, your joking? (Maximus stuttered).. Cynthia shook her head. "No Max, I'm not, Your going to be a father"! Maximus picked up Cynthia, swinging her around in his arm. "I'm so happy my darling wife! I cant believe we are going to have a baby"! (Kind Maximus said).. Kissing his queen, as he let go of her finally. "Easy Max"! (She had to tell him).. The King was just a little too excited, and was a tad-bit wound up from the resent battle, so he wasn't the gentlest being at the moment. "Oh, sorry, forgive me, I'm just so happy"! (He said). "I know Maximus, it's fine, I'm ok my love, promise! (She assured him).. "Are you happy about this my love, is this what you want"? (He asked her).. "Yes Max, I am absolutely thrilled! I actually couldn't be happier"! (She admitted, earnestly)..

The King was so ecstatic with the news that he and Cynthia are going to be parents, that he had to share the wonderful news with his friend Mateos. Maximus was making his way through all the celebrating soldiers. It was hard because they all wanted to celebrate with the King as he swam by them looking for Mateos. "Mateos"! (The King called out).. Mateos was at the other end of the battle field as he was trying to make his way to the king when he spotted him. "Maximus, my King, we did it, we defeat them"! (Mateos said). As he hugged his friend, the King.. "Yes, Mateos we did, because of you! (Said the King). You did good Mateos, I'm proud of you. You saved the Kingdom and all our people, both Mordainians and OctaGods alike. Thank you my friend, I owe you"! (Said the King). "Nonsense! (Mateos Replied). I was just doing my job.. But I thank you, this means a lot! But in all honesty, we are all alive and they are gone because of you and Cynthia"! (Mateos said). "OK, OK, we all did it.. So, speaking of me and Cynthia". (Maximus said). With a big smile on his face.. "She's with child.. Cynthia's having my child"! "Congratulations Max! (Mateos said). I'm so happy for you and the Queen, Max. you will be great parents, I believe in you"! (He told his friend).. "Thank you My friend"! (Maximus said). Just as his wife Cynthia came swimming over to them". Congratulations Cynthia, you will be a fantastic mother"! (Mateos said to her).. Hugging his friend the Queen. "Thank you Mateos! (Cynthia replied). I just couldn't be happier".. "Everyone, everyone, quiet down! Your King and Queen have an announcement". (Mateos said). To all the soldiers of the royal army.. "Go ahead my King". (Mateos told him).. "Me and Cynthia are going to have a baby.. My Queen, she is with child"! (Maximus said). As he raised his arm and Cynthia's as well, with her hand, in his. "YAAAAAAAA"!!! Everyone cheered.. "All hail the King and Queen"! Came from out the cheering soldiers.. "Long live the Kingdom of Mordainia"! (They shouted). "We are the protectors of the Tolkien Sea, forever and always"! (Said the King). As they all cheered louder and louder. "Yaaaaa"! "Here Mateos, take the Trident and hide it somewhere else now, were only you know! You can take Zar with you and the Trident, and meet us back at the kingdom! (King Maximus commanded).. I only ask because you're the only one I can trust, please Mateos!?! Will you except this mission"? (He asked him).. "I, my King! (Mateos replied). It would be my honor"! "Thank you Mateos! (Cynthia said). The Trident will let you know when it is safe for the Trident to be buried. "I, my lady"! (He replied). "Please be safe Mateos, we will look after your family until your return"! (Cynthia promised). "Thank you"! (Mateos said). Turning around and loading up him and Zar for their journey.

While King Maximus and Queen Cynthia rounded up the royal army and headed for home, back to the Kingdom of Mordainia, Mateos and Zar the trusted royal sea dragon, headed off in another direction with Trident in hand. Mateos and Zar road for three days and two nights, when all of the sudden, the Trident began to light up. "Whoa-hoo, easy boy".. (Mateos said). To Zar, as he was slowly pulling back on the reins, and lightly tapping Zar on the side of neck, telling him to slow down. "I think we are here my friend"! (He said). The Trident grew brighter and brighter until Mateos reached and Zar reached the caves of the Volcanic mountains in the abyss of the Black Sea. Mateos had to leave Zar as he made his way through the crevice until the Trident flickered and then stopped glowing completely. The Trident had guided Mateos to it's perfectly hidden location that only Mateos would ever know where it lie, hopefully for eternity! Mateos buried the Trident, then said.. "Long live the Kingdom of Mordainia".. Then swam out of the caves to Zar and they both took off for home, they road and road until the kingdom was in their sights. At least, Mateos will have a long awaited reunion with his family, his wife and daughter.

In the Kingdom, Maximus and Cynthia were planning a big celebration and feast for Mateos and all the kingdom people. They wanted to celebrate the victory, as well as the pregnancy. They also wanted to reward Mateos, by knighting him for his bravery and leadership with everything he has done, including the Trident of Tolkien Mission with the Prince. They are waiting for upon his return to Honor Mateos and the rest of the Royal Army. When Mateos, along with Zar had returned back from their mission, he couldn't wait to see his family! Mateos thought to himself.. As soon as he entered, Mateos was met with a Hero's welcome! He was met by all his friends and family, the entire kingdom was cheering him on. There were instruments playing, people singing, and the rest were chanting and cheering for him. "What's all this"?! (Mateos asked). Blushing, as he picked up his excited daughter Kylynn and hugged and kissed her and his wife Aleina! "Why it's a celebration Mateos! It's a Feast in your honor! (King Maximus explained).. Everyone is so grateful, because of you, the Kingdom is safe! You're a Hero Mateos"! (Said the King). "But I was just doing my job"! (Mateos replied). "And for that, we thank you"! (Replied the King).. "We just want to thank you Mateos! (Cynthia interrupted). Now go! Go spend some time with your family, then come to the Palace for your Knighting ceremony"! "And don't forget the Feast"! (Added Maximus).. "Hahaha"! Everyone laughed.. As Mateos gathered his family and headed home to get ready for his knighting ceremony. "Tonight, we party"! (Declared the King).. "YAAAAA"! Everyone cheered.. The King turned to all of his people and said.. "My people, Mordainians and

OctaGods alike.. I declare today a holiday! Today, the day we fought and won the our freedom! So everyone, dance sing, eat and be merry, because tonight we party! Long live the Kingdom"!! (Said Maximus). As he turned and kissed his wife. Everyone in the kingdom was so happy! They loved their new King and Queen very much!

Back in the deep dark abyss, in the caves, in a volcanic crevice, is where Mateos had left the Trident buried, the rocks and dirt was sliding down shaking loose from the volcanic eruptions. There was a light, glowing, coming out from where the Trident lay. All of the sudden, the rocks and dirt were vibrating fiercely out of control, shaking free and bearing the Trident. The whole cave lit up from the glowing Trident, like it was filled with fire! Something was happening with the Trident. Only what is it? What is going on with the Trident of Tolkien? Will the King know there's something wrong, or will they leave it there, in harms way, in risk of being found by someone else!

CHAPTER
10

MEANWHILE, BACK IN THE KINGDOM of Mordainia, Cynthia got the weirdest feeling, in the pit of her stomach. At first she thought it was because of the baby. But then the feeling got worse until Cynthia got stuck in a trans. While in her dazed state, she had a vision. In her vision, there was a bright red light! "What's wrong my dear Cynthia, are you ok"? (Maximus asked, franticly).. But there was no response, Cynthia just floated there with a blank look on her face, saying absolutely nothing! "CYNTHIA!? (Yelled Maximus). Are you OK"?! (He said). One more time, placing his hand on the small of her back. "Who me? (Cynthia finally replied).. Oh, no, nothing my dear, I, I'm fine"! (Cynthia stuttered). Finally snapping out of it. "Let's go Maximus, let's go mingle amongst our people my king"! "I, my Lady! After you.. (Maximus had replied).. But before we go, I just want to tell you how happy I am Cynthia! I love you so much, Cynthia my Queen.. I promise I will forever protect you and our child with all my might! You have made me the happiest man in all of the eight seas, and I cant wait for our little prince to be born"! (He declared).. "Or little Princess"! (Cynthia said). With a smile, playfully! "I love you too my King, and I as well can not wait to extend our family together! You have made me the happiest I have ever been in my life Max, thank you, Love you so much my sweet, dear husband"! (She replied). As Cynthia grabbed a hold of her husband, she heard a faint whisper.. "I will kill you, I'll kill you all"! She knew what she had heard.. "What did you just say"? (Cynthia said). Pushing away from Maximus. "Who me, nothing, I didn't say anything"! (Maximus replied). Cynthia looked around, but all she seen was the kingdoms people celebrating. She was trying to see where that came from but she didn't know. All of the sudden she herd it again; "You are all going to die".. (Whispered the strange voice, again).. Cynthia figured out it was just in her head and decided to just let it go for now! She didn't want to ruin the festivities.. The people deserve it, Maximus deserves it, their friend Mateos deserved it too.. The new queen decided to put on a smile and celebrate with the rest of them. It was a fantastic night with Mateos being Knighted, he is Sir. General Mateos now, and the Kingdom of Mordainia was safe and sound, once again.. But for how long!?!

Some time has passed now, since Cynthia had a vision or has herd any voices. Cynthia is at the very end of her pregnancy, she was in her final trimester so she could give birth in any day now. Cynthia had decided to not say anything to her husband, (or anyone else for that matter), about the voices she heard that day of the kingdoms celebration, no matter how frightened she was over it! Cynthia figured it was for the best.. Besides, she hasn't heard or seen anything since that day! "I Can handle my husband Maximus"! Cynthia thought to herself. Cynthia was going wait until the time was right to deal with it, like when it happened again. So Cynthia waited for the time to come, but it never did! The new Queen has gone the entire rest of her pregnancy with no problems. She didn't go into any trans state, she didn't have anymore visions, nor has she heard anymore voices! Cynthia hasn't even thought about her parents, Cyris and Elisabeth, or even Kavizious for that matter. Cynthia has only thought about her child, she was so happy that she was going to be a mother. So she has put all the bad stuff that happened in the past, out of her mind, she hasn't thought about them and everything she went through at all.. Well, until today that is!

On this day, Cynthia and Maximus were in the royal sea garden just talking, and enjoying each others company on a very nice day, down in the deep salt waters of the Tolkien Sea. Maximus and Cynthia made their way to Zar the sea dragon to say hi, and feed all the sea horses and the sea dragons in the kingdoms stables. The sea creatures loved the attention, especially Zar! Zar has been with Maximuses family for as far back as he could remember. Everyone loves Zar, he has formed special his own separate bonds with each of them, Maximus Cynthia, Mateos and his wife Aleina and daughter Kylynn as well. He too, missed King Keyira and Queen Muriel. Zar would protect them all with his life! The sea dragons loved when you rub the side of their head and necks while you feed them. While the sea horses liked to be brushed on their manes. Maximus was feeding Zar while Cynthia hummed a sweet lullaby, patting him on the side of his head and neck, when all of the sudden.. Cynthia fell into another deep trans state. Cynthia' vision brought her into a fiery cave with crevices with flowing lava and surrounded by volcano's. these deadly mountains were deep down in the abyss of the Black Sea. During her vision, the cave was completely engulfed in flames, and Cynthia was just there, floating in the middle of the flames.

At first Cynthia screamed in fear, but then quickly realized she wasn't burning! Cynthia wasn't hurt, she didn't feel any pain! Nothing was happening to her from the flames and or lava. that's when Cynthia followed the light until she came upon it. There it was, the Trident! "Gasp"! Cynthia had lost her breath for a moment. She couldn't believe her eyes, the Trident was sticking out from all the rocks and dirt that it was buried in. Except in this vision, Cynthia wasn't pregnant. She was holding her child, chanting in a language she only herd once or twice before, from when her mother Elisabeth spoke in the same tongue, when she used her black magic. It was the old language that has been dead for thousands of years. When Cynthia finally came to, she was shaking uncontrollably. Cynthia was completely hysterical, screaming and crying. "Shhhhh, Cynthia, it's ok now, your fine".. (Maximus said). Trying to console his wife, holding her tight! "It's ok my love, I'm here for you, everything is going to go just fine"! (He promised her).. Then all of the sudden.. Cynthia had her first contraction. Cynthia leaned forward, holding her stomach in pain, she was going in to labor. "It's Time Maximus"! (Cynthia said to her husband).. Cynthia and Maximuses lives are about to change forever, the two are about to become parents! Maximus was so nervous, that he swam off without Cynthia.

Later on that evening, back in the palace. Cynthia and Maximus were each taking turns holding their brand new baby boy! Maximus was so proud of the new little Prince. He and Cynthia were discussing baby names, when Cynthia said.. "Key! Let's name him Key, Max!?! It's perfect, we name him Key after his grandfather, King Keyira, and he's the KEY to the survival of both our people, because he's the first half Mordainian, half OctaGod and he just so happens to be the future King! Beside's Max, (Cynthia continued), I want to name him after your father the Great King Keyira, I want his legacy to live on my sweet Max. It's because of your father I'm alive Maximus. It's because of him, we were able to have a family, and honestly, what better way to honor him than this!? I want our son to always know that he came from a long line of great deep sea warriors my love"! (Cynthia said). She didn't want her son to thing he was born from evil because of his grandmother and father, her parents! She wants him to follow his good blood line, and to be proud he's the first Mordainian and OctaGod, ever. Maximus smiled, he thought this was a terrific idea! "Are you sure my love? (He asked her).. Because I thing this would be a great honor to my father, and I couldn't agree more. I would absolutely love to name him Key! Thank you my love"! (Maximus said). Kissing Cynthia.. She smiled, Cynthia couldn't be happier than at this moment in time! She thought to herself. "Then, Key it is"!! (He said). With pride.. "I thought you'd like that my dear Max".. (She snickered). "Ah yes, Prince Key! (He said). Kissing his son on the forehead. That's a great name, I love it! Prince Key! (He continued). Son of the Royal Family. He is, the Royal Prince, son of King Maximus and Queen Cynthia Posidian, grandson of the great King Keyira and Queen Muriel Posidian. He is the first Mordainian and OctaGod Hybrid. He is the future, the King of the great Kingdom of Modainia, the future RULER, of the Tolkien Sea. He is.. The Key to our kingdoms happiness".. (Maximus declared). On this day, the birth of his son the new Prince. "Today is a holiday, in the kingdom. For this is the greatest day of both the people Mordainian and OctaGod alike"! The King had Spoken.. (Maximus turned to Cynthia, and said.. "I love it Cynthia, I just absolutely love it! Prince Key it is then, my love". (He said). Cynthia smiled and spun her son around and around, hugging him, and she said.. Oh my son, my beautiful son Key, Prince Key".. (Cynthia said). With a such joy, and happiness. "I just cant believe how Beautiful he is Max"! (She said). Key was dark gray and had all the markings of an OctaGod, but he had a body of a Mordainian, he just seemed a little thicker than a typical Mordainian. But as far as Cynthia and Maximus were concerned, Key was perfect!

Cynthia's life of mother hood, was absolutely fantastic! She loved being a new mother, and she loved her life as Queen, and Teaching at the center, as well as raising her son, and being a wife to her husband, and also being a friend to Aleina and her family, but she knew keeping busy would help keep her mind off her parents and losing Peretta. She had to stay focused on all the new, good thing's in her life, and not all the Death and Destruction! Cynthia was so happy, she never dreamt that she would be able to raise her child, in the kingdom that she grew up dreaming to be a part of that world. Now she's the Queen of the entire kingdom and she has a beautiful family and life in the kingdom she so desperately wanted. "Peretta would be so proud"! Cynthia thought to herself.. Cynthia found and married her soul mate, King Maximus, and had his child. She never would have thought possible, back in the days of those caves, when she and her people were outcasts, tossed out into the belly of the abyss.. But now because of her husband Maximus, she is living the life she couldn't have even dreamed of. She and Maximus, were just as much in love with each other today, as they were when they first had met. Who would have thought this would ever be possible. She and Maximus, never spoke of the trans state she had slipped in, right before she went into labor. Maximus never brought it up, so Cynthia just figured it best to just leave it be, and just go on with their lives and just raise their child in the beautiful kingdom and not make any waves. Cynthia was just so happy with Maximus and Key. She knew how lucky she was that Maximus and Mateos had crashed right into her that day with Peretta, way back when. Cynthia knew how proud of her Peretta would be, with her living in the kingdom and marrying Maximus and having a child. She couldn't help it, that the thought made her smile.

Years have passed with no threats to the Kingdom. Prince Key was getting older and Cynthia hasn't heard any voices or had any visions, she hasn't slipped into any trans states. Just nothing but pure happiness with her husband and son in their beautiful kingdom with all their friends and people. Life couldn't be better. Prince Key was growing up, he had become an extraordinary young man. He and Mateoses daughter Kylynn, have become the best of friends. They were inseparable growing up together in the kingdom. They were just two peas in a sea pod. As kids, Key and Kylynn would explore all the ins and outs of the crevices in the caves inside and outside of the kingdom, in the bottom of the abyss. They were just like a young Maximus and Cynthia. Kylynn was a few years older than Key so she was always looking out for him. She had known him, his whole life because of their parents being so close. She basically had grew up in the palace, her father Mateos was best friends with King Maximus, and her mother Aleina was best friends with Queen Cynthia. Kylynns parents, absolutely adored Prince Key, and his parents thought the world of Kylynn! So they could basically come and go as they pleased with out question, as long as they were together. Needless to say, the kids got themselves into plenty of mischief together. The two grew so close because, while the husbands and fathers, were off with the Royal Army, the wives and mothers, would take their kids to the stables together, to feed the sea horses and the sea dragons. They also were brought to the center were Cynthia and Aleina, each taught a course, that both Key and Kylynn were students in. The ladies were passing their passion for the animals, and the Learning/ Training Center, down to their children.

One day, Cynthia was thinking about her beautiful life that her and Maximus had built together for their child. She couldn't help think about how lucky she truly is to have a husband like Max and a child like Key! She knew just how much Maximus adored her and Key. It's just as much as she adores her boys, Max and Key. Cynthia couldn't be happier! She thought to herself.. She just couldn't help but smile! And that's when all of the sudden she saw it! Cynthia was completely frozen in fear. She didn't realize at first, that it was only a vision.. In the vision, she seen her son Prince Key fully grown, with a fully grown Kylynn on his arm at his side. He was holding a brightly glowing red Trident in the other hand! Then all of the sudden, her vision changed to flashes of fire, and then Kavizious was stabbing her husband Maximus with the Trident. It kept flashing back and forth between the two Visions, fist of her son and Kylynn, and then too the fire and Kavizious stabbing her husband with the Trident.. And that's when she heard it, that voice! Cynthia quivered in fear.. The voice was that of Kavizious. "I will kill you Cynthia1 I will kill you all, but first I will kill your husband, and then your son. I wont stop until every single Mordainian and OctaGod is completely wiped out"! (Whispered the voice of Kavizious).. Cynthia decided that it was time to finally tell her husband, King Maximus, the truth!

Later on that evening, Cynthia finally told her husband about the visions, and the voices, she told him everything! Cynthia was crying, she was so scared for her family's safety.. "It's all my fault! (Cynthia said). I knew I could never have a normal life"! As she threw her face in her hands, crying. "No Cynthia! (Maximus replied). No it's not, it's my fault! I never brought it up again that day you had that episode, the day Key was born". (He said). "No Max, it happened before that as well. It's been happening off and on, for years now. I should have told you, I'm so sorry Max"! (She replied). "Shhhh! (Maximus had interrupted).. It's ok my dear"! the King felt so bad for his wife Cynthia! "Please Cynthia,! (Maximus begged of her).. Please don't ever feel scared to tell me any of these things again my love. I'm your husband Cynthia, I love you with every ounce of my being. You don't ever have to go through anything like that by yourself, ever again my queen"! (He promised). As he hugged his wife, embracing her, making Cynthia feel safe, once again.. "I know my love! (She replied). I wont, I promise! I'll never keep anything from you again! Please forgive me Max!? I promise I will never keep anything from you ever again! No matter what it is"! (Cynthia promised). "Well thank you, that's great and all Cynthia, I am truly happy to hear this, and I believe you, I do, but what are we going to do about the visions you already had and the voices you've already heard?! (Maximus asked her).. They have to mean something, don't they"! (Max said). "I don't know, yet! (she replied). But I sure do intend on finding out my love"!

CHAPTER
11

IT'S BEEN A COUPLE YEARS now since Cynthia and maximus, discussed the visions and the voices that day she figured out it was Kaviziouses voice she heard. Today is now Prince Key's seventeenth birthday. Which makes his best friend Kylynn twenty years old already. In the kingdom of Mordainia, when you turn seventeen, you become a man! "What's wrong Key"?! (Kylynn asked the Prince).. Key wasn't acting like his normal, usual, annoying self today, so she knew something was bothering her friend. "I don't know! (Key replied). It's just, I'm going to be a man after today, and my parents and everyone else, is going to expect so much from me, and I'm afraid I'm going to end up letting everyone down! All I want to do is be free and spend my time with Kylynn, I don't want to grow up and have the entire kingdom counting on me"! (Said the Prince). With such sorrow in his voice. "Oh Key"! (Kylynn whispered). Kylynn's heart broke her friend, the Prince. "My mother and father named me after my grandfather, the Great King Keyira! (He continued). I just know I can never live up to the name, I'll never be half the man he was"! I'm going to be King one day, and I'm going to let them down Kylynn, I'm going to, have to, let them all down"! (He cried). "Oh Max; You'll be a great King some day"! (Kylynn told him).. "I have all these unanswered questions about my mother's side of the family, Kylynn. (He told her).. I don't know one thing about that side of me! I mean, I'm the first half Mordainian and half OctaGod in hundreds of years, and I'm royalty. Do you know how much pressure that puts on me, being the symbol of hope for not just one, but for two species"!?! (Key had proclaimed).. "You cant think like that Key! Kylynn tried pleading with Key.. All you can do is be the best you can be Key, and you'll be just fine! You got the blood of the Greatest Kings running in your veins, you'll be just fine Key, stop worrying so much"! (She said). "Yah, but what else Kylynn?! (Key asked). Who else's blood do I have coursing through my veins? That is the question Kylynn! (He replied)." So what does your mother say about her side"? (Kylynn asked him).. "Nothing! Every time I asked my mother, or my father for that matter, about her side of the family, she just gets this sad look on her face, like something horrible happened Ky! (He said). And my father, well he just gets upset and yells, changing the subject, every single time I mention it.. Besides, him and your dad just keep training us with the army until we are ready to collapse, and our mothers with their courses at the training center, between the four of them, I'm going crazy Ky"! (He complained). To Kylynn.. "They just want what's best for us Key"! (She replied). "Don't you wish there was more to our lives than just preparing for battle every day of our lives"!? (Key asked Kylynn).. "Why don't we go and try and find someone who can and will tell us about your mothers past, about her side of your family then Key!? (She said to him).. I know of some OctaGods that still live deep in the caves, hidden way away from the kingdom. We should definitely go and see if we can find out who your grandparents were! (She said). "You would do that for me Ky?! (He said). You would come with me to try and find out"?! Key was smiling with such excitement. "Of course I will Key, you're my best friend, I love you Key"! (Kylynn replied). Key scooped her up, hugging and kissing her cheek, repeatedly and saying.. "Thank you, thank you, thank you"! Over and over again! "Thank you so much Ky, I honestly don't know what I would do without you"! (He said). Getting serious again. "Your welcome Key! (She replied). Completely blushing, because she had a huge crush on the Prince for years! It's my pleasure, I actually want to go"! (Kylynn told him).. "So it's settled then, we'll leave tonight! Ky, meet me in the garden, by the stables at three AM after everyone s vast asleep"! (Key told her).. "OK! (She replied). But if we do this Key, we can't get caught, my father will kill me"! (She said). "Yah Ky, He'll kill us both! (He added). Trust me Kylynn, we wont get caught! I'm more afraid of what your father Mateos would do to me, than I am of what my own father and mother, the King and queen would"! (He told her).. "Hahaha"!

They both laughed out loud for a moment. "Yah my father's pretty scary". (Kylynn said). As they continued to laugh..

Later on, in the middle of the night/early in the morning, while everyone was sound asleep, before anyone would wake for a while, Kylynn had swam out to the garden to meet Prince Key. "You ready Ky"?! (He asked). As she approached him.. "Yes"! (She replied). The Prince couldn't help but help but notice how beautiful Kylynn looked. Key had never noticed just how stunning she actually, truly was. For the first time ever, in the young Prince's life, he was speechless in front of her. Kylynn was very slender, with long flowing black hair, down to the small of her back. She had one single braid down the side of her head, that she sometimes tucked behind her ear. Kylynn had beautiful green eyes, and the most gorgeous smile. She was absolutely breath taking. Key didn't know if it was because he was now becoming a man, but Kylynn looked completely different to him now, and yet she was exactly the same she has ever been. It's just now Key is starting to notice her. "Are you ready my Prince"?! (Kylynn asked Key). With a big smile on her face. "Ye - yes, I - I'm ready"! (Replied the Prince).. Stuttering, and completely blushed. "Well ok, good. Let's do this then"! (She said). "Hahaha"! They both laughed. Key took Kylynn's hand and swam right out of the kingdom, and straight into the shadows!

Prince Key and Kylynn swam threw the pitch black dark, because of their training in their mother's courses at the training center, and the survival skills, with their fathers and the royal army. Kylynn and Prince Key, were as tough as they come. They both had extensive army combat and defense training. They both could very easily handle themselves, so their parents never worried about them when their out and about and not around. They were very trusted, so they both could not be seen for days without any suspicion. They were just about to exit a cave when they herd it. A booming voice coming from behind them, from out of the shadows, in the dark. "You want to know about your grandparents, correct my Prince?! (Said the strange scary voice).. You would like to know about you mothers past, isn't this why you traveled this far out of your comfort zone my sweet, naive children"?! "How did you know that"? (Key asked). The unseen stranger.. That's when he showed himself. This big scary creature thing, came out of the shadows, and was looking down upon them. "Who in the Sea Hell are you"?! (Prince Key demanded).. As he grabbed Kylynn and pushed her behind him, shielding her with his body. The stranger laughed. "Hahaha! You can relax you two! If I wanted you dead, I would have killed you a long time ago"! The stranger, had assured them.. "I wont ask again creature! (Key insisted). So for the last time, who in the deep dark sea, are you"?! "Take it easy! (Said the creature).. Let's just say, I knew both your grandparents"! "Who are you, really?! (Kylynn interrupted). What do you want from us, tell us right now"!?! "ME?! Who am I? (The creature replied).. My name is Kavizious! You mean you honestly don't know who I am"? (He asked). The pair of them.. "NO, Never! (Replied the Prince).. So what do you want from us"? (Asked Key). "I don't want anything from you two! Well, not yet anyways"!

Kavizious went on to tell Key and Kylynn the story of Keys mother, and her parents. He told them Cynthia's entire past. He told them all about the war and the great battle, he told them about their black magic, and how it's in his blood. "Are you ok"? (Kylynn asked Key).. "Yah, I'm fine! I wanted to know, right?! I will be just fine! (Key said). I just don't understand,why my parents would hide all this from me?! They obviously don't trust me enough to be able to handle the truth"! (Key said). "No, Key! (Kylynn said to him).. I'm sure there's a logical explanation, I'm sure of it"! "Listen Key, (Kavizious interrupted). You have the power to locate the Lost Trident of Tolkien. Together we could rule this realm! You could be what you always feared you could never be Key! (Kavizious told him).. I was sent here to protect you, together we can rule this realm. With me by your side, there would be no stopping us Key, you could be invincible. You have black magic coursing through your veins Key. It's your birth right Key! You are a Sea God, Prince Key"! (Kavizious told him).. Hoping he could trick the Prince into tapping into his dark side.. "You could make you OctaGod grandparents very proud if you. Except my offer, and let me help you bring forth your very, very powerful black magic, and embrace your evil dark side young Key, like I said.. It's your God's given birth right"! Kylynn was never so scared in her life! "We have to leave Key! (Kylynn whispered). Please Key, we have to go, NOW! This was a huge mistake coming here, and I want to go back home Key"! (Kylynn begged him).. Key was very quiet for a moment, not saying anything! He was trying to wrap his head around everything that the creature Kavizious had just told him. "Come on Key, we have to go Now"! (Kylynn demanded). Key finally snapped out of his little trans that Kavizious had over him. "Leave us alone, you filthy creature"! (Prince Key shouted).. As he grabbed Kylynn by the hand and they swam away as fast as their muscular torso's, (that were built for the deep dark, salt watery caves of the abyss), would take them! When the duo made it back to the kingdom were it was safe, they didn't say one word to each other. Kylynn just hugged Key, and nodded goodbye, as she swam away from him, leaving him alone in the garden. Kylynn had departed from the Prince, at the same exact place that the two had met earlier that same morning, very early that morning!

The next few days were very difficult for Prince Key! Now that he was seventeen, he was considered a man and he had to take on much more responsibilities. He also had to go through their ancient ritual of crossing over into manhood. The Royal Tournament of the Vflosiken Ceremony.. It's a test of skill and strength, a measurement of your hand to hand combat abilities of only the men of Mordainia. With Key being half Mordainian and half OctaGod, as well as being royalty, (The future King), they were going to expect a lot from him at the ceremony! While Key was training for his showcase in the royal coming of age tournament, you could tell something was wrong. Something was bothering him and it was very noticeable, the Prince was not acting like himself. All he kept thinking about was that creature Kavizious and what he said, if he had the Trident, then he would definitely win the tournament in the ceremony with no problem. He couldn't stop thinking that he wouldn't have to worry about embarrassing himself or his family! No one would be able to beat him if he had the Trident, he would defeat them all. "What's wrong my son"?! (King Maximus asked Prince Key).. As he was removing his helmet after their army training session, was over. "Please Key, you're my son, I know when there's something troubling you, please tell me what it is my Prince"!? (He asked Key).. "I don't know father! (Replied the Prince).. I guess I'm just feeling the stress of the ceremony and living up to grandfather's legacy"! (Key replied). "You will do just fine Key, your stronger than any soldier in our army. Your name alone brings greatness, you're a born leader Key, Even if you don't see yet, it's there my son! Deep down in your soul.. As long as you follow your heart, and learn to believe in yourself and always trust your instincts, I promise you'll forever and always, make the right decision for your people and your kingdom! As long as you believe deep down that your making the right choice, don't ever be afraid to follow your heart my son! (He told his son).. You will make a terrific King one day Key! Just know this one thing my son, I'm proud of you my son! Just always be true to your family, and true to who you are Key".. (He told his son).. "But how father"!? (He asked his father the King).. With such a depressing tone in his voice, he continued.. "How can I be true to who I am, when I don't even know who or what I am father?! My whole entire life, you and mother have been hiding the truth from me"?! Key kept right on, ranting and raving.. He kept right on and bombarded his father, the King, with his hostel questioning. "I know I have black magic coursing through my veins, I know I have evil running ramped in my bloodline, and I know my grandmother and grandfather on my mother's side, were evil sorceress and you and mother, well especially mother are afraid that I'll end up like one of them"! Key's emotions were running very high. He couldn't stop wondering about his OctaGod side of him. "Of course we are afraid for you Key, your our son"! (Said the King). Key's emotions were all over the place, racing along with his thoughts. "We love you Key, me and your mother just want what's best for you! I don't care what else you got running through your veins, because all I care is that you have me and your mother and the greatest king of all time, my father, your grandfather's blood pumping stronger through your heart and soul. So you don't have to stress out about failing, because no matter what happen, you will still be our son! You have the right to chose Key. You chose to make the right or the wrong choices in life my son! Your mother made the right choices, and believe me Key, her choices were a lot harder to make than any you have or will ever face in your entire life, and your mother, Cynthia, she's a Full OctaGod!! (Maximus said). To his son Key, the Prince.. And so did half of the kingdom. They all had choices to make, and they chose good like the rest of us! Don't you get it my son? (Max asked him).. We all can make our own choices in life Key, but it's up to you and I, to make the right decisions, and protect our kingdom and it's people, at any costs, my son"!

Later that evening, Key was at the center of the kingdom's garden with Kylynn, thinking and telling her about he and his father the King's conversation earlier. He decided his father was right! Just because his mothers parents were vicious Warlocks, didn't mean he would become one, himself.. "I don't care what that beast Kavizious is trying to tell me about it being my birth right and all, and I don't care that I have black magic powers surging through my body. It doesn't mean I have to use it for evil Kylynn"! (Key said). To his friend, as the two of them swam off, out of the garden and straight outside the kingdoms walls, to go hunt in the deep dark caves of the abyss. "Well did your father ask you were you heard about your mothers parents key"? (Kylynn asked the Prince).. Did you tell him about Kavizious"? You could tell she was very nervous for her life long friend Key's life.. But actually, to Kylynn, Key was more than a friend, he was the love of her life! She really liked Prince Key and was hoping to soon bring their relationship to the next level. Except Kylynn was nervous to kiss the prince, she had never kissed a boy before and was afraid Key would reject her, because she was a couple years older than he is, and was very inexperienced. But what Kylynn didn't know yet, that Prince Key was himself, developing feeling for her as well, Key was actually falling in love with Kylynn!

Kylynn has been in love with the Prince, for as far back as she could remember. Kylynn had always wanted to kiss him ever since they were little, but she was afraid if her father Mateos ever found out, he would forbid her to ever see him again, and she valued their friendship way to much to ever let that happen. Kylynn had always wanted to tell Key how she felt about him, but she figured it best to just leave it alone and stay quiet for now, so She would just remain Key's best friend, and keep him in her life forever!

Prince Key and Kylynn, were on their way back from their little hunting trip out in the caves, completely unaware that Kavizious was following them. He has been stocking them from a distance, from within the shadows. He has been watching Key's every move for days now, ever since he tried bringing forth the Prince's dark side. Kavizious was absolutely determined to get his slimy hand on the Trident, and he knew that the best way to accomplish this, is to go through these two kids, one way or the other. If Kavizious couldn't persuade Key to explore his dark black magic side, and help him channel it, then he would just have to kill him, and take the girl. He would use her as bait, to control her father Mateos (the only other soul in thee entire Eight Sea's, other than Key), and make him retrieve the Trident, in exchange for his daughter.

CHAPTER
12

BACK IN THE KINGDOM, IN the palace, King Maximus and his wife Queen Cynthia, were discussing their son Prince Key's behavior lately. "I'm telling you Cynthia, (Maximus said). He knows all about your father and mother, and what had happened! I know he's your son and your only trying to protect him no matter what the cost. I get that Cynthia, I truly do, but he's a man now my love, and he deserves to hear about your side of his family, from you, his mother. I know it's tough my dear, but we raised a wonderful young man Cynthia. We did a damn fine job, and I think we owe it to him to finally tell him everything and trust he'll make the right choices, just like his mother and half the kingdoms people did. (King Maximus assured his wife, Queen Cynthia).. He will take after you and I, not your mother, nor your father Cynthia, I promise! You broke the cycle, the chain of evil in your family has been busted, by you. It started and ended with your parents. (he told her).. You yourself, you proved you can make your own destiny in life.. That's why I fell in love with you Cynthia! You are truly the greatest person I have ever known, Mordainian or OctaGod".. Cynthia smiled, hugged her husband, and said.. "I know Max, my love, your absolutely right"! (She said). With a sigh ... "He's a terrific young man, because he's just like you, his father! (Haha).. They both smiled, and laughed a little. "OK, OK, I'll do it"! (She said finally).. After a long, dramatic pause.. Cynthia decided it was time to have the talk about her parent's with him. "Ok Max, I'll talk to him, I promise"! Max smiled, hugged his wife and said.. "Thank you Cynthia, my love. Your making the right decision, I assure you"! (He told her confidently)..

Over in the barn area of the sea horse's and sea dragon's stable's, Prince Key and Kylynn were feeding Zar and the rest of them, just quietly talking about what's been going on lately. "Key, I'm nervous about the disgusting beast creature from the other day, Kavizious. What if he comes back Key"?! (She asked franticly).. "He wont, I promise! (Key replied). Besides if he ever did come back, I'd kill him"! (He promised her).. "Well, have you at least told your father or mother about out encounter with that scary creature Key"?! (She asked him).. "No Ky, I didn't! (Key replied). As he stopped doing what he was doing, and grabbing a hold by both of Kylynn hands, with his own, and said.. "listen to me Ky, please!? (He said). With a look of desperation.. I'm not going to let anything happen to you! (He assured her).. But I'm also not afraid of that creature! I truly, honestly think its best, if we don't say anything Ky! We don't tell my parents, we don't tell your parents about Kavizious, at all. OK Kylynn!?! I'm serious, they will lock this place completely down! No one in, no one out. This place will be locked up so tight, and you and I will both be stuck with bodyguards! Is that what you want Kylynn?! Because I sure as hell don't"! (He told her).. "No! that's not what I want Key"! (She replied). "Good, because we wouldn't be able to do this. (He said). As he leaned in, and kissed Kylynn for the first time, ever! Key was so nervous as he kissed her for his first time, as well.. Not only was it their first kiss together, it was both their first kiss, kiss, ever! During the kiss, Key kept opening his eyes and checking if she was looking back at him, but she wasn't, her eyes were closed, Kylynn was so happy! She couldn't believe that Key was finally kissing her, she's has dreamed of this moment for as far back as she could remember. At that moment, Kylynn knew she wanted to be with Key for the rest of her life! She would die for him. "OK, ok, I won't say anything to my father Key, I promise"! (She said blushing).. Once he stopped kissing her, Kylynn was smiling uncontrollably. "Thank you Ky! (Whispered the Prince).. As he leaned in, and kissed her, again..

At that moment, Kylynns father Mateos had entered the stables. "What won't you say anything to me about"?! (He asked them). Catching the two of them of guard, both completely acting like they had something to hide. "Na - Na - Nothing sir"! (The Prince stuttered).. Key quickly answered her father Mateos, as he backed away from his daughter Kylynn as fast as he could. "Nothing huh? Well, it doesn't look like nothing"! (Said Kylynn's father, Mateos).. "Father, Stop"! (Said his daughter Kylynn).. And with quick thinking, she said.. "Don't tell you we just had our first kiss! (She said). To he father.. Is that what you wanted to hear, are you happy now father"?! Turning to Key and winking. Kylynn had succeeded in embarrassing her father Mateos. "You made our first kiss very awkward now father, thanks"! "Oh, umm, I'm sorry, I - I - I didn't mean to intrude! (Mateos stuttered).. He felt so uncomfortable, that he turned to exit. "I'll see you later on Kylynn. (He said). As he went to leave. "Sorry sir"! Key added, hoping that Mateos wasn't mad at him.. "No Key, I'm the one who's sorry son! (Mateos said). I apologize if I made you feel uncomfortable in anyway, both of you"! Mateos reached his hand out to shake Prince key's, and just as he was about to release his grip, he actually squeezed tighter, pulled the prince in closely and whispered.. "You better not brake her heart boy-O"! then he let go of Key's hand. "I wont sir, I promise"! (Prince Key, replied).. Mateos looked to his daughter, then back to the Prince. "Good! (Kylynn's father said to him).. That's all I ask son, we do this, and we'll be just fine! Do we understand each other"?! (He asked him).. "I give you my word"! (Key assured him).. Mateos nodded and left. "Oh thank the god's"! (Kylynn said). She had an instant sigh of relief once her father left, she and Key both did.

Now that the two soon to be lovers were alone again, Kylynn swam over to the Prince and kissed him. "I've been waiting a long time for you to do that"! (She softly whispered).. Key was honestly taken aback by that piece of news. "Well, Good! (He told her).. Because I'm starting to fall in love with you Ky"! (Her eyes widened).. Kylynn was shocked to hear Key say this to her. "I want to be with you, I love you Kylynn"! (Admitted the Prince).. "OH Key! (She replied). I love you too"! Throwing her arms around him, as they kissed so passionately. "Oh Key"! (She moaned). As he moved lower and started kissing Kylynn's neck. The two of them were so use to each other, that neither one of them were nervous in the least bit as he made love too her throughout the night! The two of them spent the night in the open night waters, in a secluded area of the open part of the back of the stables, where Key and Ky had been coming to be alone throughout the years, either by themselves or together. It was the most magical night of either one of their lives. Kylynn couldn't help but think just how amazing it was! It was as if he had been making love to her their entire lives. The two were so in tune with one an other, it was as if it was meant to be. The Sea God's had aligned the earth's waters, with the stars of Mid World's Universe, to bring these two together! Key just kept thinking, on how he was going to marry this girl. She would be his wife, at any cost. "I love you Ky".. (He whispered to her).. "Oh Key, I love you too"!(She replied).

The following day, Key was Training with his father, King Maximus and his head of his Royal Army, Mateos, (who is also his fathers best friend and his own mentor/ instructor, and not to mention, Kylynn's father), were out training, when he said.. "Did the King know that his son Key and my daughter were seeing each other"? (Mateos asked Maximus). As he swung his sword over his head and then into a forward motion towards Maximus. "No, I didn't"! (He replied). Blocking Mateoses sword with his own, and then returning the favor with a thrust of his own sword counter attack back at his friend Mateos. "I thought there might be something between the two, but I wasn't sure"! (Admitted the King).. "Oh yes, (Replied Mateos). I caught your son, kissing my daughter out in the stables last night". "Is this true my son, is it true what Mateos has said"?! (Asked the King).. Yes father, it's true! (The Prince admitted).. I love her! I was hoping down the way I could actually get your blessing in asking for your daughter Kylynn's hand in marriage Mateos"!?! (Prince Key said).. To the man he has known his entire life. "You know I have the utmost respect for you and your family Mateos! (Key told him).. I truly hate the way you had to find out, I would have liked it if me and Kylynn had gotten the chance to speak to you and your wife, and then also you and I man to man! (Key said). Then of course we would have came and spoke to you father, you and mother, but it just so happens that last night was our first kiss, and".. "It's ok Key"! (Mateos interrupted). Putting his hand on Key's shoulder. "You and Kylynn have my blessing! (Mateos told the Prince).. But it's not me you need to worry about Key, it's my wife Aleina, Ky's mother"! (Hahaha)! Mateos and his father King Maximus laughed.. "She's the one you should be worried about"! (He said). "Yah and don't forget about your mother"! (Added the King).. (Hahaha)! They laughed again.. "Yah you got those two you should be worried about.. Just a little word of advice, from me too you, my son"!

(Said the King).. "Yah thanks for the encouraging words guys, no really, thank you.. I truly appreciate it"! (Prince Key replied, sarcastically)..

The next few weeks, Prince Key and his new love, Kylynn, were more inseparable than ever. Their fathers were just messing with Key that day, making him worry about he and Ky's mothers, but that wouldn't be the case, Key soon came to find out.. Both sets of parents, couldn't be happier for their children. Mateoses wife Aleina, thought the sea of Prince Key and his royal family, she was so happy for her daughter and her future husband. It also went without say, just how much Key's parents thought of Kylynn and her family, they were the closest thing to family they had, and couldn't be happier that they would soon be family, after their children wed. "I'm so happy for our son Maximus"! (Cynthia said). To her husband, the King with the biggest smile upon her face. "Our son has found his true love"! The two family's were celebrating their unity through their children's new found love. "You will make my daughter Ky a very good husband Key. (Mateos said). I will be proud to call you son"! Just then, Key's father, the king, was so full of joy as he approached his son Key and Mateos and slapped them in their backs simultaneously as they were talking, and said.. "Tonight we drink and celebrate the up and coming unity of our two family's"! Then the King, pulled out his magical, water resistant, piece pipe, and with a magical water proof flame spell, he was able to take a toke and passed it to his friend Mateos. It wall the ultimate sign of respect and loyalty when you share the piece pipe with the King. "Come my family and my new family, tonight we drink and the men smoke the piece pipe of unity"! (Said King Maximus). "I couldn't be happier for our children and our family's Max". (Mateos said). To his friend the King, as he took a puff off the piece pipe and passed it back to the King. "I" (Replied King Maximus).. Taking another toke off the piece pipe and passing it to his son Prince Key. "I couldn't agree more Mateos, my friend, (Maximus admitted), I couldn't agree more"!

The following morning, Queen Cynthia went looking for her son. "There you are Key"! (Cynthia said). As she seen her son all by himself in the courtyard by the royal garden. "Good, I'm glad your by yourself my son. Are you ok my son, is there anything wrong my child"? (She asked him).. "No, no! I'm just thinking mother! I like it here, its very peaceful"! (He told her).. "Oh, ok, just checking on you my son! (She replied). I did want to speak with you for a moment though Key".. (She said). With a very serious tone in her voice.. "I think it's time you heard about my side of your family Key my son! I think it's time you find out the real truth about the OctaGod bloodline.. Come my Prince, let's talk". Cynthia was very nervous to have this talk with her son, she didn't want him to feel like he was different or evil in any way. Cynthia has only tried to shield him from the truth all these years out of love, he was her son and wanted to protect him by any means necessary! She just realized she might have kept him from the truth a little to long. Key is an adult and needs to hear everything from his mother Cynthia, only she knows the whole truth! "You know I love you Key my son, right"!?! (She began). As they swam to the middle of the kingdoms coral reef garden. "Of course I do mother! (Key replied). I love you too"! Cynthia took a deep breath and began her story.. She told Key everything! She told him about how his grandfather, King Keyira had killed her mother, after she had caused the death of his wife Muriel. She told him all about her father Cyris, and her mother Elisabeth. She told him about the spell they created for when they died, it brought them back from the after life, she told him all about the hell realm and that's where they met Kavizious. She told him how they're responsible for bringing him to our world, along with hundreds of thousands of other sea hell demons, and how they tried to over throw the King and destroy the kingdom and how she and his father had to stop them, and how his grandfather gave his life to save the kingdom and its people.. But, she told him some good things too though. She told him about how her and his father met, she told him all about Peretta and how wonderful she was, and how much she loved her. Cynthia didn't leave anything out! She even told her son how when she was a little girl and lived in the caves outside the kingdoms walls, how she would dream of being a part of the kingdom one day. As Prince Key's mother Cynthia was done telling him everything, she was crying! Cynthia was so ashamed of her past, she was so scared that her past would one day come back and harm her family, and worse of all, her son! She didn't want anything to happen to him. "I love you so much my son! (She cried). I know I shouldn't have shielded you from the truth, but I was afraid"! Prince Key paused for a moment, then threw his arms around his mother and hugged her. "I love you too! (Key replied). Thank you mother, thank you for telling me everything! I know your scared that I'll get hurt, but

I promise you, I wont let you or father down! You and father raised me right mother, I'm your son! So there's no way anyone could force me to do anything I don't want too. No one could ever make me be any other way than like you and father. I love you mother, and I promise I will make you proud"! (Key assured his mother, the Queen).. "Oh Key.. (Cynthia cried). I'm so proud of you now my son"! (She told him).. Cynthia couldn't be happier, or more proud of her son than she was, at that moment. That's when she knew, that her son Key, would be just fine in life, she knew she didn't have to worry about him, ever again. Key was a strong young man who will be able to protect himself and the entire kingdom. Cynthia could actually see it in her sons eyes. Key is the hope of the kingdoms future, and she had no doubt in her mind, what so ever, that Key can and will profile his destiny with ease!

After Prince Key and his mother, Queen Cynthia said their goodbyes for now, Key swam off to go find Kylynn, while Queen Cynthia had stayed behind at the royal coral garden, and was thinking about her and her son Key's conversation, and how glad she was that they had discussed everything. She was feeling that it actually brought her and her son closer together now. Cynthia couldn't help but smile. She was just about to leave when all of the sudden, she froze. The Queen had fell into one of her deep trans states, like before. This is the first time this has happened in a very long time! It caught her by surprise, Cynthia thought those were behind her. In her vision, Cynthia saw the magical, Lost Trident of Tolkien. It was surrounded by a very bright, glowing red light. that's when her vision went from bad to worse, it changed to the sea hell demon, Kavizious, with Trident in hand, he was attacking her kingdom and it's people, while her husband and son King Maximus and Prince Key, along with Mateos and the royal army were fighting off Kavizious and his sea hell demon army! Cynthia's vision was flashing back and forth between the glowing red Trident and the horrible war with the demon army. It was flashing back and forth so fast, and then all of the sudden it was gone, she had snapped out of her trans states. Once Cynthia had came back too, she was very dizzy and crying hysterically.. Cynthia began to scream in fear! She knew somehow, some way, that Kavizious was back, and would hurt her family! Cynthia was absolutely petrified, she screamed for her husband Maximus. Cynthia had figured she couldn't hide these visions any longer! She was hysterically crying, screaming in such fear, calling out to her husband, King Maximus, and her son, Prince Key, for help, but there wasn't anyone close enough to hear Queen Cynthia's screams!

That's when she felt it, the bone chilling, cold sensation of fear. Then she heard it, the voice sent quivers down her spine! "Hello Cynthia"! (Said Kavizious). Creeping out from the shadows.. "Oh my Gods, it, it, it cant be"! (Cynthia stuttered, in reply).. Turning around and coming face to face with her absolute worst nightmare, under the sea. "Oh I assure you my dear, it is I, Kavizious"! (He answered). "No one can hear you scream Cynthia so you might as well not even bother.. Besides, I'm not here to kill you, so you can relax"! (He told her). As he slithered his way around, circling her, like she was his pray. "What, You thought you had vanished me back to the realm of Sea Hell"?! (He asked rhetorically).. Well Cynthia, I assure you this is no dream, I have made my way back to this realm, because we have some unfinished business my child"! "Don't you dear call me that! Show some respect for the Queen of the Tolkien Sea"! (Queen Cynthia demanded).. "So you're the Queen now, huh?! Well Queen Cynthia, we have some unresolved business to attend too". (Kavizious said). "Oh yah, and what might that be Kavizious, what business could I possibly have unresolved with you, other than you not being trapped in Sea Hell for eternity"!? (Cynthia replied sarcastically).. "The Lost Trident of Tolkien"! (Kavizious answered). Cynthia's eyes widened, "I knew it"! (She said). Threw her teeth, as she shook her head back and forth. "Good, I have your attention I see"! (Kavizious Admitted). That he had noticed her change in Cynthia's demeanor. "I tried to keep you out of it for now, but I can't get your son Key to give in to his dark side, his sinister, dark magic destiny of which your parents would want of him. So it seems to me that, that would make it, your problem Queen Cynthia"! (Kavizious said). His voice getting louder and scarier!! "I want that damn Trident Cynthia, and your going to get either you son Key or Mateos retrieve it for you, and you will bring it to me! They are the only two, (in one way or another), who know where it is located.. My patients are wearing thin! (Kavizious told her).. If you want your family to live, then you will do what your told and get me that Trident or I will kill them all and then you"! (He threatened).. "I will never help you Kavizious"! (Queen Cynthia replied). "That's not a very healthy decision Cynthia! (He said). If you don't help me get that Trident, soon,

I won't wait long before I start killing your family, I'll start with your son Key and his little girlfriend. What's her name again, Oh yeah, that's right, it's Kylynn, that's her name correct"!? (Kavizious said). In such a crude, sarcastic, tone.. "I assure you Cynthia, I am not bluffing! You have two days, to deliver me the Trident! Then I start killing your family and your people". (Kavizious promised).. "May the Sea God's smite you back to Sea Hell Kavizious"! (Cynthia hexed him).. "Hahaha"! (Kavizious laughed). "I'm from Sea Hell my dear, and I promise you, I will bring the Sea Hell realm to you, and unleash it upon your kingdom, and the entire Tolkien Sea. Either get me the Trident, or face the wrath of your consequences"! (Kavizious promised). As he disappeared back into the shadows. Cynthia broke down crying hysterically again. "I knew it.. She thought to herself out loud.. I knew my family would never be safe"!

CHAPTER

13

LATER ON, BACK AT THE kingdoms palace, Cynthia was trying to figure out what she should do. She had decided not to say anything yet, she was going to try and figure it out on her own. Deep down she knew she couldn't wait to long though, if she couldn't figure it out soon then she would have to come clean to her husband and son. "I just don't want anyone to get hurt, I know I can take care of it own my own"! (Cynthia said, to Aleina).. She was confiding in her friend, about what had just happened to her. "I have to handle this situation without them Aleina, I cant let them get hurt because of my parents. There's just no way I can tell Maximus yet, I will if I cant do it on my own first, but for now I cant! What should I do Aleina"? (Cynthia asked her).. "You need to tell Maximus Cynthia, you cant keep this from him. He and Mateos can help, they can protect us, Your husband is the King Cynthia, he will know what to do". (She replied). Aleina wanted her to tell her husband King Maximus so he and her husband Mateos could handle the situation, besides, she didn't want to have to keep anything from her husband Mateos. Aleina was not good at keeping secrets. "No Aleina! (Cynthia Demanded). Don't you get it Aleina, they will go to war! Our husbands have already survived two of these demon wars, I cant let them a third time Aleina, they might not make it this time, and I know I don't want to lose my husband or child so I have to stop Kavizious on my own, before anything happens. I'm going to go kill Kavizious myself, I'll create a spell to send him back to hell for good, I just need to find one"! (Cynthia said). "Well then, looks like I'm going with you then Cynthia, me and you will just have to go kill this beast together because you cant go alone, I wont let you"! "You're not coming with me Aleina"! (She replied). "yes I am Cynthia, it's either I'm going with you or I'm telling my husband, and you know he will tell the King". (Aleina threatened, but only out of love).. "You cant come with me Aleina it's just to dangerous"! (Cynthia said). "YES I AM Cynthia! (Aleina yelled at the Queen).. Listen to me Cynthia, I love you, and I love my family. If I let you swim off by yourself and you don't succeed on killing Kavizious, well then not only do I lose you, my best friend, but then he's coming for the rest of us and without warning so both our families will die and that's just not going to happen.. I don't care if you don't think its safe for me to go with you Cynthia, there's just absolutely no way I will ever be able to continue living without my husband or daughter, so either way, I'm coming with you, and that's that! It's not safe any way you look at it, so please just let me help you Cynthia?! You have a better chance with me by your side and you know that! Our husbands trained us well with the royal army, you know we can do it, but only if we do it together Cynthia"! (Aleina pleaded with her).. Cynthia could see what Aleina was thinking, she knew if she didn't let her friend Aleina go with her, than she knew she would absolutely tell their husbands. She knew Aleina was way too scared for her to let her do this on her own. She was going to have to give in and let her friend come with her and help. "Fine you little, Ahhhhhh" (Cynthia let out an aggravated grunt).. "Yeah, yeah, yeah, I know, I know, I'm a bitch! (Aleina interrupted her).. But I'm a bitch that can help you Cynthia, and you know it"! (She told Cynthia). "Fine Aleina! I said You can come, jeeshhh! I mean what else do you want me to say Aleina, you can come, (Cynthia told her).. But.." Aleina swam over to Cynthia and hugged her.. "But what"? (Aleina asked). As she finally let go from hugging the queen.. "But. (Cynthia began again).. We need to come up with a plan! Your going to have to follow my every move, and follow my instructions to the tee, I'm serious Aleina! (Cynthia commanded). I can't lose you! I would never forgive myself"! Cynthia had the saddest look on her face when she said that. "I will Cynthia, I promise! (Aleina replied). Nothing will happen to me with the plan we come up with! Besides, I'll be with you, you'll make sure nothing happens to us, I just know it. Not to mention that I've trained more than half my life, in hand to hand combat with my husband Mateos. (Aleina said, proudly)..

Plus, you've seen me with a sword Cynthia, you know how good I am! Not to sound self centered or anything, but I'm probably the best swordsman in the entire kingdom! Well, swordswoman"! (She corrected herself).. With a playful smile and shove in the shoulder, trying to lighten her friend, the Queen's mood a little bit. There are no two stronger woman, under all of thee entire Tolkien Sea, than Queen Cynthia and her best friend Aleina.. "We will kill this Sea Hell Beast, Kavizious"! (Aleina assured her).. "Yeah we will.. (Cynthia had replied).. But how, is the question Aleina"!

Meanwhile, on the outskirts of the kingdom, deep within the dark caves, Key and Kylynn were on their way, looking for the Lost Trident of Tolkien. Key needed to find the lost Trident and kill Kavizious with it, before the beast could hurt anyone that he loved. "We have to find this Trident before Kavizious does Ky"! (Key said). "We will Key, I just know we will! (Kylynn assured the Prince).. I believe in you Key, I always have, and I always will"! (She said). With a smile that formed across her face, as she looked into Keys eyes. Key looked a way real quick as if someone called out to him, "What is it Key"? (Kylynn asked). "I just have this feeling in my gut Ky! (Prince Key admitted).. It's like I know exactly where to go. I feel like the Trident is calling to me, I feel like I'm being drawn to it like a magnet. It's like it wants me to find it"..

By this time, Prince Key and his love kylynn, were as far away from the kingdom than they ever have been, ever, in either one of their entire lives! "I'm scared Key"! (Whispered Ky). As she nervously, grabbed the Prince's arm, and squeezed tightly, pulling him in close to her. "It's not that much farther form here, I promise Kylynn! (The Prince promised).. I can feel it!! (He said) Speeding off up ahead.. We're almost there Ky"! But what the two young lovers didn't know was that Kavizious had been tracking their every move! He followed them, he knew they would lead him to the Trident.

CHAPTER

14

BACK AT THE KINGDOM, KING Maximus had noticed something wasn't right. "Something's wrong! He thought to himself.. My wife the Queen and my son the Prince, have been goon all day, and that's not like them"! The King knew that they were not together either, because he had seen his son the Prince, with his girlfriend Kylynn and they were heading off together to be alone, but he did not know the whereabouts, of his wife Cynthia. Just then.. The Kings friend Mateos had come rushing over to the King, frantically screaming to him. "Maximus my King, my wife and daughter are missing! They both have been gone all day, and that's not like either one of them, never mind both of them at the same time. It's just not like them Max"! (Mateos said). To King Maximus.. The King was in a state of shock, when he finally snapped out of it, he answered; "I Mateos, I hear you my friend!(King Maximus replied).. My wife and son are both missing too Mateos"! (Maximus said).. "But, I did see our children Key and Ky together, heading off to be alone. So I know their ok, I believe"! (He told his worried friend).. "So, that must mean our wives are off together then Max. The Gods only know doing what though! (Mateos interrupted). So what do we do Maximus, its your call my King?! I mean, where could they possibly be, they have to be together, don't you think Max"?! (He asked the King).. "Oh They're together alright, which means their safe and no need to worry, yet"! (Replied the King).. Mateoses thoughts were racing a million miles a minute. "Calm down my friend! They are all very strong, my son is with your daughter and you and I both trust him enough to keep your daughter Kylynn protected, and your wife Aleina and my Cynthia are as tough as they come, you know they got each others backs"! (The King assured his friend Mateos).. "I know Max, your right, thank you my friend"! (Mateos said). Feeling a lot better now that he talked to his friend Maximus.. "Let's just be cautious and go look for them, gather the men and gear up! (Commanded the King).. We're going to go get our families back. We will find them Mateos, I promise you"! (Maximus said). "I, my King! Where do you think our wives are Max, where could they possibly be"?! (He asked the King). "I'm not quite sure, but I think I might just know. I have a funny feeling their were they shouldn't be! (King Maximus responded).. Quick Mateos, we haven't much time. We have to go, now! Round up the men"! "What, what is it Max, please"!?! (Mateos pleaded, with his friend).. "Something my son had said to me the other day. I think we might have a visitor amongst us, Again"! (Said the King). "GASP!! You don't think"?! (Mateos said frantically).. "Yes Mateos, Kavizious is back"! (Said the King). "So what, you think Cynthia and Aleina went to stop him"? (Asked Mateos). "Yes"! (He replied). And possibly the kids too"! "We, we, we have to stop them Max"! (Mateos stuttered).. "where did you bury the Trident Mateos?! We are going to have to go get it to save our families and defeat Kavizious! We have to get to it before he does Mateos"! (Maximus said). "Are you sure my King, are you absolutely sure you want to do this"?! (Mateos asked him).. "No, I really don't Mateos, but our families are in grave danger, we have too"! "Let's go men, hurry up, we have to move"! (Mateos ordered his men).. As they exited the Kingdom on their Sea Dragons and Sea horses. "Lead the way Mateos, lead us to the Trident".. (said the King).. As he road up on the side, past his men to the front of the troop to lead his men into battle if need be!

Before they left to find their families and bring them home, King Maximus addressed the royal soldiers along with the people of the Kingdom. "I think it's time we get and keep the Trident with us my people, and keep it at the Kingdom from here on out! (Admitted the King).. Every single time we bury it, we have to go get it again to either use it or protect it. Well not any more, this time we get it, AND WE KEEP IT!! We will protect it with our lives! We will use it to get rid of our enemies once and for all! (Declared the King). I the King and Mateos, will lead our men at the head of the brigade, as we head off on our journey to save mine and

Mateoses families, and hopefully kill Kavizious for good.. But to do that we need to go get the Trident, and only Mateos knows where it is. We will go get it, the Trident will protect the kingdom and all the people, as long as we protect it, and keep it safe! We keep it out of harms way, the Trident will keep us out of harms way. We need to keep it out of the hands of our enemies, times have changed! It's time we except the Tridents power, instead of being scared of what might happen! We need to embrace it into our lives. (Declared the King).. We the people will protect the Trident with our lives, and in return, it will protect us"! "Yaaaaaa"!!! Everyone cheered as the King, along with Mateos and the Royal Army, disappearing into the shadows of the caves, as the rest of the royal soldiers locked down the kingdom and went into extreme defense mode, no one would be able to get in, nor out of the kingdom, it was virtually impossible!

Maximus and Mateos, road ahead of the small army of Mordainian and OctaGod soldiers, riding on their royal sea horses and sea dragons. "Will will locate the Trident and find our wives and children Mateos"! (Maxims assured his friend).. "I, my King"! (He had replied).. But what King Maximua and Mateos didn't realize was that they were about to go up against an Army of crazy Sea Monkeys that Kavizious had assembled previously. Kavizious has been obsessed and determined to crush this pathetic realm of insignificant sea creatures, as he would call them!

Meanwhile, Key and Kylynn were almost to the Trident, when they heard it. They heard the cries os Kylynn's mother Aleina. She was screaming her name, over and over again! "Kylynn, where are you Ky? Kylynn please, it's your mother, I love you Ky.. Please Kylynn, were are you"!?! She was calling out for her daughter.. That's when they came across them! "Oh my Gods, there you two are! Thank the Gods your alive"! (Aleina said). Once she and Cynthia seen their two children. "Mother"! (Young Kylynn replied).. As she swam over and hugged her mother. Queen Cynthia embraced her son, Prince Key as well. "What are you two doing way out here Key"!? (Queen Cynthia demanded).. "What am I doing here? What are you two doing out here mother"?! (Demanded the Prince).. "OH my Gods! (Cynthia cried). He came to see you didn't he Key"?! (She asked her son). "What, who?? I have no idea what you are talking about mother"! (Key said). Fully aware of what she was speaking about. Knowing exactly that his mother had meant Kavizious! "Who, what? (She mocked). Cut it out Key! You damn well know who I mean! Kavizious! He had came and seen you, didn't he Key?! Why didn't you tell me my son, you should have came to me Key, I could have helped?! He didn't talk you into getting the Trident for him, did he"?! (She asked frantically).. Hoping that was not the case! "No, absolutely not! (He replied). How could you even ask me that mother, of course not"!?! "He would never my Queen! He was just trying to protect us and all of the Kingdom from that Monster"! (Kylynn interrupted). As she was sticking up for Key. "I was just doing what I thought you and or father would do"! (Said the Prince). "Oh, and what may that be"?! (Asked the Queen).. "Exactly what you and Miss Aleina are doing right now mother! Just as you are on your way to kill Kavizious, so are We"! The Prince had outed, them all.. "I have a plan.. I'm going to go get the Trident before Kavizious does, and send him back to sea hell with it.. But your going have to trust me mother, you too Miss Aleina! I am going to trick Kavizious into thinking I want to explore my evil dark side, and that I will give him the Trident! That's when I kill him with it"!! (Said the Prince). With confidence.. "Key, do you have any idea how ridiculous that sounds?! (Cynthia shouted). Kavizious isn't from this world my son! He's a hell demon from a sea hell realm, you cant kill him Key, he's already dead"!

(Clap - clap - clap).. They all turned to see who was clapping when all of the sudden, Kavizious appeared from up out of the shadows, he wasn't alone either! He had a few of his soldiers with him, some of his sea monkey minions. "Now that's a good plan kid! (He said to the Prince).. But there's just one minor problem with it, It wont work! Good try though".. (Kavizious snickered). As his sea monkey minions, surrounded Cynthia and the others. "So let me see if I understand this correctly". (Kavizious said). Circling the Queen and them as if they were his pray. "You were going to try and kill me yourself, you and your little girlfriend? (he asked the Prince). And you, Queen Cynthia, you and your little friend were going to try and send me back to my realm? Hahaha".. Kaviziouses laughs faded away, and this look of death and destruction came over his face, and with a booming voice that sent shivers down everyone's backs, he said.. "I'll NEVER go back, and this world will soon be mine!! You know something Cynthia, I'm very disappointed in you! I thought you would be somewhat of a challenge for me. Guess I was wrong! (He said, to the Queen).. No, your not wrong, you were right Kavizious, I am a challenge! Cynthia, had snapped right back at him.. Taking Peretta's knife from her hair, and in one quick motion, she was behind one of Kaviziouses sea monkeys, and with the blade to his throat, she applied pressure, and slit it. Cynthia then stuck her blade into the heart of the next closest minion, as the sea creature collapsed. Cynthia picked up his spear that he had dropped, She wasn't done! She cocked her arm back, and with all her might, she heaved the spear into another charging soldier of Kaviziouses. Kavizoius let her go for a mew minutes, until she nearly killed his entire search party. A mistake that he couldn't let continue. Kavizious rushed at Cynthia, and pinned her up against the side of a cave. "That's quite enough"! (Kavizious Commanded). Making Cynthia drop the spear she had just picked out of the minions chest she threw, to the bottom of the abyss. "Leave my mother alone you coward, or"! (Prince Key shouted).. As he tried to brake free from the grasp of two of Kaviziouses soldiers. "Or what"!?! (Kavizious asked Key).. As he turned and slithered his way to the Prince. "Maybe I should just kill your girlfriend and her mother first, right now in front of you and your mother"! (Kavizious threatened). "Stay away from them Kavizious"! (Key demanded). "Why, I don't need them to retrieve the Trident"! (He said to Key).. "If you touch one hair on either of their heads, I swear I will die before I would ever get you the Trident. I will kill you and myself with my bare hands"! Key had threatened the hell demon.. "Hahaha.. (Kavizious laughed). I want that Trident Key"! (Kavizious said). As he tightened his grip around Prince Keys throat. "No Stop, leave him alone"! (Queen Cynthia cried).. "I'm not through playing with your boy yet Cynthia"! (Kavizious said). As he took Cynthia's knife from Peretta, out of one the dead sea monkey soldiers, and swam over to Kylynn's mother Aleina and put it to her throat. "Noooo! (screamed Kylynn). Please, leave my mother alone"! (She pleaded). While she was squirming, trying to brake free. "Shhhh, It's ok my dear"! (Aleina cried). While pleading with her daughter Kylynn. "Don't do it Key, if you know where the Trident is, don't tell him! My life's not worth the lives of everyone else's life"! (Aleina assured the Prince).. "Shut up"! (Kavizious demanded). Smacking Aleina in the side of the face with the butt of Cynthia's knife. "NOOOO! (Kylynn screamed out).. You Bastard"! "Key, dig deep down and use the magic that's within you my son. Your black magic is very powerful.

There's something more within us my child, especially you! Our magic isn't the bad black magic you think, trust me Key, focus on the Trident and banish this disgusting monster"! (Cynthia said).. "Enough! (Kavizious shouted). Slapping Cynthia right across her face.. He then turned to Key and said.. "I'm going to go ahead and start killing them one by one, if you don't tell me where the God damn Trident is! (Kavizious told him).. TELL ME WHERE THE TRIDENT IS, NOW"! (He screamed at him).. "NOW KEY, DO IT NOW"! (His mother, Queen Cynthia shouted).. The Prince looked at his mother and nodded, he closed his eyes and began to concentrate on the Trident. "What are you doing"?! (Kavizious demanded). When Key didn't answer him, Kavizious grabbed a hold of him and slammed him right against the big rocks of the cave wall, making him fall to the sea floor of thee abyss, making Key break his concentration. "NOOOO"! "Key are you ok"?! "You Monster"! (Everyone was screaming in panic).. "Hahaha"! (Kaviziouses minions, the sea monkeys laughed).. While Key lie struggling to gather himself. Kavizious swam over to the Prince, snatching him up by his throat and said; "Now, lets try this one more time! Where is the Trident Boy-O, tell me where it is NOW"! (He said). Squeezing his hands harder around Keys throat.

All of the sudden, just then, King Maximus, along with Mateos and the royal army, came swarming out of the shadows, attacking Kavizious and his minions with such force and swiftly contained them. King Maximus and his best friend Mateos, came soaring down from above, as they both leaped off their sea dragons. The King drew his sword, swinging it into the face of Kavizious, making him drop the Prince to defend himself against the King's advances. "Thank you Father"! (said the Prince). "Here Key, catch"! (said his father).. As he tossed his son the Prince his second sword. "Free your mother"! (He told him). Key caught the sword, freed his mother Cynthia, and the Queen and her son the Prince, joined his father, King Maximus, and battled Kavizious, side, by side, by side. While Mateos and his men, battled the last of the sea monkeys that were their with Kavizious. Mateos broke off from his men and freed his wife and daughter, grabbing them and swimming off into a cave, bringing them to safety. "Are you ok my child"?! He asked his daughter Kylynn as he hugged her so tight. "Yes Daddy, thank you"! (Kylynn replied). Mateos then turned to his wife Aleina and said.. "And you Cynthia are you ok my love"?! (Mateos asked).

His wife as he gently stroked her face, so happy they were ok! "Yes my husband, my dear sweat husband.. I am fine now that you're here"! (She replied). Throwing her arms around her husband, hugging and kissing him. "I'm so sorry Mateos, my love! (Cried Aleina). I'm so sorry I didn't tell you what we were up to Mateos, I should have been honest with you". (She said). "Its ok Aleina, all that matters is that you guys are alive. I love you and Ky so much, I don't know what I would ever do without either one of you"! (He replied). As Mateos hugged and kissed his wife and then daughter one more time, his daughter Kylynn was crying with joy because she felt safe again, now that he was there. "Thank the God's you showed up Father"! (She said). "Stay here and protect your mother Ky, I have to go help Maximus and his family"! (He ordered is daughter).. "I father.. (She replied). Be careful"! "I mean it Ky, you stay right here and make sure your mother and you are safe! I cant be worrying about you two while trying to help the King save his family and kill this hell demon.. I'm serious, you stay put"! (He demanded his wife and daughter, but mostly his daughter).. "Yes father, I promise"! (She replied). Taking her mothers hand and swimming deeper into the caves, seeking more protective shelter. "I love you both"! (Mateos said). Swimming off back to the battlefield in the opposite direction of his two girls, to help his friend, the King.

When Mateos had returned to the battle, well what was left of it, his soldiers and sea dragons, had already torn through Kaviziouses minions, the sea monkeys. They were no match for the Royal Army and their sea serpents. Mateos and his men, along with the sea dragons had joined King Maximus and his family, Queen Cynthia and Prince Key, take on Kavizious as they would try and keep him from escaping, so they can banish his ass back to sea hell for good. Queen Cynthia was chanting a spell, while Prince Key focused on the energy of the Trident and while King Maximus and Mateos were battling Kavizious, the soldiers and sea dragons, made sure they had every way in or out of this area was completely sealed off, there was absolutely nowhere to go! "Ahhhrg"! (Kavizious screamed). Charging forward attacking the King. "I'm going to kill you"! (He said to Maximus).. Maximus drew his sword, blocking Kaviziouses advances with ease, causing more frustration to Kavizious, as Mateos attacked him from the other side. Maximus, Mateos and Zar had circled Kavizious like he was their pray for once! As Mateos went in first, swinging his sword over his head and down towards him, Kavizious grabbed his sword by the blade with one hand and swinging Mateos, sword and all, right into Zar, their most loyal sea serpent, making them crash into the side of the rocks. "Now it's just you and Me"! (Kavizious said). To King Maximus.. Maximus nodded as he gripped his sword tight. Kylynn had snuck back and was hiding, watching what was happening. "I have to do something! She thought to herself.. I just have to help"!! She swam out from the shadows, grabbing a sword off one of the dead sea monkey soldiers that was laying there. Just then, her father Mateos was gaining his balance from when Kavizious had tossed him and Zar like they were nothing. "Father, Catch"!! (Screamed Kylynn). As she threw the sword to her father, and forcing Kavizious to turn his attention to her for a split second, allowing King Maximus and Mateos to attack from separate directions. King Maximus had thrust his sword forward, slicing Kavizious in his mid section, while Mateos sliced him down his back, forcing him to fall forward toward Zar, and the royal sea dragon took his tail and whipped the beast sending him flying across thee abyss. Kavizious turned too flee and as he and two of his minions, fought their way out of there, Kavizious turned and said.. "I'll be back! (Kavizious threatened).. I promise you, I will be back"! King Maximus and them were able to keep Kavizious and his men from finding the Trident for now, but for how long!?! Kavizious had retreated back into the shadows, where he has been plotting his attacks. Kavizious lost one out of the two minions that were left as they fought their way out of there. So he and only one sea monkey had made it out of that battle with their lives. "Gather the rest of the sea monkeys! (He demanded of his minion).. We are going to need a lot more soldiers next time! We have to get the portal open and call in the rest of the sea hell demons from the sea hell realm! (Kavizious said). With a smile.. Its time to release hell upon wretched sea..

King Maximus was so relieved that he and his friend Mateoses were able to save their families before anyone was seriously hurt! "Are you ok my love"?! (He asked his wife Queen Cynthia).. Pulling her in closely, hugging and kissing her. "Thank the Gods you guys are ok! (He said to Cynthia and Key).. I don't know what I'd ever do without you two, you guy's are my whole world! So what in the Gods name were you two thinking!?! Not only did you put your own lives in danger, but you put Mateos family in danger as well! I want to know please, tell me what you were thinking"!?

(Demanded the King).. "Its ok my lord! (Mateos interrupted). Their all safe and that's all that matters"! King Maximus turned to his friend and said.. "And how is your family, they are all ok I hope"?! (Asked the King).. He was sincerely concerned.. "Yes my King! (Mateos replied). A couple bumps and bruises, but everyone's good Max"! (He said). As his wife and daughter came back out from the shadows of the cave and hugged Mateos, after Kylynn went back and got her mother Aleina, who also didn't stay put. When Ky went back for her mother, Aleina was chasing down one of Kaviziouses soldiers and was repeatedly stabbing him when she finally tracked the creature down. "Like mother, like daughter"! (She said). As she shrugged and swam past her daughter Ky! Kylynn couldn't help but shake her head and laugh. King Maximus then turned to his son Prince Key and said.. "You fought well my son"! (Declared the King).. As he stuck out his arm to his son, Key then extended his and he and the King locked arms, each others hand grabbing and locking on to the forearm of the others as they shook. King Maximus then took his forehead and pressed it against his son's and said.. "I'm proud of you boy-O, You protected your family and your people. You will make a fine King"! (Maximus declared). "But you and the ladies are going to have some explaining to do when we get back to the kingdom! Like why you all almost got yourselves killed"! "Yes father"! (Key replied). "But first.. I think there's something you would like to say to Mateos for almost killing his entire family"! (Said the King). Prince Key nodded and swam over to Mateos.

Mateos was over speaking to his wife and daughter, when the prince came over to check on them. "Is everyone alright"? (Asked Prince Key). "Yes my Prince, everyone's fine"! (Mateos replied). "Good, glad to hear that! Listen Mateos, I would just like to say".. "No Key, its ok my boy, everyone's fine, that's all that matters"! (Mateos said). He stopped the Prince in mid sentence. "Yes Mateos! (Interrupted the King).. He does"! "No, my fathers right! (Key said). I would really like to take a moment and say this to you and your family, if I could Mateos, please"! (Asked the Prince).. Mateos smiled and nodded yes.. Prince Key took a deep breath and said.. "I'm so sorry Mateos, you too Miss Aleina, I'm so sorry that I put your daughter in harms way! (Key said). I was just trying to protect the kingdom and I wasn't thinking clearly. I promise I will never go off with her and do something like this on our own again! I never should have made Ky keep anything from you, and for that I am truly sorry"! "No Key! (Interrupted Kylynn). I wanted to go! (She said). I wanted to do this, nobody made me do anything, Key you didn't make me do it. I made him take me with him Father, its not his fault! (She said). To her father and then turning to the King. "I'm so sorry King Maximus, but its not your sons fault, I made him take me! So if you guys are going to be mad at anyone, be mad at me"! (Kylynn demanded). Sticking up for her love Key. Kylynn then swam to the Prince, wrapping her arms around him, crying, burying her face into his chest. "I love you Key. (She whispered). I love you with all my heart"! "I love you too"! (He replied). As he gently stroked her face and hair. "I love you too Ky"! "I'm sorry too Mateos! (Queen Cynthia said).. I never should have taken Aleina along with me"! "You stop that right now Cynthia! (Said Aleina). I wanted to go!! She didn't make me do anything, I wanted to go Mateos.. I knew we had a better chance together, because I knew I could help her. I'm so sorry my love"! (She said). Turning to her Husband Mateos, hugging him when she said it.. "And you my King! (Aleina said). As she turned her attention to King Maximus.. I am truly sorry we kept this from you, it was clearly a mistake! I swear to you, it will never happen again, I can assure you my lord"! (Aleina told the King).. Facing towards Cynthia, giving her a look as she said it. "All is forgiven! (Said King Maximus).. But for now on, We work together to protect our people and the kingdom! No more keeping anything from your husbands, fathers, wives and especially your King, EVER"! (Declared King Maximus).. Everyone agreed with their King and his wise words of wisdom and forgiveness.

King Maximus was a special King, he had a heart like no other, filled with loyalty, love and an instinct to protect everyone! "Oh Max, I love you so much"! (Cynthia said). Kissing him on his cheek, as he was adjusting his armor and putting his helmet back on.. "I know my Queen.. (He replied). I love you too! Everyone, mount up, we are heading back to the kingdom"! (King Maximus ordered).. The royal army, as everyone was getting on their sea horses and sea dragons. The King turned to his friend Mateos and said.. "What do you think we should do about the Trident Mateos, my friend?! We need to figure out this Kavizious situation"! "I, my lord"! (Mateos agreed). "Heyah"! (Called out King Maximus).. As he snapped the rains on Zar, his sea dragon, as they all road off, following their King, one, by one, by one, into the shadows..

CHAPTER

15

WHILE THEY WERE RIDING BACK to the Kingdom, Key approached the front of the brigade and road up along side of his father, King Maximus and said.. "Father, I have a plan"! At the same moment, Queen Cynthia almost fell of her sea horse while getting sucked into one of her visions.. It was just for a flash, a quick moment, but she knew right there and right then, that they were to listen to her son, Prince Key, and trust whatever he says that he and or they, need to do from this moment forward, whatever Prince Key says, goes.. And she made damn well sure that her husband King Maximus and the rest would do exactly what he says!! "What's your plan my son"?! (Said the King). Looking to his son, then to his friend Mateos, and even then to his wife the Queen. King Maximus wasn't quite ready to trust the Prince fully yet, but he was willing to hear his son out and see what he had to say". Prince Key took a deep breath, looked at his mother, Cynthia nodded, giving her approval, then he looked to Mateos, who also gave him the go ahead nod. He took one last little breath, exhaled and said.. "Please father, you have to trust me! We only have one shot at this. We have to get the Trident before Kavizious does! He has been watching our every move, except right now father. We have a small window of opportunity to where I brake off and go get the Trident without him knowing, because he's coming back! I know where the Trident is, its like some force is drawing me to the Trident, but if we are going to do this, I have to go now my King! Please, father, I can do this!! (He said with confidence).. You have to trust me"! (Prince Key asked of the King).. King

Maximus looked to his wife to see what she thought of their sons plan, and then too Mateos, they both nodded in agreement with the prince's plan. "If I brake off now and retrieve the Trident and catch back up with you before you get back to the kingdom. I have to do this father, for the kingdom"! "Ok! (Replied his father).. But your taking Mateos with you! He's the only one else who knows where the Trident is, just incase, and I trust him to watch each others backs"! (Said the King). "I"! (Replied the Prince).. Kylynn had made her way up to the Prince and said.. "I'm coming with you and my father Key"! (She interrupted). "No your not, you need to stay with them Ky"! (Said her father Mateos).. "I! (Said the King). I need you with us young Kylynn".. (He told her). "Fine! (She replied). Be careful"! To Key and her father Mateos, blowing each of them a kiss then falling back into line. "Ok then, its settled! We will go get the Trident and meet you back at the Kingdom, or hopefully before". (He said). "I! (Replied the King).. Be safe! Watch out for my boy-O Mateos"! "I!! (Mateos replied). As Mateos and the King Locked arms, Mateos said to him.. "Please, get our families home safe my lord"! "I! (Replied the King).. On my honor"! "Be careful Key"! (Kylynn said). As she kissed him goodbye. Key then turned to his mother and blew her a kiss. Queen Cynthia smiled back at her son, knowing he was going to be just fine, as he and Mateos speed off into the shadows of thee abyss.

Meanwhile, deep down in another part of the abyss, deep in the pit of the Triangle of Death, Kavizious was licking his wounds. He had retreated back into the dark caves, he has made his home. For now anyways.. "You failed me"! (Kavizious screamed). At his head minion in charge, Banta. He was his sergeant at arms of the sea monkey soldiers in Kaviziouses army. Kavizious swam over to Banta and snatched him up by his throat. As he hang in the hell beasts hands, cowering in fear, all the other sea monkeys scattered for cover. "When we get my hell demon army through that portal, then you'll see what a real soldier does, and if you don't get me that Trident, then you wont make it to see them come through this portal and take over the Tolkien Sea". Kavizious tossed the sea monkey by his neck, into the cave wall, and grabbed one of Banta's men that was hiding from him behind one of the big rocks next to where he was just tossed, and as he picked up the frightened sea monkey, he turned to Banta and said.. "This is your last warning Banta, there wont be another"! That's when Kavizious lifted the minion up over his head sideways and ripped him right in half. "If you ever fail me again Banta, I will kill each and every one of you little bottom feeder's, until I wipe out your entire species"! (Kavizious said). In such a deep dark sinister voice, that made Banta cringe. Kavizious wanted the Trident so bad, he could feel the power radiating off the Trident. "We are not that far from where they buried the Trident, I can feel it"! (He said). Kavizious was intending to use the Trident to open the portal in the Triangle of Death, where he himself had once came through from his sea hell realm. He was determined to unleash his kind, their entire hell realm, upon this world. He was planning to lead the biggest army to battle, that this beautiful world with all its mystical and magical beings, had ever witnessed! The darkness that he will bring forth through the portal, will come with so much death and destruction, it will completely engulf the waters in Mid World's Ocean, it will destroy the entire Tolkien Sea, and all its creatures. "Go! Go now, take these pathetic minions with you and get the rest of your people and get me that Trident Banta! It's time to open the portal and pay a visit to the Kingdom of Mordainia"! (Kavizious commended). Banta bowed and exited, gathering up the few sea monkey soldiers that retreated from battle and survived. Banta and the minions, swam off as fast as possible, out of the caves and away from Kavizious, heading back to their home to get the rest of their kind and retrieve the Trident.. But, while on their way, they were to spy on the King and Prince, not knowing yet and or why, that they had separated, off in different directions.

King Maximus had led his family and thee others, safely back to the kingdom. "Man the battle stations! (Commended King Maximus).. I want this kingdom locked down, no one in, no one out, except Prince Key and General Mateos! (Said the King to his royal army).. We need to be ready, they will be approaching the kingdom fast, and they will most likely have the enemy right behind them! We must get them through safely, while keeping out the hell creatures and their allies. We must protect our people and our Kingdom at all cost"! (Declared the King). "You heard the King, sound thee alarms, I want this kingdom completely lock down and sealed tight men! (Said the lieutenant of the royal army).. He was General Mateoses next in command. King Maximus trusted the royal lieutenant very much.

Over in the near distance, Queen Cynthia could see her friend Aleina, nervously pacing back and forth, almost swimming in circles muttering to herself. "what is it my dear"? (She asked). "I'm just so worried Cynthia, I really hope they make it back safe. They need to make it back safe, I-I-I just don't know what I would do"! (Cried Aleina). "I know my dear! (Cynthia said). As she consoled her friend. I promise you Aleina, they will be here soon, just fine and will have the Trident! You just need to be ready for when they do get here. I need you to focus Aleina, OK!?! It's Key and Mateos, two of the strongest, bravest, soldiers ever to come from this kingdom! They will both protect each other with everything they have"! (Cynthia said to her).. "I! (She replied). I know my Queen! I'm ok now, thank you Cynthia my friend. I understand it's not just my husband, that it's your son too, but Key means a lot to us too, you know that! My sweet Ky loves him dear, and I thing the sea of him"! (Aleina told the Queen).. Hugging her one more time.. That's when King Maximus approached the ladies and said.. "Come ladies, help me and young miss Kylynn put the sea horses and dragons in the stables"! (He said to her and Mateos wife).. "Yes my love"! (Cynthia replied). Looking to Aleina. "I! (She nodded). I'll be right there, just give me a moment. (Aleina responded). As the sirens sounded and the royal soldiers and the people of the kingdom were rushing around, getting into their positions, getting ready for battle and protect their kingdom. Aleina took a deep breath, gathered her thought and caught up to her daughter Kylynn, who was with the King and Queen at the stables.

Meanwhile, Prince Key and General Mateos had made their way to the cave where Mateos had buried the Trident of Tolkien. As they approached the cave and dismounted their sea dragons, Prince Key was getting off of Zar, the most trusted serpent in all of the kingdom, Key noticed something was wrong. "what's that bright red light coming from within the caves Mateos"?! (He asked). "I don't know my Prince! (Mateos replied earnestly).. But that's where I definitely left the Trident"! "Well lets go get the Trident my friend"! (Prince Key said). As he and Mateos drew their swords and entered the cave, one, by one. Prince Key and General Mateos both believed that when they reached the caves of where the Trident was, that they would surly be met with a fight, but when they finally reached the brightly lit heart of the cave where the Trident was, nothing! Just the glowing Trident, partially buried. Key put his sword away, with Mateos following suite. General Mateos, picked up the Trident and handed it to the Prince. "Here Key, this belongs to you"! (He said). Prince Key nodded and when he took the Trident of Tolkien in the palm of his hand and closed his fingers around it, gripping it tight, the Trident stopped glowing. "I don't understand! (Mateos said). I know I buried the Trident really good! How did it come free"?! He wondered. Prince Key looked over where the Trident was hidden and said.. "It shook free Mateos! Look around, we are surrounded by active volcanic caves that erupt lava, and shake all the loose rocks, and the Trident is very powerful General. It made sure I could find it, it's been calling to me Mateos, the Trident had led me here to it. Even if you weren't here, I would have found it. It's like I'm drawn to it, and it's drawn to me. Not saying I'm not glad you're here with me, watching my back, because I am! Lets just get that covered".. (Prince Key said).. With a playful smile, winking to Mateos. "OK well, enough horse play, lets get us and that Trident out of here"! (Mateos said). "Right behind you General"! (Said the Prince).

Just when Prince Key and General Mateos turned to leave, Key was just about to put the Trident his back holster when all of the sudden, the Trident started vibrating and lighting up again, a bright Red. "What's going on"?! (Mateos asked). "I don't know"! (Replied the Prince).. Key placed the Trident, holding it out standing straight up in front of him when the bright red light that was lighting up the top of the Trident, started to form on Prince Keys hands. "What's happening to your hands"?! (Mateos asked). Worried about the Prince.. "I don't know"! (Replied the Prince).. All of the sudden the whole Trident lit up red. The light then traveled from Key's hands, to lighting up his arms next, then to his torso. The red light then went up to his head and then down to his tail fin, then back up to his hands, then back out to the Trident. That's when all of the sudden, the Trident shook so violently, that it was hard for the Prince to hold on to, and that's when this bright red beam of light came shooting out of the top of the Trident, blowing a hole right through the top of the cave, and went right through the entire sea. It shot up and out from the floor of thee abyss, and went as far up to the top of the salt water where the land creatures explore, and beyond. It shot up out of the water of Mid World's Ocean, the Tolkien Sea (thee Eighth Sea), and shot up very high, into the very dark night sky, right in the heart of Mid World! Prince Key and General

Mateos were in complete disbelief in what had just occurred. "What in the Sea God's name was that Key"?! (Mateos asked). Completely shocked at what he had just witnessed. "I have no idea Mateos! (Replied the Prince).. But I feel so powerful right now! I mean I never felt as good as feel right now. Something happened Mateos, I can feel it, it's a part of me"! (He said). With a smile.. "It is a part of you Key! (Mateos replied). You, you, you're the chosen one Key"! (He stuttered). In the ancient legends, it states that it has been thousands of years since the Trident had picked a chosen one. "The Trident has waited all these years for the chosen one, and that is you my Prince, the Trident chose you Key! (He said). With pride and joy.. Now come on my Prince, we have to get out of here"! "I"! (Prince Key replied).. Putting the Trident away as it stopped glowing and Prince Key and the General, fled off on their sea serpents, as fast as they could, out of the shadows of the caves, heading back to the kingdom, before Kavizious knew that they had split off from the rest of the Mordainians and OctaGod's, to retrieve the Trident.

General Mateos and Prince Key, were a little more than halfway back home to the kingdom when all of the sudden, they were attacked by a few of Kaviziouses minions, the sea monkeys. "Mateos, watch out Mateos"! (Screamed Key). As one of the sea monkey soldiers swam out from the shadow, and was coming up on Mateos when the Prince noticed and shouted, but he was too late. The sea monkey had managed to grab Mateos right off of his sea dragon from behind, before he had a chance to react. Right before the sea monkey soldier had a chance to swim off into the dark shadows of the abyss with the General, Prince Key took the Trident out of his holster and aimed it forward and with his mind he willed a bright red bolt of lightning out of the top of the Trident. Careful not to hit Mateos, shooting the bolt at the minion hitting him, making him explode instantly, and "Poof", just like that he was gone, and Mateos fell, but before hitting thee abyss floor, his serpent had rushed to his aid and broke his masters fall. "Who's next"?! (Key shouted). As loud as he could, aiming the Trident at the last couple of lone sea monkey soldiers for Kavizious. The minions chose to live, for now and fled back to tell their master Kavizious. "We have to get out of here before they reach that hell beast Kavizious"! (Said General Mateos).. "I! (Replied the Prince).. We have to go now"! (Said the

Prince). Snapping the rains on Zar, his sea dragon and they two started to head back to the kingdom, once again.

While the pair were almost all the way back to the kingdom, those lone few minions had made it back to their master Kavizious the hell demon. "Sir, Prince Key and General Mateos have the Trident! They separated from the others and snuck off and grabbed the Trident and are heading to meet the others, back at the kingdom, and they're almost back there sir"! (Said the minion). "What you want we should do our lordship"?! (Asked Banta). Kavizious thought for a moment and said.. "Round up all your men and stolen serpents. We will head them off before they get through the gates of the kingdom. It's time we bring the fight to them! (Kavizious declared). Once I get my hands on that Trident, I can bring forth a hell like no other upon this realm, the likes of which this world has never seen! I will crush the Kingdom of Mordainia, and rule the Tolkien Sea"! (Kavizious said). "Oogh ough, augh augh".. (Screamed the sea monkey's).. All the sea monkey soldiers were swimming around in a frenzy, screaming in excitement, creating all types of commotion. "Silence! (Kavizious demanded). It's time to move out"!

Kavizious and his small army of sea monkey minion's headed out of the shadows and straight into the open waters. Kavizious and his soldiers, swam off towards the kingdom they went, in full force. "I want that Trident, by any means necessary"! Kavizious reminded his men.. "I want that portal open at all cost"! (He said). There will be no stopping Kavizious once he opens that portal and brings forth his brethren from the sea hell realm! "Do not let anything happen to that Trident or I'll kill each and every last one of you nasty little algae eaters! Kavizious threatened Banta and the rest of the sea monkeys.. You're lucky I took pity on your people and allowed you all to live this long! I should of just killed you all Banta.. Don't make me re-think my decision". "Yes your lordship"! (Banta replied). All the sea monkeys follow one sea monkey, and that was Banta. Banta was the one that they all followed without question. Banta was very cunning. He would do whatever it took to insure the survival of his people. Including, fighting for the wrong side! Banta or any of the other sea monkeys, just didn't care about anyone or anything, other than their own kind! "Go Banta, go now and get me the Trident"! (Kavizious commanded). "Yes my lordship"! (Banta replied). As he swam off away from Kavizious, and up to his men. "No Mistakes"! (Banta said). To his sea monkey klan.. "Kill everyone and everything, and get me that Trident, at any and all costs! I don't want a single scratch on it, or it's your head"! (General Banta threatened).. As the sea monkey soldiers, swam off to battle, one, by one, until it was just Banta and Kavizious left. Banta turn to Kavizious, he tightened his armor and swam off with Kavizious following suite, as they were on their way to the Kingdom of Mordainia!

CHAPTER

16

MEANWHILE, OVER IN THE KINGDOM, Queen Cynthia, along with Kylynn and Aleina, were waiting by the front gate for their men to return with the Trident and save them all from this hell demon. "LOOK! (Kylynn shouted). It's Prince Key and father"! (She said). With a smile, pointing too them, as they road up on the kingdom from out of the dark shadows. "Oh thank the Sea God's"! (Queen Cynthia sighed in relief).. "Wait, look behind them in the distance, there in the shadows, their being followed and their coming up on them fast"! (Aleina was frantically shouting).. "Quick Key, hurry, hurry Mateos, please father hurry up, quick my son"! Queen Cynthia and her friend Aleina, along with her daughter Ky, were screaming.. They were waving their arms and frantically swimming back and forth trying to get the Prince and Generals attention. "Quick, open the gates and be ready to shut them as soon as they are through! Go, do it now. Open the gates"! (Commanded the Queen).. Right behind Prince Key and General Mateos, was Kavizious and what looked to be thee entire sea monkey klan, as they appeared one after the other. "LOOK Max, they have the Trident, but look what's chasing them"! (Cynthia said). Pointing to Kavizious and his minions that were coming up behind his son and best friend. King Maximus had come back with his royal soldiers behind him, to the front gates where the woman were waiting for Key and Mateos. "Cynthia my love, take Aleina and young miss Ky to safety! (Commanded the King).. Let me and my soldiers handle this, please"!?! "I, my King"! (Cynthia replied). Grabbing Aleina and Ky's hands and swimming behind the royal army, as the soldiers formed a defensive formation. "Hurry up, get in here now"! (Yelled King Maximus).. Prince Key and General Mateos, were riding as fast as they could. Young Prince Key was pushing his sea dragon Zar to his ultimate limit. The Prince and General made it through the Gates and dismounted their sea serpents, screaming.. "Shut the Gates"! The royal guards quickly shut the gates, before any enemy could infiltrate the kingdom. The royal soldiers, opened fire upon Kavizious and his minions, as they approached the Kingdom of Mordainia, on their sea horses and a few stolen sea dragons, they acquired from the royal soldiers they killed that were riding them. The royal kingdoms, defensive fire power was too much for the sea monkey soldiers. It stopped them dead in their tracks and pushed them back, retreating, seeking cover behind anything they could. As the royal armies magical fire power, rained down on them, picking them off one, by one. "What are you doing you fools?! Get through there and get me that Trident"! (Kavizious had demanded).. "But sir, we are out gunned, it's a slaughter, we have to retreat! (Said Banta). I'm losing to many men"! "Fall back, Retreat"! (Banta commanded). While he and his men, flee from the kingdom, they were still getting plucked off as they scattered, fleeing, like the cowards that they are. "This isn't over! (Kavizious promised). You think you won because you have the Trident. I'll be back for the Trident, and kill each and every one of you"! (Kavizious shouted). "Over my dead body Kavizious! (The King shouted back).. Now go on and get out of here while you still can"! (He told him).. "I'll be back, I promise you that"! (Kavizious said). Then he and his whole army, was gone!

King Maximus and Queen Cynthia, were so proud of their son! They knew they put their trust in the right man, to take that journey with their son. "We are forever grateful to you Mateos! (Said his friend, the King).. We are forever in your debt". "It was an honor to ride side by side with the prince"! (General Mateos replied).. "Thank you for watching my sons back and keeping him safe Mateos"! (Queen Cynthia said).. As she gave the General a hug. "Actually, Young Key saved Me! (He had told them).. "We are so proud of you my son"! (King Maximus told the Prince).. Locking arms with his boy, nodding and smiling. "We love you so much Key"! (Queen Cynthia said).. Pulling her son away from the King, and hugging him, while crying tears of joy.. "I'm just glad Mateos and I, got the Trident"! (Said the Prince). "Well I'm just so damn proud of both of you"! (Said the King). Mateos had went on to tell them all about their findings. He told them how the Trident had chosen Key, and that their Prince, Prince Key, is the chosen one! When Mateos was done, Key went to hand the Trident over to his father, the King. "No my son! (Replied King Maximus).. It seems it's your destiny, you're the chosen one my son, you keep it".. Prince Key held the Trident in his hands, just looking at it for a moment, silent. "I don't know what to say"! (He replied). "He's right my Prince! (Mateos said). You and that Trident are meant as one! I seen it with my own eyes Key. The Trident guided you right to it and you right back here. I've never seen anything like it, other than when you got close to it, and then when you touched it for the first time, it's like it synced up to your soul Key". (Mateos told him).. "I always knew you were special Key"! (Said the Queen). "Ok my people! (Said King Maximus).. It's time to prepare for war! We are going to bring the War to Kavizious while he is weak, while he is few! We strike him before he figures out how to open that portal without the Trident and brings forth more of his kind to our realm, and destroys our kingdom. He must be stopped. We have to protect our people and our kingdom by any means necessary! We will hit him with the Trident, and we hit him now"! (King Maximus commanded).. "I my King"! (Mateos agreed). As he swam off to round up his soldiers and prepare for battle. "We have one more fight my people! (King Maximus declared).. Our Prince has the Trident, and he is the Chosen One! We will bring the fight to him and end this now, before he brings the War to us"! The royal army was ready for war!!

"I know where Kavizious is"! (Said Prince Key).. Looking up from the Trident finally. The Trident began glowing red and vibrating, Again! "He is in thee abyss of the Triangle of Death"! (He told them).. "Oh my Sea God's"! (Queen Cynthia gasped in fear).. "What is it mother"?! (Prince Key asked).. "That's where your grandparents spell had opened the portal and brought forth all those sea hell demons from the hell realm. That's where Kavizious came through from! He's trying to open the portal! (Cynthia realized). We have to stop him Maximus"!! (She said). Swimming over to her husband and buried her head in his chest, as he wrapped his arms around his Queen, consoling her. "This isn't good Key! (Said the King). "I know father, but I know where he is, and I'm going to go stop him"! (Prince Key declared).. "The Trident is telling you where Kavizious is"?! (He asked the Prince).. "Yes! (He replied). I cant explain it father, it's just when I'm holding the Trident. Anything I think in my head, it's like I know the answer instantly! I can see him at the abyss of the Triangle of Death. (Key replied). It's like mothers visions without falling into a trans state. Even when I'm not holding it, it just draws me to it, wherever it may be, I can go right to it without even knowing where it is". As soon as Prince Key finished that sentence, his mother, Queen Cynthia right on cue, slipped into one of her trans states.

The King and Prince, rushed to her aid. "Mother, Cynthia!! (They both cried out).. As they swam to her in a panic. Prince Key held his mother up from falling over, while King Maximus held his wife's hand, calling out to her, seeing if he could get through to her and snap her out of it. "Cynthia my Queen, can you hear me my love"?! (He kept asking her).. "Stop father! (Said the Prince). Don't snap her out of it, she could be injured, you have to let her go through the process and focus in her trans state"! (He said to the King).. "What do you mean my son, why not"?! (his father demanded).. Maximus was so clearly upset and confused, he was absolutely horrified for his wife. He didn't understand yet the trans state that produces Cynthia's visions would come to be tool that she can use to help them. Prince Key knew though! "It's very dangerous to bring someone back from a trans state to soon. It's impossible to bring her back without freaking her out father. (Prince Key explained).. She could get extremely hurt, or even worse, she could die"! (Key said). That's when all of the sudden, Cynthia had snapped out of her trans and was coming too. "Cynthia, thank the Gods! Are you ok, my deer"? (Asked the King). As he swam over to his wife, helping her keep her balance, she replied.. "Yes Max, I'll be fine! (She assured him).. But".. "But what Cynthia? (Maximus asked her).. What is it my love, what did you see"?! Completely worried about what she was going to tell them. "He doesn't need the Trident to open the portal at the triangle anymore. (she told them). We have to do something Max, we have to stop him"! "Wait, what do you mean he doesn't need the Trident anymore Cynthia"?! (Asked King Maximus).. "He still needs it to control all the creatures and the sea, but not to open the portal. He figured it out somehow, I seen him opening the portal, without the Trident. (She said). Key, when that light shot out of the Trident, back at the cave with you and Mateos went and retrieved it, well it triggered the portal in the abyss of the Triangle of Death, and somehow opened the portal from the sea hell realm. It gave Kavizious and the other sea hell demons full access to our waters in Mid World! (Queen Cynthia told the King and Prince).. They will destroy our world if we don't stop them, especially if Kavizious gets his hands on the trident. Our world as we know it, would be over"! "So what are we going to do"?! (Asked Prince Key).. "Wait, there's More! (Said Queen Cynthia). When the beam shot out of the Trident, it didn't fully activate the portal at the triangle of death, because the cave blocked it some what, but its opening and closing, giving access to two to three hell demons are crossing through to our world"! (She told them). "when is this"? (Asked King Maximus).. "NOW! (She replied). It's been opening every hour on the hour since the Trident lit up, and shot a beam out of light from out of it, through the cave"! (Queen Cynthia told them).. "We have to stop Kavizious and shut down the portal, I can use the Trident to shut it down and send back them hell creatures"! (Prince Key declared).. "Yes, it's the only way Maximus! (Prince Key's mother, Queen Cynthia agreed).. But we have to send Kavizious somewhere else! We can banish his seal hell demon soldiers back to their sea hell realm, but just not Kavizious, he has made it back here three times now, that we now of, we have to send him somewhere he cant get out of"! (Cynthia said). "Purgatorseas! (Said King Maximus). We banish him to sea purgatory, that will get rid of him"! "He's right Key! (Cynthia said). "Ok then, lets go banish these sea hell bastards, and shut this portal down for good"! (Announced Prince Key).. With a smile on his face, locking arms with his father the King.. "let's save our people and our Kingdom"! (Declared the King).. "I! (Key replied). What do you say Mother, you and Kylynn's mother Miss Aleina, can conjure up some spells and use you magic to help defeat them"?! (He asked her).. "If you use the Trident and after you banish him to sea purgatorseas and lock the gates behind him, then shut down the portal, it just may work! (She said). I can conjure up some spells to get rid of Kaviziouses sea hell demon soldiers and then we get Kavizious and shut the portal down at the Triangle of Death for good! (She told them). Turning to her son and saying.. "It's your destiny to save our people and our world my son"! (She said). As she hugged him so tightly.. "We do this together, as a family"! (Said the King).

Just then, Mateos returned. "All set my lord. (He said to King Maximus).. The Troops are ready to go, and the kingdom is completely locked down tight and secured. No one in, and no one out. Once we move out"! (He told Maximus).. "I! (Replied the King).. Let's gear up and get Zar ready for Battle, tonight we ride! Mateos, get the sea dragons ready, we are going to need them for this battle! We got some demons to send back to Sea Hell.. (Demanded the King).. "I, my lord"! (Maximus replied).

The King and Prince, with Trident in hand, led the cavalry of the royal army, along with Mateos and of course the three women. The King figured instead of putting up a fight, he would give in and let Queen Cynthia and Mateoses wife and daughter Aleina and Kylynn. They would never have gotten out of there without the ladies, so they devised a plan for the girls to use their black magic and spells to help defeat Kavizious and the rest of the sea hell demons, and close the portal in the deep dark abyss of the triangle of death. King Maximus knew that with the girls black magic and spells, along with his son Prince Key and the Trident, along with Mateos and his royal army, and of course Zar and the rest of the royal serpents, it wouldn't be easy but they could definitely defeat Kavizious and the rest of those damn sea hell demons. The King and Queen came up a strategy for battle against the demons. The Queens visions gave them all a sense of calm. Her black magic was very strong and she learned how to fully control it. She even helped Aleina and Kylynn practice their control of the black magic arts. Besides, Prince Key had become one with the Trident, he and the Trident were radiating with power. He has been learning to control its power more and more every second, the more time that passed Prince Key was getting stronger and stronger, but as time passed more and more sea hell demons crossed through to this world. Even though the men would have wanted the women to stay back at the kingdom where it was safe. Once they knew it would never happen, the devised the battle plan around the girls black magic and spells. Besides, not only was Cynthia a great sorcerer, she along with Aleina and Kylynn were fierce worriers. They believed that they were all in this together, which meant that they live as one, they fight as one, and if need be, they would die as one. As they road off out of the kingdom, disappearing into the shadows, one by one, through the caves, Kylynn road up along side her father, the King and the man she loves, Prince Key and said.. "Besides, us girl's can fight better that you men. (She said). Playfully, with a smile. You know you men need us"! (Ky said). Lightning the mood. "Hahaha" They all laughed.. "OK ladies, stay low and keep your eyes open, stay focused! (Said the King). And don't be a hero! Do not take on Kavizious alone, anyone! (King Maximus demanded).. Let's kick some demon ass"! "Woo-hoo"! Everyone cheered as they road off to battle. Each and every one of them were ready to die for one an other if need be. That's how much they all loved each other and their sacred kingdom.

As they exited the mouth of the cave, following behind a very confident Prince Key and his Trident to the dark abyss of the triangle. The King and Queen couldn't be prouder of their son! Prince Key knew exactly where to go, the Trident was like a built in locater. It was directing him to find Kavizious, but first it was bringing him to close the portal and then they can destroy the sea hell, demon army and their leader.. But what they did not know was that Kavizious had sent a troop off demon soldiers and sea monkey minions to the Kingdom of Mordainia to destroy as much as possible. He sent them there to do damage and destruction. They were to cause complete chaos and mayhem.. But the kingdom was prepared for all attacks! The whole entire kingdom and its borders were so very well protected. The Royal family, along with General Mateos had trained the kingdoms people to protect themselves and their way of life. Everyone of the kingdoms people had their own assignments, based upon their skill set. Anyone of them would give their life and die for their home and each other, for that's how much it had meant to them. They would protect one another by any means necessary. Even the children have their own little orders, to help protect the kingdom. When King Maximus and Queen Cynthia opened their training facility, the entire kingdom was trained in self defense and other training. Even Cynthia taught a hunting and trapping course to the young-ins of the kingdom. They were all trained in hand to hand combat, and also, sword fighting. The entire kingdom ad come together and worked as one, as they prepared for this battle. Everyone knew that if they had to work together, if they wanted to continue living in their beautiful kingdom with a King and Queen that absolutely loved and adored them all so much, then they were all going to have to pull together and do their fare share to defeat Kavizious and save their world as they come to know and love.

CHAPTER
17

THE KINGDOM OF MORDAINIA, WAS a fortress. It was completely locked down and secured, the kingdom was protect in and around the premises. As the kingdoms people were ready for war, but so was Kavizious. The King and all the rest of the royal army with Mateos and Prince Key along with his Trident, were riding along side him as they lead the pack to battle at the Triangle of Death, or (thee Triangle of Fire).. Whichever you prefer! This dark part of the abyss, has many different names. Ever since Key and Mateos fount the Trident and it shot the bright light out of the cave and triggered the portal in the Triangle of Death, two to three sea hell demons would slither their way through the portal from their sea hell realm. Every hour on the hour, the portal would open, there would be a huge triangle of fire glowing so bright in the middle of the abyss in the deep dark salt waters of the Tolkien Sea, in Mid World's mystic Ocean. As they were approaching closer to the Triangle of Fire, the Trident would lit up and started vibrating. "This is it everybody".. (Said the Prince). "Stay focused men and ladies! (Said the King). Be very alert and keep your eyes opened for Kavizious, STAY AWAY, he will kill you"!

Back at the kingdom, Kaviziouses men were closing in on the outskirts of the kingdom, when they were ambushed. There were soldiers from the kingdom's royal army, lying in wait. They were ready and awaiting for the demons to arrive, so they could attack. As soon as the Kavizious men, the sea hell demons and his sea monkey minions entered the cave that led to the kingdom, the exit and entrance were sealed off, and that's when the royal army made their move and attacked. As they were locked in combat, the kingdoms people, opened fire upon the minions and demons, blasting them with fiery balls of magic, and blazing fast and deadly arrows that Queen Cynthia, along with Miss Aleina and Kylynn had made with the Queen's incredible black magic spells. Her skill level with the black magic art was like no other. She had figured out how to use the art of black magic for good, and to use it against evil. While the minions and demons got bombarded by the fiery spells that Cynthia had conjured up, as soon as the hell demons got hit, they would burst into flames and then poof, they were gone, but the sea monkey minions would stay there flopping in agonizing pain, shrieking while burning to death. Even the kingdoms young were loading up the catapults with queen Cynthia's magic spells, and firing upon the enemy. "Good job everyone, the King and Queen would be proud"! (Said Gerald). Sergeant. Gerald was Mateoses sergeant at arms, in charge of the kingdoms Defense. "Quick! (Commanded Sergeant Gerald). Detonate the explosives now, trigger the back, front and sides, DO IT NOW"! "KABOOM - BANG - BABOOF"!!! Three major explosions in a row went off. After all the smoke and dust settled, the entire kingdom erupted into cheers. "YAAAAA"!! (Everyone shouted). "Seize fire, seize fire"! (Commanded Sergeant Gerald).. They had succeeded in protecting the kingdom, all the sea hell demons and the sea monkey minions were stopped. Not one of them even made it through the gates of the kingdom before they were either killed or sent back to Sea Hell.

As soon as Prince Key and them had reached the bottom of thee abyss in the Triangle of Death, they were met by an awaiting Kavizious and his army of sea hell demons and his sea monkey minions. Prince Key came to a screeching holt, stopping everyone behind him. Queen Cynthia closed her eyes and raised her arms above her head and using her magic, she mouthed the words to one of her spells and she sent a shockwave that had spread across thee entire area, wiping out the first few waves of demon soldiers, killing hundreds of them instantly. That's when the royal army soldiers started taking out all the sea monkeys, killing any minion they could. While King Maximus and General Mateos, with swords in hands, were tearing through the gigantic sea hell demons, along with Zar and the other royal sea dragons biting through their enemies like nothing. Kylynn and her mother Miss Aleina were fighting the hell demons together as a team, swinging each other around. One would grab a hold of a demon from the front, while the other one comes up, and strikes from behind. They were very fast and very deadly together, Mateos was proud of his girls, both his wife Aleina and daughter Kylynn.. "Haha".. (Mateos laughed). As he watched them enjoying themselves, smiling and giggling. Mateos shook his head and laughed, then he continued on with his own little tag team fighting style with his friend King Maximus. They kept right on attacking the hell demons and minions, together with all they had, every ounce of energy and might that they could muster up. They kept right on loping off their enemies heads, and piercing as many hearts as they could, or at least were most of their hearts should be.. "Quick Key, do it now! (Shouted Cynthia). Use your Trident, concentrate, my son, do it now"! So with Trident in hand, Key concentrated on killing the sea monkeys and banishing the sea hell demons, Key jumped down from his faithful sea dragon Zar, gripping the Trident tight with both hands and with a mighty thrust, Prince Key jammed the Trident down into the ground at the bottom of thee abyss when he landed. It was like an atomic bomb went off, shaking all of the oceans waters, and even shook the lands in Mid World. All of the sea hell demons instantly burst into flames, killing them slowly, and blowing up the Triangle of fire in the middle of thee abyss. There was a huge explosion, cutting off access too and from the hell realm, completely destroying the mystical portal. "NOOOOOOO"! (Screamed Kavizious)..

As King Maximus and them were fighting the rest of the sea monkey minions that were still alive, Prince Key seen Kavizious swimming away in his peripheral vision. Kavizious swam off real fast, and disappeared into the shadows, and into a near by cave. Without hesitation, the Prince took off after him, giving chase. He was not going to let Kavizious get away. All you seen was a bright light, trail off into the cave and disappear, as Prince Key with trident in hand, glowing and vibrating, following after the evil sea hell creature that has been tormenting his family for years now! Prince Key was so focused on killing Kavizious, that he was falling victim to his own anger, that fueled his fire of hate inside of him for this despicable lost soul, who tried tricking the Prince into crossing over to his dark black magic side. Prince Key was so outraged that he almost fell for Kaviziouses lies to get his claws on the Trident of Tolkien. Key looked down at the Trident, gripped it tight and screamed out in anger. He sped off like a lightning bolt shooting through the deep dark sea, and disappeared into the cave after the sea hell beast.

"Oh Max, he's gone"! (Queen Cynthia said).. "Who's gone"? (Asked the King).. "Key, he went after Kavizious"! (She replied). With such fear in her voice! "Kylynn said she seen a flash of light disappear into that cave over there after Kavizious. It's him Maximus, He took Zar Max"! (She pleaded). With her husband the King. "OK, Cynthia you and Ky stay with miss Aleina and finish off these nasty little sea monkeys, and me and Mateos will go after him"! (Ordered the King).. "Thank you Max! Please go get our son back, but don't forget that Kavizious has to be sent to sea purgatory, (purgatorseas), so he cant get back here. Key can use the Trident, he just needs to focus Max, please go help our boy". (Queen Cynthia said). Kissing her husband goodbye. "I! my Cynthia, I will. Mateos, lets go"! (Said King Maximus).. While he and Mateos jumped on their sea dragons. "We have to go help my son kill this filthy sea hell scum". (He told him).. "Well then, lets go help Key get that slimy sucker then"! (Mateos replied). "Be careful my love"! (Aleina said). As her and Ky, came over to wish Mateos and the King luck. "He-yah, yah"! (Called out the King).. Snapping the reins on his sea dragon, and he and Mateos disappeared into the cave after the Prince and the sea hell demon, Kavizious.

Meanwhile, way deep in the caves, Prince Key was riding on Zar, the most trustworthy sea serpent in all of the deep dark ocean. Key was around Zar his entire life, his father King Maximus, raised Zar since he was hatched. Zar has been the royal sea serpent since way back when King Keyiera would ride him. He was part of the royal family, everyone loved and adored him, especially Prince Key. He and Zar had such a special bond, Zar would do whatever it took to protect the Prince. Cynthia knew that Zar would keep her son Key safe. As Key and Zar were tearing through the caves as fast as they could, Prince Key had the trident in one hand, and the other one, at the ready, to grab his sword from out his holster as soon as he located that slippery sea snake, Kavizious. Prince Key and Zar had road so fast through the caves, that they were almost at the end of Mid World's abyss. They had made it to the end of the caves, and when they exited the mouth of the cave at the other end, all of the sudden, Kavizious was lying in wait, above the caves entrance. As soon as they passed through the opening, Kavizious lunged down, knocking

Prince Key from his sea dragon Zar, making them both go crashing into the rocks, knocking the trident loose from Key's hand. With a blink of an eye, Kavizious bolted to the Trident, and as soon as he picked it up, Prince Key lunged forward at the beast, slamming him up against the cave wall. Prince Key and Kavizious were struggling over the Trident. "Let it go boy-o"! (Kavizious demanded). "Never! (Key replied). It's mine, you let go"! As he turned to the side, and whipped Kavizious in the face with the Princes tail. Kaviziuoses hands came free from the Trident and Key secured it tight. "I see the trident has gave you strength"! (Kavizious said). To the Prince.. Prince Key didn't respond, he just closed his eyes and began chanting.. "Bazandia, Kazadineana, Zeezazuzsaka"!!! When all of the sudden.. A bright red light up the top of the Trident, then the light moved down to the whole Trident, then lit up Keys hands, then the bright light lit up his entire body. The light then, shot back out his hand and onto the Trident and then.. "Poof"! The bright red light, shot out the top of the Trident, out into a ring like pattern, extending outwards as far as you could see, spinning around, and around until, a huge explosion so fierce that thee entire ocean floor and the caves walls, all shook so hard, and with such force, that it shook the loose rocks free and they all came crashing down. That bright red light, shot out the top of Trident, sending a voltage bolt through Kaviziouses body, zapping him with such shocking power, that it sent him flying backwards through the water and into the pile of big rocks on the abyss floor, that fell down from the big shockwaves. Just then, King Maximus and best friend General Mateos, came flying out of the mouth of the cave, on their sea dragons. "Key! (Shouted out the King).. Thank the Gods your ok my son"! As Mateos was coming up on the side of the King, Prince Key shouted.. "LOOK OUT"! Kavizious had come to, and shot up from underneath Mateoses sea dragon, snatching up General Mateos and disappearing into the dark shadows of the caves. "NOOO"! King Maximus and Prince Key, both screamed at the same time.. As they both looked at each other and took off after their friend and beast. The King and Prince had jumped on Zar and another sea dragon and sped off into the mouth of the cave as fast as they could. They both gave chase into the bellows of the dark abyss' caves, of Mid World's Ocean.

CHAPTER

18

KAVIZIOUS HAD MADE HIS WAY through the heart of the caves, deep within the small dark crevices with Mateos wrapped up under his arm. Kavizious was twice the size of Mateos and them. Kavizious had bound, gagged, and tied up the general, before he ever knew what hit him. He had made it quite a good distance away from where he had snatched Mateos from the Prince and King. Kavizious took Mateos back to where he had been hiding out and building his army, plotting his rein in these mystical waters of the Tolkien Sea. Now he was broke, his army has been disassembled completely! The only move that Kavizious had left, was to stay one step ahead of them, and hope that the Prince makes a mistake and he can get his slimy sea claws on Key's Trident, before they get a chance to banish him again. The Trident was guiding Prince Key and King Maximus too Kaviziouses whereabouts.. That's when, the King and Prince came upon his hideout, as soon as they turned the corner in the cave. "Wow, look at this place father".. (Said the Prince). "Yes my son, I see it! (Maximus replied). This has to be where Kavizious was building his sea hell demon and sea monkey army! Keep your eyes open and be very careful my son". (He said). "I! (Prince Key replied).. You too father, he's around here somewhere father, I can feel him"! (Key told his father).. "But what about Mateos, is he still alive"? (Maximus asked his son).. "Yes, he is definitely alive! (Prince Key replied). Key had figured that he needs him alive, he's no good to him dead. He is going to try and use him to trade with me for the Trident"!

That's when all of the sudden, they heard this big booming voice, but could not see where it was coming from. "A trade you say!? Interesting"! (Said the voice). It was Kaviziouses. "Now that's a splendid idea. Now here's what's going to happen, Your going to hand over the trident or I'll kill your little General Mateos here! (Kavizious threatened). If you hand over the Trident, I'll give you back your friend, and I promise I will not kill you, right now anyways"! Kavizious would absolutely kill Mateos if the Prince doesn't give him the Trident. "Don't do it Key"! (King Maximus pleaded). "Hahaha"! (Kavizious laughed out loud).. But then his voice got serious again.. "Quiet Maximus! (He demanded). This is between me and your son, Prince Key"! "Like sea hell it is you savage"! (King Maximus snapped in replied).. "Shhh, it's ok father! I have this under control, please trust me, I know what I'm doing"! (Prince Key assured hi father).. "Just follow my lead.. OK Kavizious, you win! (Said Key). Now bring out Mateos and show yourself, and you can have the Trident". "Hahaha! (Kavizious laughed again).. You think I'm stupid boy-o"!?! Kaviziouses voice deepened again.. "Put the damn trident down, and you and your father, King, Race Traitor, can push back away from it, and I'll bring out your little friend"! (Demanded Kavizious). "OK,OK,OK! (Prince Key replied).. But he better be alive and well Kavizious"!! (Key also demanded).. "No son please, don't"! (Begged the King).. Prince Key looked over to his father and motioned to the left of him, with his head, to the big pile of rocks that shook loose and formed, from the big blast that the trident had created a little while earlier. King Maximus finally figured out what his son, Prince Key had planned. King Maximus smiled and exhaled in relief. He knew everything was going to be ok, and he needed to trust his son. "OK Kavizious, he's right, you win"! (Said the King). "Good! Now tell your boy to drop the Trident and back the sea hell off, slowly"!

Prince Key slowly put the Trident down on thee abyss floor, and when he did, it instantly stopped glowing. As soon as he let it go, he and his father Maximus, slowly back up away, towards the big pile of loose rocks. That's when Kavizious, slowly crept out of shadows, with Mateos tucked up under his armpit, all bound, gagged and tied up, still. As soon as Prince Key had visual on Kavizious and Mateos, he was about to spring into action, but it was too late. Within a split second, Kavizious in one fair swoop, he dropped General Mateos, picked up the Trident and with a shock to all, that the prince just did not see coming, and before anyone could react to it, Kavizious lunged forward as fast as he could, "NOOOO"! (Key had screamed).. But before he could stop him, Kavizious rammed the Trident, as hard as he could into the chest of King Maximus, puncturing his lung, instantly filling up his insides with blood. The Trident lit back up, but not red this time, this time it was a deep dark purple, glowing from the entire trident. As soon as he jammed the trident into the King, it lit up that deep dark purple, then made a pulse, explosion. The noise was so loud and powerful, it sent Kavizious flying backwards, crashing into the side of the cave wall, making huge boulders come crashing down on top of the sea hell beast, completely covering him.

Back over in the battlefield, back at the other end of the caves, where the King and Mateos left the women to finish off the sea monkey minions, they had completely killed or chased off every last one of those nasty little suckers, and were helping hail the wounded soldiers with their magic, that's when all of the sudden Cynthia screamed and dropped to the ground. "NOOOO! (She cried out).. Something's wrong, I can feel it.. It-it-it's Maximus, something happened to my husband"! (She said). Miss Aleina and Kylynn rushed to their friend Queen Cynthia. "What is it Cynthia, what are you saying, are you sure"?! (Aleina asked). "Oh my Gods, NO,NO,NO, this can be right now! (Cried the Queen).. Yes, I can feel it, I don't know to explain it, but something wrong Aleina. I need to go find my husband and son"! (Queen Cynthia said).. So frantic that Aleina and Kylynn were starting to worry about Mateos and Prince Key. "Quick mother, we have to go find father and Key"! (Said Kylynn). "I! (Her mother Aleina said).. Let's go Cynthia, we have to go find our men"! The three woman grabbed their sea horses, and disappeared into the shadows, leading into the mouth of the cave, where they entered so fast, one, by one, by one …

Back in the heart of the caves, where Kavizious had just murdered King Maximus, Prince Key swam over to his father and grabbed a hold of him and the Trident and yanked it right out of the King's chest, holding up his father, and gently resting him onto thee abyss sea floor. "Oh father, I am so sorry, please don't leave, me"!?! (Cried the Prince).. When all of the sudden, he heard a faint murmur. "I-I-I love you Key, my son".. (Whispered the King).. With his dying breath! "Please father, hold on, please!? I will use the Trident to save you, hold on"! (Said Key). As he closed his eyes and gripped the Trident, begging for his fathers life, but it was too late! King Maximus reached his had up ever so slow, and gently stroked his sons face, before his arm went completely limp, and came crashing back down to the sea floor. "NOOOO"! (Screamed the Prince).. The trident lit back up red, and "BOOM"! Another explosion. Prince Key's powers are getting stronger, and stronger.

Just then, Cynthia, Kylynn and miss Aleina, had just arrived. "No-no-no! Oh Max, my love".. (Cynthia screamed). As she fell down from her sea horse, scooping up Maximus in her arms, crying and screaming, while Aleina and Ky untied Mateos. "Oh Max, What happened Key"?! (She asked her son, the Prince).. Kylynn was consoling the Prince. "It's all my fault, it's my fault Kavizious killed him"! (Cried the Prince).. "It's not your fault Key! (His mother replied).. It's Kaviziouses! He's the one that killed your father Key, not you"! (She said). While she and Ky took turns, hugging the poor, grief stricken prince Key. "It's all my fault"! (Key said, ashamed). "Stop that right now Key! (Mateos demanded). I was there, I seen what happened, it wasn't your fault Key, I can promise you that"! Queen Cynthia, kissed her dead husband King Maximus on the cheek one last time. She wiped her tears and slowly arose, she turned to her son Prince Key, she grabbed him by his hands and said.. "You're the King now Key! Wipe your face and make your father proud my son.. "So where is that piece of slime now Key"? (Cynthia asked). "He's over there under that big pile of rocks"! They all rushed over and started pulling the rocks off of the sea hell beast. "Quick Key, you need to use the Trident and banish Kavizious to sea purgatory (purgatorseas). Remember the magic spell chant"! (She reminded him).. As they were digging out the beast, Queen Cynthia turned to her so and said.. "Give me a minute with him before you banish him to sea purgatory for ever Key"! (Cynthia demanded). "I"! (King Key replied).. They where going to have to banish Kavizious to purgatorseas, in-order to keep him gone from this realm for good. He knows how to get out of sea hell, so they had to devise another plan and figure out how to get rid of a creature that will not die, because he is already dead.

Once they had uncovered Kavizious from the falling rocks and debris completely, he was barely conscious. "He's hurt"! (Kylynn said). "Everyone, move out of the way, I'm about to get rid of this scum, once and for all". Key raised his Trident up over his head, and was just about to sent Kavizious to purgatorseas, when all of the sudden, Cynthia started losing it. She began screaming and yelling. "You slime"! (She cried). While punching Kaviziouses broken down body, in the face and chest, over and over again. Mateos grabbed Cynthia and shouted.. "Now Key, do it now"! Prince Key closed his eyes and with two hands he lifted the Trident up over his head and began chanting ... "Pergatnahanana, pantinitisistias, parazanernizkiavanieza, atwanapertatinatoriza"!! And then jammed the Trident downward in a thrusting motion, and slammed it into thee floor of thee abyss! The Trident of Tolkien lit up a very bright red and started vibrating, and then out shot a beam of fiery red light and shot straight up and out the top of the cave, and hit all three points of the Triangle of Fire, one, by one, by one, forming a fiery triangle shaped portal directly in the middle of the deep dark abyss of Mid World's Ocean, deep, deep, down in the Tolkien Sea. That's when a beam of light shot straight down to Kavizious, from the triangle and forming a bright red ring of light around his body lifting him up off the ground and spinning him around and around, faster and faster.. That's when Kavizious started to come to! "Wait, what the, what's going on"?! (Kavizious demanded). Kavizious looked down and seen Cynthia and Maximus staring up at him, as he was being sucked up into the fiery triangle of fire portal, while he himself was glowing a magically bright red. "NOOOO! (Kavizious screamed). I'll be back, don't you worry about that, I promise, I'll be back, and I will kill you all. I will kill every single one of you"! (Kavizious threatened). "No you wont, I guarantee it"! (Prince Key replied). As Kavizious was sucked away, into the portal in the Triangle of Death, and then.. "POOF"! Just like that, Kavizious and the fiery triangle shaped portal, were gone!

There was an eerie feeling in the abyss, Kavizious and the Triangle of Fire were both gone, and everyone's ears were ringing from the blast earlier. Even the bright red light on the Trident was gone. All that was left, was a broke down, bunch of heroes, so distraught from losing their husband, their father, their best friend and their King, King Maximus Posidian.. But they had finally defeated the sea hell demon beast, Kavizious. They had defeated all the sea hell demons, the sea monkey's had retreated in defeat, and they got back their stolen, brain washed sea dragons, that Kavizious had taken control of.. But the win, had come with a very high price. Maximus was a terrific King, who was loved and respected by all of the kingdom and throughout thee entire Tolkien sea. So now instead of celebrating their major victory over the hell beast Kavizious and his demon army, they are morning the loss of their beautiful, beloved King! Key and Mateos, picked up Maximuses limp body and gently placed him on Zar, and draped a cloth over him that Kylynn had in her satchel, hanging over her sea horse. Even the sea dragon Zar was visibly upset over the King's death.

It was very slow going, heading back to the Kingdom. Mateos led the way, while Key and the ladies, tried comforting his mother, Queen Cynthia. Cynthia was in complete shock over the death of her husband. All the way back to the kingdom was very, very quiet, except for the faint whimpering cries from the Queen. It was a very eerie quest back home to the kingdom. The whole lot of them were in complete disbelief. Cynthia was absolutely crushed and Key knew he was going to have to be strong for his mother. As they made it back to the kingdom, the royal water trumpets and horns were blowing, all of the kingdoms people were so happy to hear the water trumpets sounding, because it meant that the Prince And them were just outside the kingdoms walls and were about to be home from battle, that they had won. Except, no-one knew the tragedy that had occurred with their King. Thee entire kingdom was awaiting at the front entrance of the kingdom, to celebrate their arrival, and welcome their heroes back home.. But instead of celebrating, all the cheering and clapping had quickly came to an end, and turned into cries and many, many tears of sadness and sorrow. Once they all seen the body under the white cloth, draped over the royal sea serpent, Zar. Their were whispers from the crowds of people when they realized that King Maximus was not amongst the living, which brought them all to one conclusion. They had lost their beloved King!

CHAPTER

19

As the entered the Kingdom, General Mateos and Prince Key, now King Key, couldn't help but notice how good the Kingdom looks. The people of Mordainia, along with the royal army, did a terrific job protecting the kingdom. There was not one casualty in or away from the kingdom, other than the royal soldiers they lost on the battle field, and of course, their King. When Kaviziouses hell demons and sea monkey minions showed up and tried to do damage to the kingdom, the people of Mordainia, were ready for them! The Kingdom was well prepared and completely ready for anything that they have possibly thrown at them. The entire kingdom has been trained in combat and defense so well, that nothing could ever defeat the people and or royal army of the kingdom. They defeated Kaviziouses troops on more than one occasion, and that made them feel so strong and powerful. They wanted so bad to celebrate with their king, but now they were morning him. It's a sad, sad day in the Kingdom of Mordainia. Sergeant Gerald swam up to General Mateos and Prince Key, grabbing stuff from off their shoulders and out of their hands, he was helping them to carry their armor, when he asked the question, that he already knew the answer too, but hoping and praying to the Gods, that he was wrong.. "Is that King Maximus under their"!? (Gerald asked). "Yes Sergeant, it is"! (Mateos replied). Mateos stooped and addressed the people. "It's a sad day in the Kingdom, we have lost our King! Prince Key is our new King now and we will have the coronation coming up soon, the day after Key's eighteenth birthday"! (General Mateos declared).. Their were a mixture of cheers and jeers. Most everyone was happy and clapping for the Prince, but they mostly crying and consoling one another, because they were all so sad about the loss of their King. They were all trying to hug the Queen and Prince, to give their condolences. The King was so beloved amongst the people of the kingdom. It's because of King Maximus and Queen Cynthia, the Mordainians and the OctaGod's were all living together, peacefully in Kingdom. It's because of them they had such a good life in Mordainia. You could see the pain and sorrow in everyone's faces, as Zar passed by them with the King's dead body draped over him, under the white cloth.

The very next day, they had a huge funeral in the kingdom for their King. The entire Kingdom was in attendance. "your father would be so proud of you Key! (Mateos assured him).. I hope you do know this Key"!? "I know Mateos, thank you"! (Key replied). As Mateos put his hand on Key's shoulder, and gave a little squeeze. "He was so proud of how you have turned out son"! (Mateos told him).. The Prince smiled and nodded. "After your birthday tomorrow, we can have your coronation to become the new King, Key"! (He told him).. "Yes, and I'll step down as Queen, so you can take over as complete ruler of Mordainia! It's what your father would have wanted my son! (Queen Cynthia announced).. So that way, once you and Ky wed, she can be your Queen. I do not want to be the one who ends up being in the way of that"! "We will talk about this later! (Demanded the Prince).. Can I please just bury my father today and deal with everything else tomorrow please, thank you.. But yes, I will except my fait as the new King. I will honor my fathers wishes"! (Key said). The Queen smiled. That made Key happy, that he made is mother smile. Key sway over to his father's body and whispered.. "I love you father"! As he kissed him on his forehead and swam off, back over to his mother Cynthia's side, and hugged her as tight as he could.. "He loved you so much Key"1 (Cynthia told him).. "I know mother, he loved you too"! (Key answered). "That he did my son, that he did! He will always be with us, in our hearts Key"! "I know Mother, I know"! (He said). Wiping his tears from his and his mothers faces. Everyone came and paid their respects to the King, and said their goodbyes to their King, in their own little way. Some cried, some talked about things they remembered and loved about the king, and some were so shocked, that they just stayed silent, not knowing what to say.. Queen Cynthia was trying to stay strong for her people, but everyone knew just how crushed she truly was!

King Maximus was Cynthia's one and only, true love! She fell so deep in love with him, she absolutely adored him so much, and he her. Maximus was absolutely infatuated with Cynthia from the first time they met. She and Key, were King Maximuses whole world, and he and Key were Cynthia's.. But now she had to let them both go! Not only did she just lose her husband, she is also losing her son. She's not losing Key in the same way as her husband Maximus, but she is losing him none the less, just this time, it was to another woman and thee entire kingdom. She was going to have to relinquish the throw as leader of Mordainia so that her son could be ruler and also take Kylynn as his Queen. She Knew it was what's best for the kingdom that she loved so deer. Cynthia was a little concerned however, that this all might be just a little to much for her son to handle, right after his father just passed. That was until Kylynn had swam on over to comfort the Queen. Kylynn took her hand and placed it over Cynthia's and squeezed ever so lightly. She gave Cynthia a smile, letting her know that everything would be fine, she knew Ky would be there for her son, and have his back no matter what! Queen Cynthia knew right then, that everything would be OK. Kylynn Loved Key with all her heart and would always support him. It was time for Cynthia to move aside, she raised a fine young man, who hasn't realized it yet, but he will soon be fallen in love with a beautiful girl. She knew that her time has passed, and a new era has begun. Young miss Kylynn was a terrific young lady, and her son Key was a very lucky man to have won the love and affection of such a catch, General Mateos and miss Aleina had done a fine job in raising her. Kylynn loves Cynthia's son so much that it shows, you could see the glow of young love, radiating off of her, it reminded the Queen of a young Cynthia and Maximus. Some how the Queen just knew that she would never have to worry, that Kylynn would be by Key's side through thick and thin, the good times and the bad. Kylynn has loved Prince Key since as far back as she could remember, and it gave the Queen such a piece of mind, knowing that her son Key had actually found his one true love, his one and only soul mate, just like his mother and father did. He too, now knows what it's like to love someone more than life itself..

After everyone in the kingdom said their prayers for their fallen King, and they all had said their goodbyes, his best friend General Mateos addressed the people of the kingdom. He talked about how much the King would be missed, and talked about how he and the king had met, and what they had gone through, growing up together. How they fought and protected each other, their entire lives. "I loved King Maximus so much, he wasn't just my friend, he was my brother and I will never forget him! I am truly sorry for your loss Cynthia and Key, my Queen and Prince, me and my family love you and the entire kingdom very much. I owe Maximus my life, and I will forever serve his family, I promise you this on my life! I just want to say one last thing, I know how proud my friend was of his wife the Queen, he loved you so much Cynthia, he was so proud that you were the one that was able to help him bring the Mordainians and OctaGod's together again. King Maximus had fought hard to protect all of you, he literally gave his life! He truly loved this kingdom and all it's people so much. King Maximus sacrificed his life for you, for me, his wife, his son, my wife, my daughter, he sacrificed himself to save the entire Tolkien Sea! We owe him everything! Max was the greatest man I have ever known in my entire life. He absolutely cherished his home, and every single one of us"! (Mateos said). Taking his hand and pointing around to everyone.. "But Maximus did not die in vain! He saved all of us and our home. He died to preserve out way of life that he and Queen Cynthia have made possible for us all. So when you think of your late beloved King, I want you to smile, and remember just how much he loved you! I know I will forever be grateful". (Mateos said). Looking up and after taking a deep breath, Mateos spoke again from his heart.. "I pledge my life to this kingdom, and I vow to forever watch over your family my King. I will fight until my dying breath to protect the kingdom and all of you I was proud to call Maximus my King, and I damn sure will be proud to call his son Key, my King, as well".. "YAAAA"! Everyone clapped and cheered.. After Mateos was done with his eulogy, he swam over and hugged and kissed Queen Cynthia and hugged and shook Key's hand. As Mateos turned to swim off, he was greeted with his own hugs and kisses by his wife and daughter Aleina and Ky.

Queen Cynthia was the last to address the people. Everyone understood her pain and felt so bad for their Queen. They all knew just how deep in love the King and Queen were. She started by saying.. "I would just like to thank you all for coming and showing your love and support for Maximus and our family. As Mateos stated earlier, my husband King Maximus loved this kingdom and all of us so, so much. In two days my son will be sworn in as King, and I will be relinquishing my power and seat at the thrown so that my son Key can be complete ruler of the kingdom and all of the Tolkien sea. This way the Queens thrown will be opened if and when my son chooses to take a bride. I just know that Key will make as terrific a King as his father was! It's what Maximus would have wanted, and I intend to honor my late husbands wishes! I just know you will make us all proud my son. Your father loved you so much and I know you will miss him, I know we all will miss him. Maximus was my.. (Cynthia paused). Maximus Is my whole world"! Cynthia began to cry.. She felt she had began to lose it a little bit, so she decided she need to be alone for a few, and swam off. "Thank you all for coming"! (Key quickly said).. As he followed suit, after his mother.

At the end of the King's funeral, Maximuses body was burned in a very old magical ritual. Only Mordainians and OctaGods partake in this enchanted after life ceremony. They started this ritual thousands of years ago, so no other sea creatures could eat or take the bodies of their deceased, loved ones. So an ancient OctaGod, created a magical spell that could burn and cremate the remains under water, deep down in thee abyss of Mid World's Ocean.. But they created this ritual in such a beautiful way that it was an honor to go through this process when you pass on. It was a glorious sight to behold. It was an absolutely honorable tribute to their fallen. The King's funeral ended with a chant from all of the kingdom. Everyone gathered around the King's body that was lying over a beautiful bed of sea weeds and sea flowers, with a silky white cloth draped over him. As the kingdoms people began their chant, under the King's body, the bed of flowers burst into flames, catching the white cloth and then his entire body was engulfed in flames and it was breath taking. The inner base of the flames where the body was lying, was a beautiful greenish color, and as the flames expanded up and out, the colors changed from green, to pink, to orange and then to a deep bright red. As the King's body burned away into the night sky, with such beautiful colors surrounding it, Key had persuaded his mother to come back for the ritual. Key was comforting the Queen, he was holding her in one arm and the Trident in thee other. Cynthia reached up grabbing her sons hand, gripping it so tightly. Cynthia knew that life was going to be so tough without her husband, King Maximus. It was going to be tough without her soul mate around to share her life with, but she knew that her son Key would need her to stay strong for him. He is going to have the weight of the entire sea on his shoulders, and it was going to be tough enough on him, without his mother flaking out on him. She couldn't lose it completely, she didn't want her son nor the people of the kingdom to lose faith in their way of life. She wanted them all to still feel safe, even though Maximus was gone! Soon they will all have a new King and he will need all the support he can get. Cynthia understood the more confident she was in her son, then the more faith the people will have in Key's ability to lead them and protect the kingdom.

CHAPTER
20

THE FOLLOWING DAY WAS KEY's eighteenth birthday. He and Kylynn were out in the royal sea garden. Directly in the middle of the kingdom, there was this beautiful coral reef garden right in front of the sea stables, where a young Kylynn and Prince Key use to sneak off too, but now their all grown up and they don't have to sneak around anymore! Kylynn has been awaiting for Key to be of age so they could wed, she has always wanted to be his wife. She has loved Key forever now, Kylynn never took another mate, ever! She has always held out for Key. As far back as Kylynn could remember, she has loved the prince and wanted to be with him. She was so happy that the two were in love. As Key and Ky were discussing everything that has been going on lately, and everything that has happened, Key took Kylynn by her hand and swam off, through the coral reef garden very slowly, almost at a stand still. Key put his arms around Kylynn, pulling her in closely to him and said nervously.. "I've always thought I'd have you around in my life, you have been my best friend for as far back as I can remember, I've always loved you Ky, I just didn't realize how much! I thank the God's you didn't just give up on me and move on. Now that I'm a man, I can actually see how much I want to be with you and I can actually appreciate your stunning beauty. My heart skips a beat every single time you are near me, I love you Ky, now and forever".. And as he leaned in and kissed her, he whispered.. "I love you so much Ky, will you do me the honor and take my hand in marriage, will you be my Queen Kylynn"?! (He asked her). "Oh Key! I been waiting my whole entire life for you to ask me this question.. YES! Yes Key, I will marry you and be your Queen, my King"! (She replied). Throwing her arms around Key, kissing and hugging her soon to be husband. "If I'm going to be King, then I'm going to need a strong beautiful Queen by my side"! (Key stated). "Oh Key, you have just made me the happiest girl in all of the oceans"! (She told him).. Kylynn couldn't wait to rush home and tell her mother and father the good news, that Key had just proposed to her.

Later on that evening at Key's birthday party in the palace with he and Kylynn's families and all their guests were celebrating, Key and Kylynn told them all the great news. This was a truly joyous occasion, with the engagement, the eighteenth birthday and tomorrow Key will be sworn in as ruler and king of Mordainia. "Well Key my son, You are officially a man now. Your father would be so proud of you, he always was proud of you"! (Cynthia said). "I know mother, I know"! (He replied). For that brief moment in time, they had put their grief aside and forgot all about their horrific loss they all had just suffered, and were actually happy! The Queen actually felt a little joy and happiness, that she so much deserved, even though it was just for a short period of time. Cynthia had lost her soul mate, her husband and her best friend, Key had lost his father, his mentor, Mateos had lost his best friend and his brother, and the entire kingdom has lost their friend, their King, who they absolutely adored and he did them.. But for these few moments in life, everyone was happy. There was love in the waters and hope for the future, except..

What nobody had known was that when Kavizious stabbed King Maximus with the trident, he released a spell, he had conjured up with his black magic. He had placed his spell in the wound of the King when he stabbed him in the chest. The spell lied dormant in the chest cavity of King Maximus for twenty four hours. When it was finally released, it seeped out of King Maximus during his funeral, and made it's way to the closest sea creature. It was almost gas like, when the spell was inhaled into the lungs of the poor unsuspected soul and seeped into his blood stream, making him completely engulfed in rage and hate. Whatever the creature see's and hears, so could Kavizious from the other side, stuck deep within purgatorseas. It just so happened the spell ended up taking control of a loner, OctaGod named Takine. Takine never liked to be around crowds of people, but he had the utmost respect for King Maximus and had to pay his respects before they burned the body. So while life was starting to look good for the future of the kingdom, so they thought. Its seems that Kavizious has an angry insider in the kingdom while he would build an army and search for a way back to Mid World's Ocean, in the Tolkien Sea (thee Eighth Sea).

It was finally here, the coronation, swearing in Prince Key as the new King, King Key! Key had the two woman he loved the most in thee entire sea, by his side, Kylynn and his mother. He couldn't be happier. "I am so proud of you my son"! (Cynthia said). "Me too Key"! (Kylynn added). Giving him a hug. "You look so handsome Key"! (Ky told him).. "Stop, your going to make me blush"! (Key replied). "Thank you for being here for me guys, I really appreciate it"! (He told them).. "You'll be just fine! I'll see you out there my son"! (Cynthia said). Kissing her son on the cheek before swimming away. Cynthia is the one who is going to present Key with his fathers crown and name him the new King and sole ruler of Mordainia. Cynthia has denounced her position of Queen and ruler of Mordainia. She has moved aside to allow Key to take full control of the Tolkien sea, as he takes his rightful seat at the thrown. Besides, Cynthia wanted Kylynn beside Key, as his Queen. She knew they would be perfect together as King and Queen, but deep down, she knew she was truly doing it because she didn't have it in her to rule over the kingdom properly without her husband Maximus by her side, she was completely empty inside and figured it best to let her son begin his new journey in life. A little soon than she would have hoped, but she knew it was for the best of the people and their kingdom. It was time for the new generation to put their mark in this watery world. After the ceremony swearing in Key as new King and sole Ruler of Mordainia, Cynthia slipped into another trans. This particular vision was so surreal, she has never had one feel so incredibly real before. When she finally came too, she was so frightened, she was in shock! Cynthia couldn't believe what she has just seen, it was Kavizious. He was in purgatorseas, and he has created an army unlike any world has ever seen. He was heading back to Mid World's Ocean, and he was pissed. He some how found his way back to their world, and he did it without the Trident to open the portal, he had found another way, and he has help from a more powerful being than even him. "This is not good"! Cynthia had thought to herself.. She looked around and seen her son and all of the kingdom so happy, she couldn't ruin this for them, not today anyways. It was going to have to wait, they deserved a win and she couldn't take that away from them. "Thank you for the most perfect day mother"! (King Key said to Cynthia).. Cynthia Smiled and said.. "Good, I'm glad your happy my son"! Pushing down the terrifying horror that was to come and bottling it up, deep down inside, keeping it to herself!

Meanwhile, over in another realm, in Purgatorseas, the sea hell demon Kavizious, was controlling the mind of Takine, the lone OctaGod back in the Kingdom of Mordainia, in the realm of Mid World's Ocean, deep down in thee abyss in the bottom of the Tolkien sea. The spell has soaked into this poor, unsuspecting soul. Kaviziouses spell on Takine, had him planning and plotting against the new King Key and his kingdom. Takine has been watching Key and Kylynn, spying on them, and Kavizious has been monitoring from Purgatorseas. He has also been watching Mateos and Aleina, he has even been studying the movements and the ways of the royal army. He has even been watching Cynthia, who has seemed to have forgotten all about her vision at her sons coronation. Kavizious was smiling as he looked at a beat down, broken Cynthia. Takine has completely mapped out all their schedules, their hobbies, down to their dirty little forbidden secrets! Takine knew everything about everyone.. Deep down in the bowels of Purgatorseas, Kavizious was trying and trying to find his way back to the realm in which he's been trying to destroy, since the first time he has ever entered that realm. He vowed to build an army bigger and better than he ever has, and get back to Mordainia to destroy them all once and for all. Kavizious will not stop until he brings death and destruction upon all eight seas.. But this time, was going to very difficult. Kavizious has never been banished to the purgatorseas before, it was going to be a difficult task, even with a man on the inside, completely devoted to his every command. Takine would however, prove to be very useful later on..

CHAPTER

21

IT HAS SEEMED LIKE ETERNITY, since Kavizious has been banished to Purgatorseas, but in actuality it has been over two months that have passed since the battle that killed King Maximus. Even though nothing has changed, and he hasn't gotten any closer to finding his way out of this nothing realm, Kavizious would never give up! He will never stop trying to get back and reign hell upon the Tolkien sea. Kavizious has been a hell demon for over a thousand years now, he has nothing but time to plot his revenge, he's a demon, he's already dead!

Thousands of years ago, when Kavizious was a alive, way back in a different time, Kavizious was a God of war. His King was a vicious creature who sought out death and war, he pillaged and plundered any and all civilized societies he came across, and Kavizious was his second in command, he was the head of his army. Kaviziouses whole life and afterlife for that matter, has been nothing but war! Death and destruction was all he was good at, it was all he knew. Kavizious had led his troops to war, thousands of times, he has had hundreds and thousands of battles, many, many times. He has pillaged and plundered hundreds and hundreds of kingdoms and small villages too. He has taken the lives of millions of sea creatures, good and bad. Kavizious was a cold blooded, savagely calculated killer, he was pure evil. So when he finally got killed in battle, his soul went directly to sea hell, where it's nothing but torture and war. Kavizious was right at home in the sea hell realm. Kaviziouses soul, strived in sea hell and has quickly risen through the ranks of the sea hell demon army, and soon was the head of all the hell demon soldiers, where he continued to torture poor lost souls damned to eternity. Until the day he met Elisabeth when she died and her soul was sentenced to his sea hell realm. Kavizious could see the evil radiating off of her, he could see the evil black magic oozing out of her pores. Kavizious knew the moment he met Elisabeth that she would be the key to getting him out of this realm, and back into the battle waters where he belongs.

Kavizious pledged his loyalty to miss Elisabeth and she vowed to get them both out of sea hell and bring him to her world where she would have him rage war upon her home seas, deep down in thee abyss of Mid World's Ocean, the Tolkien sea (thee Eighth Sea). Where she would have Kavizious lead an army for she and her husband Cyris, against King Keyira and his kingdom. Elisabeth figured with his help, they could get the Trident of Tolkien, and rule thee entire Eighth Ocean, there would be no stopping them! There was just one catch though.. They had to wait for her husband Cyris to die and get sentenced to eternity in sea hell. Elisabeth created a black magic spell, that would allow her to brake free from sea hell, but it would only happen if and when her husband Cyris dies and crosses over into the same realm as her. Elisabeth told Kavizious all about the spell she had conjured up before she died. Both she and Cyrises bodies would be protected by one of her black magic spells, until she and her husband could get back to their vessels. She had told him, how once Cyris is in sea hell and they locate him, a portal in the Triangle of Death would open up and they could cross through the Triangle of Fire, but she would need his help to locate the entrance to the portal from within this realm, in sea hell. She continued to explain that it would only work if Cyris is evil enough to be sent to the sea hell realm, and how they could help make that happen while speeding up the death of her husband Cyris, in the process! They would just have to wait to see if they didn't take action, and Elisabeth didn't want to take that chance, she had made sure that Cyris would avenge her death, and if one of the battles he would soon be in, didn't take his life, then Elisabeth would use her black magic to help secure his death. Either way, he wouldn't be living too much longer, but in the meantime, she and Kavizious would devise a plan and build their sea hell demon army! When they finally were able to activate the portal and cross back through, Elisabeth kept her word and brought Kavizious back with them. Even though Elisabeth and Cyris used Kavizious for their own selfish needs, he was set on carrying out their wishes and bringing the Kingdom of Mordainia to its demise! Ever since Kavizious first past threw the portal into this new world, he got back the thirst for war and death, he wanted to get back there as fast as he could, its all he can think about. Kavizious knew if he could get their from the sea hell realm, then he could definitely get there from the Purgatorseas realm! He will not rest until he gets back to the Tolkien sea realm, and finish what he started.

Back in thee abyss of the Tolkien sea, Takine was out and about in the caves on the outskirts in the waters near the kingdom. He was searching for ingredients for his black magic spells to try and get his hands on the Trident of Tolkien and get his master back to this world, somehow. I will get that portal open and bring you back home my lordship"! (Takine said). Out loud to himself.. But he was actually speaking to him master, Kavizious. Takine has found a nice secluded place to work on his black magic spells and potions. Kavizious was working through Takine in this world, while figuring things out in purgatorseas. Anything and everything Takine could hear and see, so could Kavizious. His spell as turned Takine into a clone of his master, Master Kavizious. So when Kavizious was busy in Purgatorseas, Takine would still be working on things back in Mordainia. He thought exactly what Kavizious thought, Takine would soon become a very big problem for the new King and Queen. This spell that Kavizious had casted upon Takine, not only gave him the power to telepathically communicate with Kavizious anytime either of them wanted or needed too, it also gave him the power and strength of a sea hell demon, but in the body of an OctaGod. It was a very lethal combination. Takine still had his own thoughts and ideas, but now they were filled with hate and anger. While Kavizious searched for a way out of purgatorseas from within, Takine Conjured up spells to try and help him get the Trident free from the new King, it was seeming nearly impossible, until Takine had an idea. "It wont be long now my lord! (Takine said). It's easier for Kavizious and the demons to get from the sea hell realm and the Purgatorseas realm, to the realm of Mordainia, because they didn't need vessels. The only time you need a host vessel, is if and or when you go back to the world in which you once were among the living. That's why Elisabeth needed to preserve her and her husbands bodies, once their souls left their original vessels. If she didn't, then they would only have a short period of time to find and secure a host vessel but as long as they could get a hold of someone, they wouldn't need their permission to take control of their bodies either! "Soon we will open the portal and bring you back to the abyss, my lord. I have a plan"!

Kavizious has been busy for months now, recruiting lost souls in purgatorseas to come join his demon army, and reign hell down upon the kingdom of Mordainia. Kavizious had come across all types of frighteningly scary creatures, stuck in this nothing world. Now that Maximus was defeated and out of the way, and Cynthia was depleted, Kavizious could beat them, by striking King Key and General Mateos, but he has to strike hard and fast! Before King Key figures out the true potential of the Trident. Once Key truly masters the Trident, it will be too late! Key will be more powerful than he could ever imagine. It seems that the trident has chosen Key, there hasn't been a chosen one for over four thousand years, its going to prove difficult to get the Trident from Prince Key. The Trident of Tolkien is the most powerful object from any world and could do tremendous good, or it could completely destroy anything and everything. If he waits to long to attack, he wont be able to defeat the Morainians and OctaGods, there will be nothing he could do.

Kavizious promised the vicious creatures of Purgatorseas a way out of this nothing world, and a life of war and revenge in a sea of magically adventurous, blood quenching times. "I have always been second in command, following out others orders. No more! (He said). I'm in charge now"! As Kavizious rounded up soldiers from this world, one, by one, he had made sure they knew his qualifications and not o ever cross him. He told them all about the hundreds of Wars he won, the thousands and thousands of battles he had concord. Kavizious had millions of kills, all for others greed. "I have fought and killed in life and in death, for someone else's gain! (Kavizious confessed). NO MORE! (He screamed). I am offering you freedom and revenge! Freedom from this nowhere, nothing world, and revenge on worlds that felt you not worthy to be a part of and forsaken you to this dreadful existence.. All you have to do is pledge your loyalty to me, and I will lead you into battle once again. We will reign down death and destruction upon the Kingdom of Mordainia like they have never witnessed before now. We will kill every single creature in all of Mid World's Ocean, and together we will rule over the Tolkien sea"!

Kavizious has built a following of soldiers and is training them for battle, against the Mordainians and OctaGods!

Kavizious has thousands of sea demon creatures, that have been stuck in this gods forsaken realm, ready to come forth and unleash their horror upon King Key and his Kingdom, except for one thing.. Kavizious nor Takine haven't figured out a way to open up the triangle of fire portal to the Triangle of Death. "I got threw from sea hell, I can get there from here too! (Kavizious said to Takine)..You need to figure it out Takine, get me through the portal and do it soon, or else"! (Kavizious threatened)..

Kavizious had noticed this one particular demon over all the rest. "I was listening to what you were saying, I think we might be able to help each other out! (Said the creature). My name is Kyzer"! Kyzer was just a little bigger and a little meaner than the rest of the other demons, Kavizious had come across in the realm of purgatorseas. Kavizious had instantly taken a liking to Kyzer. He had told Kavizious about a creature that has been in purgatorseas longer than anyone else in there. "He should be able to help you get what you need to get back to the world you keep speeking about". Kavizious told Kyzer he would like him to lead his army once they get through the portal. "You will be my number two Kyzer". (Kavizious told him).. "I"! (Kyzer replied). Kavizious told Kyzer all about Takine and what he had him doing over in the other realm, while awaiting his return. "With you and Takine, along with all the demon soldiers we will bring forth with us, we will be unstoppable"! (Kavizious declared). "If you can get us out of this world and through this portal of fire you speak of, then I will have no problem following you into battle my demon brother".. (Kyzer replied). "Good, it's settled! Once I get the portal open, we will crush King Key and all of Mordainia!

Kavizious had gathered hundreds and thousands of vicious, demon soldier creatures, to build his new army with and he has found the perfect general to lead them into battle with him. Kyzer has brought forth more than enough demon soldiers for Kaviziouses army. Every single one of these evil lost souls, wanted a way out of this nothing realm. They would do anything to get through the triangle of fire portal. Kavizious knew he would be able to control his new soldiers with ease. Purgatorseas was home to the most lost souls that ended up, stuck in this most horrible after life! Kavizious could and would mold these creatures into anything he desired, and all he desired was war! Kavizious began his plan by implanting seeds of hate and anger against the Kingdom of Mordainia, all his beliefs and logics. Kavizious planted a little seed of black magic into his control spell, which made every single demon, obey his every command, with just a thought. Except Kyzer, he did not cast his spell upon him. He wanted him to have his own free will, so he could have another opinion from someone in which he trusted. For some reason Kavizious took a liking to Kyzer. He reminded him of a younger self. Kavizious knew he would need Kyzer's knowledge and help. Incase he missed something, hopefully Kyzer would catch it. He knew they were going to make a good team. He just might actually be able to finish what was started so long ago!

CHAPTER

22

Back in the Kingdom, Cynthia, the King's mother and their close friends, Mateos and his wife Aleina, threw a little get together for King Key and his soon to be Queen, miss Kylynn. They had absolutely no idea that Kavizious was plotting his return, he would be back to try to destroy them and they didn't have a clue. Cynthia had completely forgotten about her vision she had when she slipped into that last trans. They had no idea that he had eyes and ears in the kingdom. This get together was to unite the two families together as one finally. They have always been close, but now thanks to Key and Kylynn have fallen in love and are due to wed, they will actually be family and all of them couldn't be happier. It couldn't have been a better day in the kingdom and Cynthia couldn't have been happier for her son and soon to be daughter.

The following day, Cynthia was so happy! She was out and about in the royal reef garden, humming and smelling all the pretty sea flowers. Cynthia was actually like she once did. For the first time since her husband King Maximus died, she actually felt a sense of inner peace. She started to feel like she and her son just might be ok, and the kingdom will flourish.. Cynthia was deep in thought and didn't notice Takine, over at sea dragon stables, watching her.. But Mateoses wife Aleina did. She noticed a strange man watching her friend in the sea garden. Aleina went to go meet her friend Cynthia at the sea garden, like she usually did, when she noticed her being watched. Aleina stopped dead in her tracks when she seen him hiding, watching her friend. She took cover on the other side of the reef, and spied on him, while he spied on Cynthia. Aleina couldn't help but get goose bumps all over her body and shivers down her spine when she got a good look at him. He had this empty, evil look upon him, that just didn't sit right with her.. But she couldn't just leave to go get help and just leave her friend alone with this guy near. She couldn't just leave her alone with this strange creature watching her. She needed to make sure her friend was safe.

Back over in the purgatorseas realm, Kavizious was watching Cynthia through Takines eyes. He couldn't wait to get to that world and get his hands on Cynthia. Kavizious had just finished conjuring up a black magic spell that would allow him to actually communicate to Cynthia while she was stuck in one of her trans states that she slips in and out of. "Next time she slips into her trans state I will be waiting, I want her to know I am coming! I'm coming to kill her and her son! I want her to know I'm coming with an army like no other, I want her to know its because of her we are coming to unleash hell upon her family and kingdom".. And right before she was about to leave the royal garden, Kavizious got his wish and was able to finally speak to her and tell her he is coming for them, and this time he has help! Cynthia snapped out of her trans and broke down hysterically! Aleina watched in horror as her friend was gasping trying to catch her breath. It was so hard for Aleina to stay put and not blow her cover. She needed to find out who this OctaGod was that was spying on her friend Cynthia, and why!

Aleina waited for the creature to turn and leave, before she swam over to help her friend.. "What just happened Cynthia, who was that watching you and why"?! (Aleina questioned). "Watching me, who was watching me"?! (Cynthia asked Aleina). "I don't know, but I know what he looks like and we will find out who and why! (Aleina had promised).. But for now, lets get you home my dear". "Please Aleina don't tell my son, or your husband. I need to figure this out on my own Aleina, please"!?! (She begged of her friend).. "Ok Cynthia I wont, but we will figure who and what this creature was and wanted, and if its something real bad, then I'm going to Mateos and Key! (Aliena said).. But for now, you need your rest Cynthia. We will finish this conversation tomorrow". "I! (Cynthia agreed). Thank you".. "Don't worry Cynthia, we will find this creature and figure this all out, if it's the last thing we do "!

CHAPTER

23

A FEW DAYS HAD PAST before miss Aleina and her friend Cynthia could speak upon what had happened that day back in the royal reef garden, and what they should and would, do about it. "When I was in the garden that day, I fell into one of my trans states, that's why I didn't notice the creature watching me Aleina"! (Cynthia said). What was it Cynthia, you seem really nervous about what you seen"?! (Aleina asked her friend).. "Its not what I seen Aleina, its what I heard! (She replied). It was Kavizious! I couldn't see anything, but I could feel his presence and hear him clear as day, like he was right inside my head Aleina. I was frozen in fear"! "Gasp"! Aleina was shocked to hear it was Kavizious.. "What did he say Cynthia"?! (She asked). Miss Cynthia took a deep breath and told Aleina what Kavizious had said.. "He's coming back Aleina, and this time we wont be able to stop him! He said he doesn't need the power from the Trident this time, and he is gathering up an army of demons from every possible realm, that have been sentence to eternity in Purgatorseas. They are coming to our world and unleashing dome upon our seas, without mercy"! (Cynthia said). Shaking as she finished telling her friend everything he said too her. "We have to tell Mateos and Key, Cynthia, we have to go tell them now"! (She said). "No Aleina.. (Cynthia demanded). We cant! Aleina, you know that I get these clips of the future, and sometimes they come tuition and sometimes its just a dream. I don't know yet, if he actually contacted me, Yet! First we find out who that was watching me that day and why. If Kavizious did make a spell to get into my subconscious, then this creature will be

135

connected somehow. If not, then it was nothing and there's no reason to alarm our children, you know they will put everything on hold, including the wedding! We don't want to do that Aleina, we will figure it out first, then if he contacts me, we will tell Key and Mateos, deal"!?! (Cynthia asked of Aleina).. "I! (She replied). Well lets go find this creature then, I'll never forget that face watching you Cynthia! So what's the plan"? (Aleina asked). "We go find that Creature you seen watching me.. First we ask, then we make him talk"! (Cynthia replied).

Later on that evening, Cynthia and Aleina were searching the kingdom for Cynthia's stalker for hours and nothing. "Arrrrg! (Aleina sighed). Its no use Cynthia, it's getting late and we aren't going to find him"! (She said). So very frustrated.. "Ok Aleina, but I just want to check one more place, I wish we thought of earlier, we need to go check the caves! I have a funny feeling he's hiding something and if that's the case, then the caves would be the best place to do so! Please, please, just search the caves with me and then we will head back, but we have to find out Aleina"!? (Cynthia asked of her).. "I swear, you get me into more mischief, Ok Cynthia, fine"! (Aleina agreed). As they both gave a little smile. "Well, you coming or not"?! (Cynthia called out).. As she sped off ahead of her into the caves. "Hey wait for me"! (Miss Aleina called out).. Picking up speed, as she swam after her friend into the deep dark watery caves.

Cynthia and Aleina searched through the caves, looking for any signs of black magic or just anything linking them to the creature from the reef garden. "Who do you think it could have been watching you, what could possibly be the connection between him and Kavizious"? (Aleina asked). "I do not Know Aleina, but we will, soon! I can feel a presence of black magic here"! (Cynthia stated). As they pushed through to the next cave, the came around the corner and something caught Cynthia's attention. "Look Aleina"! (Cynthia said). Pointing to a small opening in a crevice, deep within the cave. "Come on Aleina, we got to go there"! (She said). Squeezing through the small entrance with miss Aleina following right behind. "WOW! What is this place Cynthia"! (Aleina asked). "It's some kind of conjuring room, a spell lab. Someone's been casting black magic spells in here"! (Cynthia said). "It has to be the creature from the reef Cynthia, I just know it"! (Said Aleina). "I guarantee it's whoever you seen watching me back at the garden, and somehow Kavizious is involved with him. He has help here from the Purgatorseas realm, I don't know how though, we have to find him Aleina! Quick, we have to go"!

Cynthia knew they needed to get out of there, before the creature returned and caught them off guard in his hide away. She knew he had the advantage and they would be killed or captured. As the two swam back to the kingdom out of the caves, Aleina asked Cynthia why they left in such a rush. "What's going on Cynthia"! (Aleina demanded). "Kavizious is controlling this creature from Purgatory. I don't know how or what's happening yet but we are going to find out and stop it! You will recognize the creature that you seen that day right"!?! (She needed to know).. "Yes! (Aleina replied). I'll never forget that face Cynthia. (She assured Cynthia).. I do know I have seen him around the kingdom before, he is always alone, by himself. He's one of us, he is from the kingdom of Mordainia, but he isn't a Mordainian, he's an OctaGod and very creepy looking, and very scary"! (She said). "Ok Aleina, I think I know what to do, I have a plan to catch this slimy sea slug"! (Cynthia declared). "But you don't understand Cynthia, I didn't recognize him that day because there's something wrong, he's more off than he ever was because I would have noticed something like that, he looked pure evil Cynthia, he scared me"! (Aleina said). "That's because he's under Kaviziouses power, he is controlling him, he must have conjured up a spell and released it before he was banished somehow. Come on Aleina, we are going to have to find away to reverse his spell, we need to brake the link in the chain that controls him, before he and Kavizious figure out how to open the portal in the triangle of death! We will find him tomorrow, you can point him out to me when you see him, if he is from the kingdom, then he will have to be there tomorrow at the mandatory defense meeting, which Kavizious would want to know our strategies, so he will definitely be there. I think I have a plan! Your sure you can point him out right Aleina, this is very important"!?! (Cynthia said). "Yes Cynthia but what about Mateos and Key? We have to tell them, this is way to dangerous Cynthia! It's Kavizious, w - w - we cant go up against him alone"! (Aleina stuttered). In completely and utter fair.. "NO Aleina, we cant! They will stop the wedding and both our families futures depend on this wedding, we cant ruin this for them, you know Key will stop the wedding and he and your husband Mateos will stop at nothing to protect the kingdom from Kavizious! They will spend every waken second dedicated to killing him and nothing else. You cant Aleina, I'm sorry! I have a plan though, and it will work, I promise! But I'm going to need your help Aleina, my friend, please?! I know what to do Aleina, we have to create an old spell my mother taught me when I was a child, it was to protect our family if anyone ever took control of one of us! Please trust me Aleina, ok"!?! (Cynthia asked of her friend).. "Fine, I wont say anything, but only until after the wedding, and if we are getting in way to deep then I'm going to have to do what's right Cynthia, but yes, I'm with you"! (Aleina agreed). "Thank you Aleina, now lets go conjure this up. We are going to need a few things". (Said Cynthia). "Well in that case, follow me"! (Announced Aleina). Cynthia smiled and followed Aleina, this time..

As the ladies conjured up a spell to brake the control spell Kavizious had on Takine, they still didn't know exactly who he was yet, or where he was. Even though they were done with the spell they still needed Takine, to see if it works. They looked all through the kingdom and the surrounding caves, but he wasn't there, but they now Know he is! They figured out it was Takine, when he was the only one from the royal kingdom, that didn't attend the kingdoms defense meeting. "Well I was wrong about Kavizious wanting to know our defense strategies, guess Kavizious and Takine have other plans.. We have to find him and brake this spell Aleina, where in sea hell can he be"!?! (Cynthia cursed). As they continued through the caves after destroying his spell room when he wasn't there either, but what they didn't realize, was that he wasn't at any of these places, because he was in the deep abyss of where the sea monkey's dwell, in their own hidden territory, way deep down under the volcanic lava filled waters, under a slew of the nastiest sea creature to ever swim the waters of Mid World's Ocean. Takine was rounding up soldiers for his armies return. "Master Kavizious will spear all your lives when he returns to this realm, and if you do not join him, he will have his sea demon soldiers from all over, from the worst realms and banished to the worst of the worst eternity, and they are coming! He wants your decision by his next contact and I have to tell him yes or no".. (Said Takine). The sea monkey's had no choice, and their leader, Lord Banta agreed to follow Kavizious and Takine's wishes. Lord Banta knew that if he disobeyed their request, that Kavizious would not stop until he had killed every last one of them, wiping out their entire species. He just couldn't say no!

Takine had left the kingdom for his journey to the sea monkey's territory before the brake of dawn. He had taken a sea horse from the royal stables and when he made it to the sea monkey minions territory, he had to make through the series of tunnels, deep down under the bottom of thee abyss, deep down within the triangle of death. Under all the thousands and thousands of sharks lurking there, Great whites, hammer heads, tiger sharks and even bull sharks all roam directly above them. They sometimes, on occasions, would feast upon the sea monkeys, that were caught slippin.. This was the absolute worst place to live in Mid World's Ocean, it was complete Sea Hell on the dark ocean floor, and Takine wasn't scared in the least. When Takine reached the entrance of the minions domains, he was instantly surrounded and brought deep down to where lord Banta and the other elders were. Where they asked why he was there and decided whether or not to kill him, until he pulled out a big satchel of gold, and then he told him why his master had sent him. When Takine had left the kingdom before anyone had the chance to notice he was gone from the kingdom, but Cynthia and Aleina knew. He was the only person in the entire kingdom that didn't show up to the meeting. Takine had no idea that Cynthia and Aleina where on to him, searching for him, he never seen Aleina the day he was watching Cynthia in the reef garden. Although they knew that Kavizious had a spell over Takine, they didn't know just how to what extent and how much power and control he actually had on the sea creature, or how much of this was fueled by his own desire! They had no idea that Kavizious could see and hear whatever Takine could, when he is powering the spell, at will. They had no idea that when Takine was watching Cynthia in the sea garden, so was Kavizious!

Before Takine had left the minions, he told them.. "Me or Kavizious will be in touch, We will contact you when it is time. We are going to war against King Key and the kingdom of Mordainia, but this time we are coming with an army this world has ever or will ever see.. This time we guarantee we will be victorious, I know how to retrieve the trident of Tolkien and we will use it to destroy them, once and for all. You will have your people ready for when we contact you Banta, and we will be contacting you, soon"! (Takine told him).. "I, Takine, we will be ready, I will make sure of it"! (Banta replied). "Good, because I don't want to have to kill you by pulling your head right off your body, and beating your top soldier to death, with your body"! (Takine promised). "gulp"! You could see the fear in Banta's eyes when he said that.. He knew he wasn't lying. "You can tell Kavizious we will honor his wishes Takine, I give you my word"! As Takine turned to leave and head back to the kingdom, he said.. "Not that you had a choice, but you made the right decision Banta".. And just like that, he was gone!

CHAPTER

24

BACK AT THE KINGDOM, THE two ladies were laying in wait, just outside the kingdoms walls, waiting for Takine to return. The friends had figured out that their was a sea horse missing from the royal stables and was waiting for him to return, and sneak the animal back in before anyone had noticed, but he didn't count on these two, foiling his plans, he had no idea that the girls would be on to him. It wasn't until real late that evening, when Takine snuck back into the Kingdom and returned the sea horse to the stables. He was in and out within minutes, and disappeared into the shadows of the caves, heading to his hidden spell room, but what he didn't know was Cynthia and Aleina were hot on his trail, following him back to his hideout. The girls knew they had to fight black magic with black magic, but they were going to have to cut him off before he made it into the spell room and seen it destroyed. They had to cut off the connection to Kavizious and they had to do it now!

Back in the palace, King Key and Kylynn were awaiting their wedding day. Cynthia and Aleina met their children and Aleina's husband Mateos at the palace, acting like nothing had happened. They never once let on that they had kidnapped the sea creature Takine and dosed him with their black magic spell that Cynthia had conjured up. They had attacked Takine deep within the caves, and he is now tied up and stuck in a black magic spell the girls had made especially for Takine. Cynthia and Aleina couldn't help but feel a little bad that they were keeping this from their loved ones.. But for now they were keeping this between the two of them, at least until after the wedding anyways. "May we have everyone's attention please, me and Ky have something to tell you all. There's a reason we told you all to come here, well I'll let Kylynn tell you. (Said Key). Go ahead my dear".. "I'm pregnant, me and Key are going to have a baby"! (Kylynn said). With the biggest smile, holding her stomach, as King Key held her. "Congratulations"! (Said Mateos). Hugging his daughter and shaking Key's hand. Cynthia and Aleina were so happy for their children and as the were all celebrating the good news and congratulating key and Ky with hugs and kisses, Cynthia gave Aleina the look, the look letting her know that they need to get bake to the spell room and finish what they started with Takine, and stop Kavizious, once and for all. They need him out of their families lives and that was final.

Aleina could spend a lot of time with Cynthia without raising any red flags, because Mateos and King Key have been quite busy, training the soldiers of the royal army, and Kylynn was so occupied between the baby and planning her And King Key's wedding. So no one even noticed when the ladies had left, back to the cave's to Takine and his spell room. When they returned, Takine was stuck frozen in a holding spell that the girls had put on him. He has stuck in a magical bright ball of light and was suspended up off the ground, rotating around and around, bound, gagged and tied up, completely detained. When the release him, he will be completely free from Kaviziouses spell and they will be able to question him and see where his loyalties truly lye. When they unlocked him from his spell and un-gagged him, but at first they did keep him blindfolded, bound and tied, just incase. "What have you done!?! NO, NO, NO, when he goes to contact me and cant, I am doomed, we are all doomed! (Takine Shouted). What is going on, who are you people and what did you do to me, why cant I contact my master"!?! (Takine demanded answers).. "I'll tell you everything you want to know Takine, but first your going to answer a few of our questions you slimy sea snake! (Cynthia shouted). As she smacked Takine so hard, upside his head with a hardened lava rock. "What do you want to know"? (He replied). Completely in submission. "What does Kavizious want from you, and what is his plans, and what have you already done for him"!?! (Cynthia demanded). "HAHAHA! (Takine bellowed). You guys have no idea what's coming, do you?! Master Kavizious had me recruit the sea monkeys and he has gathered the most evil sea demons from the Purgatorseas realm, and is working on getting him and them back to this world from the realm it which they wont be stuck for long either, you cant stop Master, he will come, and unleash a plague upon this world like no other, and either you bow to him, or you die"! (Takine told them).. "When's your next check in with Kavizious"?! (Aleina asked Takine).. "Tomorrow"! (He replied). Cynthia pulled Aleina to the side and whispered.. "We have to figure out how to make that spell work, when Kavizious goes to contact Takine, he will get through but it wont be Takine that he's talking to, it will be me. We have to beat him at his own game Aleina, I have to figure out if he knows another way to get back to this realm, because if he doesn't have Takine or his little sea monkey minions, well then, he will not be able to get near the Trident of Tolkien from where he is"! (Said Cynthia). "I"! (Aleina replied). "Bad news Takine! (Said Cynthia). Looks like your hanging here for a few days, until we can figure out what to do with you"! (She told him).. "You cant just leave me here"! (Said Takine). As the two ladies re-gagged him, and exited the cave. "We will work on that spell, and be back here in time tomorrow for Kavizious to contact Takine. I cant wait to see his face when instead of Takine, he see's me"! (Cynthia said). With a smile, as she and Aleina sped off back to their families in the kingdom, with a plan to stop Kavizious and save their children's future, and it just might actually work!

Back over in the realm of Purgatorseas, away from the realm of the Tolkien sea, aka, thee Eighth Sea.. Kavizious was done recruiting his demon army and was ready to contact Takine and make sure he had made good with end on his end back in the Eighth Sea.. "Know I will make sure him and the sea monkey minions get me that Trident so I can get back and destroy the Kingdom of Mordainia".. But when Kavizious went to make contact with Kavizious, he couldn't. "What in the sea hell is going on, why cant I get through to Takine"!?! (Kavizious had wondered).. And then that's when he seen it, Takine locked in a spell rotating up off thee abyss floor, bound, gagged and blindfolded. "Hello Kavizious, guess who"?! "CYNTHIA! What do you want little girl, you shouldn't have tried to upset me, you will not like me when I'm angry Cynthia"! (Said Kavizious). "This ends now Kavizious! (Cynthia said). Why cant you just leave my family alone Kavizious, why do you want to destroy us and our kingdom so badly?! You don't need to do this Kavizious, we can come to some type of agreement or understanding, please, I beg of you"!? (Cynthia tried pleading with him).. But she knew she wouldn't get anywhere with the sea hell beast, but she was buying time while Aleina was following directions to one of Cynthia's spells, trying to magically incapacitate Kavizious while he was stuck in Purgatorseas. Cynthia taught her friend Aleina the spell earlier, she had faith in her, that she would be able to do it, except it wasn't working, she couldn't get it to work through Cynthia and Kaviziouses connection. "Hahaha! (Kavizious laughed). Your friend isn't strong enough to brake through my black magic shield I have created Cynthia, but to answer your question, there is nothing you say or do that will keep me from coming to your realm and killing everyone and everything"! (He told her).. "But why"? Cynthia really, really, wanted to know.. "Because that's what your mother Elisabeth and your father Cyris wanted, and you can guarantee that when I get out of this nothing realm that your son forsaken me too, I will bring sea hell and purgatorseas to take control of the eighth sea. You might as well just open the portal yourself and pledge your loyalty to me and I'll let you serve as my slave"! "Hahaha" (He laughed). After he finished saying what he wanted to her. "Well there's one thing your forgetting Kavizious. (Said Cynthia). I have Takine and I cut off your connection to him and this world, so once I'm done here with you, that's it, it's over! You wont be able to sea or hear anything from this world ever again, so enjoy eternity in the middle of nowhere"! (Cynthia said). As she cut the connection that magically linked them together. "Do you think it was a good idea to attack him like that at the end Cynthia, because we don't know what he has done while over there. Just because we cut off his link to Takine and this realm, we don't know how far he has gotten to getting back here Cynthia"! (Said Aleina). Cynthia turned to her friend and said.. "Yes we do Aleina, he has nothing and he can not get back here without help from this side and we stopped that! It's over Aleina"! (Cynthia told her).. "So what do we do with Takine"? (Aleina asked). "We keep him here until after the wedding and then we turn him over to Mateos and he goes to trial for helping Kavizious and betraying the kingdom".

Meanwhile, over in purgatorseas, Kavizious was beyond pissed! He was so mad that grabbed a pergatorseas demons, and as he tried swimming away from Kavizious real quick, Kavizious snatched him up, he picked the smaller sea demon up over his head and ripped him in half.

Kavizious continued his little tirade, snatching up any demon he could and completely tearing them apart, screaming and cursing, destroying anything and everyone near him. Until his second in command, Kyzer, entered and said.. "Enough Kavizious! We are going to need these demons when we get to our new world"! (Kyzer said). Calming down his master.. "There's someone I think you should meet Kavizious. I will take you to thee elder of purgatorseas. He will be able to help us, he has been in this realm longer than anyone and if there's any way out of here, he will know it, but it's a long journey so we are going to have to go now my lord"! (Said Kyzer). "Elder"!? (Asked Kavizious). Much calmer now, than he was when Kyzer first entered and told him enough, but he has calmed down dramatically now. "Yes my lord! (Kyzer replied). "The ancient roomers speak of an old timer called Zantar. Zantar has been here since the beginning of time. Roomer has it, that he was actually the first lost soul ever! He was the first sea demon in purgatorseas that was banish from any realm to eternity in this lost world Kavizious. It has been said that he is the gate keeper to purgatorseas, he decides if a soul stays lost here forever or sent down to sea hell. If he is the decider, then we can have him open up the portal and send us to the realm of Mid World's ocean, the Tolkien sea"! (Kyzer told Kavizious).. "And what if this gate keeper Zantar says, No"?! (He asked Kyzer).. "Well, then we make him"! "Hahaha"! They both laughed. "I will round up a few demon soldiers and we will start this journey my lord. It's going to take us month's to get to the gate keep of purgatorseas"! "I! (Kavizious replied). I will make Cynthia and her son Key beg for death"!

CHAPTER

25

BACK IN THE WATERS OF Mid World, there was a wedding taking place. The new King is about to have a new Queen. King Key was the luckiest man under the seas and he couldn't be happier. "We will go check on Takine later this evening after the ceremony and everything Aleina, ok"!? (Cynthia said). To her friend and now family member, Aleina. "I, Cynthia"! (She replied). The entire kingdom had come to watch their new king take his new bride, their new Queen, Queen Kylynn. "Oh Key, you have made me so happy! I love you Key, my King". (Ky said). To the love of her life. "I love you and our unborn child so much Ky, I promise to forever love and protect you both"! (Key replied). "I now pronounce you husband and wife! Here is your new King and new Queen of Mordainia, King Key and Queen Kylynn Posidian"! "YAAAAA"! Everyone cheered, as the new King and Queen hugged and kissed their parents goodbye and waved goodbye to all of the kingdoms people, as the headed to the palace for a brief little, very low key, honeymoon.

As Cynthia and her friend miss Aleina, met at there usual meeting spot in the royal reef garden, they made sure the cost was clear and they started to head off into the caves, outside the kingdom, but what they didn't know was that Aleina's husband Mateos had grown suspicious of his wife and friend Cynthia and he watched as they disappeared into the shadows of the caves. When Cynthia and Aleina had made it to Takine's hidden spell room, the girls were shocked and stunned to learn that Takine had somehow broke free from his magical restraints and has disappeared. "Where did he go Cynthia, were is Takine?! Oh my Gods, this is bad Cynthia, this is real bad! We have to tell Mateos and Key"! (Aleina cried). "Yes Aleina, I agree. Lets go talk to your husband Mateos". (Cynthia declared). That's when Mateos seen something at the mouth of the caves, it was Takine. "What is Takine doing coming out of the caves"?! He thought to himself. Mateos waited for Takine to leave the cave and swim off, before he went in after his wife and friend.

When Mateos entered the caves, he made his way deep into the system of the caves, and that's when he found it, it found them.. "What's going on here you two, what is this place"?! (Mateos asked). As he entered the spell room of Takine's. "Mateos! What are you doing here"?! (Aleina asked). As she and Cynthia both looked at each other in complete shock. "You first! (He replied). Whats going on, and why did I see Takine fleeing from the caves"?! (He demanded). "Wait you seen Takine, where"?! (Asked Cynthia). "Will someone please tell me what in the sea hell is going on here"?! (He asked loudly).. "We were just about to come to you and tell you everything Mateos, I promise"! (Aleina admitted). "Well tell me now then"!?! (Mateos demanded). Aleina took a deep breath and she and Cynthia began to tell Mateos everything! They told him all about The day it all began back in the royal reef garden and how Cynthia fell into a trans state, and how Aleina caught Takine watching her and how they need to figure out if her trans and what she heard and felt was real or not, and how they needed to track down Takine and save their children's wedding. They told Mateos all about how they figured out it was him, and how they captured him and broke his spell that Kavizious had over him. They even told him how Cynthia spoke to Kavizious, and everything that was said.. "I'm sorry I didn't tell you Mateos, please forgive me"!? (Aleina begged). "It's not her fault Mateos, I made her stay quiet, it's because of me that she didn't so please if your going to be mad at anyone, then you should be mad at me! (Cynthia said to Mateos).. But we did it for our children, and we stopped them. As long as we find Takine and get him to the dungeon and keep him from fleeing to the sea monkeys territory then we have nothing to worry about. There's absolutely no way for Kavizious to open the triangle of fire portal, without the Trident and there's no way to do that from his realm and if he doesn't have Takine nor those nasty little things, his sea monkey minions then there's NOTHING he can do now Mateos"! (Cynthia declared). "I! (Mateos replied). So lets go get that traitor Takine then"! (Mateos said). "Your not mad"?! (Aleina asked her husband).. "No Aleina, I'm not mad!

Your heart was in the right place. Besides, I know Cynthia can be very persuading"! (He said). As he smiled and then hugged his wife. "Now lets go get this bastard traitor, Takine"!

Meanwile back in purgatorseas, Kavizious and Kyzer were already on their way to find the elder. Months and months have gone by in the realm of purgatorseas, while only days have gone by in the realm of Mid World's Ocean, the Tolkien Sea (thee Eighth Sea). "So what's your plan Kyzer? I'm counting on you here"! (Said Kavizious). "Well, the way I see it is that he's been here for a very, very long time, and if we offer him the same position that he keeps now, except he does it from the realm of Mid World. We offer him partnership in ruling this new world along side you and I"! (Said Kyzer). "Yes, and if he declines, well then it's like you said, we make him open his realm gate, right Kyzer"?! (Kavizious asked). "No Kavizious! (Kyzer replied). We only have one shot at this and yes, if he declines then I will have every single demon ally in purgatorseas, fight to the end with us, but we wont win Kavizious! (He told him).. The only chance we have, is to make him an ally too Kavizious. His black magic power is like no other, he can open up any realm in any world he so chose. If we can convince him to join us, we wont just take over the world in Mid World, that will just be the first of the beginning, of many, many realms. We can take over every single sea world in every realm Kavizious, but there's one problem"! (Kyzer said). "Yeah, what's that"? (Asked Kavizious). "Well, he doesn't take to well to deceit. He will know if we lie to him, and if he doesn't like our offer, he will either kill us all, and trust me, there is a way to kill something that's already dead.. Or, he will banish our souls to eternal damn nation, in his sea hell lock box, that he wears, wrapped in chains around his chest and waste. We will be slaves of his and locked away for eternity in his lock box of hell. So when we reach his domains, you offer him the same job he has, except we go to the realm of the Eighth Sea, in Mid World's Ocean, and you tell him why you want to take over the Tolkien Sea and that we will be his partners and we will get revenge on every single sea world abyss, in every single sea realm. He can take us there, and we will destroy them and rule them all". Kavizious smiled after hearing what Kyzer has told him. "I knew I liked you for a reason Kyzer"! (Kavizious said). Kyzer grinned and the demons continued on their journey through the realm of purgatorseas. It has been months now since the began this mission, and it will be many more months, until they are only half way to their final destination.

CHAPTER
26

Back in the kingdom, Mateos and the ladies were tracking Takine, they couldn't let him get into the royal stables and take either a sea horse or worse, a sea dragon and seek refuge with the sea monkeys, they had to find him and stop him from doing anymore black magic and putting the kingdom in imminent danger, but Takine was nowhere to be found, it was just as they feared, Takine had stolen a sea horse from the royal stable and is probably half way across thee abyss, on his way to the bottom of the Triangle of Death, deep down in the sea monkey's territory. "We have to go tell you son King Key, Cynthia! (Mateos said). I have to sound the alarm, I have to take the royal army and stop him before he reaches the triangle"! (Mateos told them).. "I"! Both Cynthia and Aleina agreed..

Meanwhile, back in the palace, the King and Queen were awaiting their baby and enjoying the married life, when they heard the siren sound.. Just as they went to find out why, in entered their parents.. "We need to talk, and fast my King"! (Mateos announced).. Mateos and the ladies, all explained what was going on and how it all came about. "I'm so sorry my son, but its not their fault, its mine! Miss Aleina was just following my instructions, and Mateos just found out right before he sounded the alarm Key"! (Cynthia told the King and Queen).. "Round up the troops General, we must cut off Takine before he makes it to the triangle, we can not let him reach the sea monkeys territory! (Demanded the King).. I never liked Takine, I always knew there was something fishy with him, always"! (King Key said). As they were gearing up, to go catch Takine. "Here's Zar my son, you guys might need him! Besides, he knew you guys were leaving and he was all wound up, he wasn't going to let you leave without him". (Cynthia said). With a big smile as she handed over the reins to Key. "I wouldn't leave with without you big guy"! (Key said). Patting his long time friend, his loyal sea dragon Zar. "You and I will speak when I return mother"! (Said the King). "Yes Key, I'm truly sorry, but my heart was definitely in the right place son"! (She replied). "Yes but you still withheld crucial information from me mother, I'm the King, how do you think that makes me look! It makes me look weak, that's how it makes me look! I don't have time for this, we have to go catch this traitor Takine".. "He-yah, yah"! (Said the King). As he snapped the reins on his sea serpent Zar and he along with Mateos and a couple dozen royal soldiers, sped of on their sea dragons and sea horses and out the front gate, one, by one, by one and disappeared into the shadow, and "Poof" just like that, they were all gone, into the dark caves of thee abyss of Mid World's Ocean, the very mystical, and very, very magical, Tolkien Sea..

King Key made his mother Cynthia and Mateoses wife Aleina, stay back at the kingdom and help his pregnant wife, Queen Kylynn around the palace. She was very close to her delivery date and Key didn't want her alone, just incase. "How are you feeling my dear"? (Cynthia asked Ky).. "I'm great, just anxious! I cant wait to be a mother". (Kylynn replied). "Yes now that the wedding and coronation, are behind you and you guys are King and Queen, which I still cant believe by the way, now you two can focus on the baby and enjoy being a family in this beautiful kingdom". (Aleina said). With a big smile, as she hugged her daughter. "I just hope Key and father, find this Takine and safely bring him back home. I don't want anyone else getting hurt, and I cant raise this child without either Key nor father". (She said). To both her mother and miss Cynthia. "They will be fine my Queen, I promise"! (Cynthia assured them).. But for now, all they could do, was to hold tight and wait for their men to return safe, with the traitor, Takine.

Takine was very slick, he had a head start and he remembered everything from when he was under Kaviziouses spell. "All I need to do is get to my masters minions, I can recreate his spell and make contact with master Kavizious once again"! He thought to himself out loud. "Hahaha"! (He laughed). As he raced threw thee abyss, not knowing that King Key and General Mateos were hot on his trail. "Where is he Mateos?! We have to capture Takine and bring him back to the Kingdom, we can not allow him to make contact with Kavizious, Mateos, we just cant"! (Said the King). The King was nervous as they were getting closer to were the Sea monkeys dwell, and there is no sign of Takine! King Key resorted to using his tridents magic to locate the traitor Takine. Key raid his trident out in front of him and as the top of it was glowing a bright red, King Key said.. "He's almost there, quick Mateos, we have to hurry"!! (Said King Key).. But it was too late, Takine had made it to the territory of the sea monkeys, where he will be able to work on his spells to contact his master, Kavizious, and with help from his masters minions, to gather his ingredients and everything he may need. "This isn't good Mateos! What are we going to do now"!? (Asked the King). "I Know what to do my King, we have to stop him, and we will. (He replied). We cant just let him go, you and I both know, he will bring Kavizious back to this realm giving the chance. We are going to have to go into the sea monkeys territory and kill him Key, and I know just the man for the job"! (Mateos said). "You don't mean".. (Said Key). "Yes, yes I do! Quick back to the kingdom, (Mateos ordered). I'm sorry my King, but this is one mission you cant come with, the kingdom and my daughter need you! "He's not going to like this anymore than I do Mateos"! (Said the King). "Me and thee assassin will handle this my King. I'm sorry, but your going to have to, sit this one out my King"! (Mateos said). As they all headed back to the kingdom.

General Mateos knew exactly who to get for this particular mission, an old war hero named Burke. Burke was the kingdoms most fierce deep water warrior, he was who the king sent inn, when he needed to send a message, and boy did Burke ever deliver. He could and would, take out an entire kingdom before anyone even realized he was there. Burke was the greatest assassin in the kingdom ever! He could slip in and out undetected and leave in his wake, nothing but death and carnage, that is until a rival general from a far away kingdom, sent an assassin of his own, too murder Burke's wife and young son. The assassin paid with his life, when Burke returned and found their mutilated remains.. But since that day, Burke never spoke another word. He quit the royal army and just sat in the royal garden, day after day, after day. Now, once again his services are needed to help save the kingdom that he so loved, and Mateos is banking on him still loving his kingdom, he just figured with the right nudge, he could snap hi out of this, seeing how the assassin who killed his family, would soon be crossing over realms and invading his home with many, many demons. This is one fight, they cant allow him to bow out of.

When Mateos and the King, made it back to the kingdom, along with the other royal soldiers, they had no idea what had taken place in their absence, Queen Kylynn had just given birth to she and King Key's child. "Key, father, I would like to introduce you to the first member of our family, with both bloodlines. Here is the kingdom of Mordainia, Princess Rylee"! King Key couldn't be happier, as he hugged his new baby girl, passing her back and forth with Mateos. "We really have to stop Takine now Mateos"! (Said the King). "I, my lord"! (Mateos replied). "Go ahead and go find Zokan, I'm sure he is in the royal reef garden. "I"! (Answered Mateos). Before he handed his granddaughter to his wife Aleina, and swam off.

CHAPTER
27

MEANWHILE, OVER IN THE WATERS of the sea monkeys territory, Takine was talking to Banta. He was telling him everything he needed to recreate master Kaviziouses contact spell. "You will bring me these things before King Key and General Mateos come here looking for me"! "Hahaha! They wouldn't dear to come into these waters! Trust me Takine, you are safe here. You will be able to work your black magic spells without interruption, and anything else that you may need, you just tell my men and they will get you whatever it is you need". (Said Lord Banta).. Takine felt right at home in thee abyss of the triangle, more so here, than he ever did in the kingdom of Mordainia. "I should have left there a long time ago"! He thought to himself out load. Takine worked day and night on his potions and black magic spells, until.. "POOF"! There was a small explosion and then a magical cloud of smoke, followed by Takine shouting.. "I did it, I did it! I have recreated Masters spell"! (Takine announced). "Hahaha"! he laughed out loud.. "They will regret the day they ever crossed me"!

Back in the royal reef garden, Mateos was explaining to Burke, the severity of their mission! "I cant Mateos, I'm sorry"! (Burke said). "So that's it then huh, your just going to waste away here forever, until you die of old age?! Tell me Burke, what good does that do, nothing, absolutely nothing, Burke! If you continue to live this way, then your wife and son had died in vain"! Mateos couldn't even finish that sentence before Burke had his hands wrapped around General Mateoses throat, squeezing and lifting him up slowly. "Go ahead Burke, kill me, that will be the only sign of life from you in years"! (Mateos said). While he was loosing consciousness. Burke finally released his grip and Matoes fell to thee abyss floor. "Leave Me Mateos, leave me while you still can"! (Burke said). Unbelievable Burke, your kingdom needs you! This could be your opportunity to actually do something worth living for"! (Mateos said). Before he swam away from Zokan and the royal reef garden. Mateos knew that what he said would bounce around in Burke's head and that he would eventually come around. He just had to devise a plan and figure out a point of attack. "Now, how are we going to get into the sea monkeys domains"?! He wondered as he swam to the war room to brief the king and ready his men. The royal soldiers would have to accompany him and Burke too the triangle of death, but they were going to have to wait for them while the two generals, went on their recon mission into very hostile waters.

Over in the Palace, King Key was explaining the situation to the ladies. He had told them all how Takine had made it to the sea monkeys domain, and what Mateos was planning on doing about it.. "But Key, Burke hasn't gone on a mission since".. (His mother Cynthia, interrupted).. I know, but Mateos thinks it will work and I trust him, it will work. After Burke roughs him up a little bit first"! (Key said). With a big smile upon his face. "I can only imagine what he's saying to thee Assassin Burke, to get him interested in the mission"! "Oh my Gods! (Kylynn said). Stop Key, you'll scare my mother"! While picking up Princess Rylee and began breast feeding her. "Oh trust me Ky, I know how your father is"! (Aleina replied). "Hahaha"! Everyone had a good laugh..

While they where back in the kingdom trying to figure out their next move, Takine has already made his.. "You, minion, come here and drink this"! (Said Takine). Handing the sea monkey minion, a magic spell potion he had just concocted. "Good, drink, drink up all of it minion"! (He demanded). The masters minion, took the potion and drank it.. All of the sudden, the sea monkeys eyes rolled into the back of his head and began violently shaking, his eyes turned a dark red. "Master Kavizious, is it you"?! (Takine nervously asked the minion).. "Yes Takine, it is I, Kavizious ! How are you contacting me, Cynthia captured you and cut our contact! You are weak Takine! So what does she think she can use you for, what could she possibly use a double traitor like you Takine"!? "No my master, you have it all wrong! I broke free from Cynthia and fled the kingdom. I am with

Banta and his klan back in the Triangle of Death, my lord! (He told him)..
I have recreated your spell, well sort of. You are transmitting through one
of the minions now my lord"! (Takine said). "Excellent, Takine! Maybe
your not as weak as I thought, just maybe! You keep working on spells and
a way for you and Banta to get the Trident, not to open the portal, but to
make sure there are no problems. I have put together the biggest army off
sea demons and are on our way to find the elder of purgatorseas, he his the
realms gate keeper and we are on our way to find him and have him join
our army! The reckoning is coming Takine, do not let me down! Make sure
you fix these spells, so I can contact you Takine. I will check back with you
and Lord Banta in a few days, I expect results! (Kavizious had demanded)..
And then he was gone! The sea monkeys eyes changed back and he began
shaking, again.. Takine turned and left to go find the Lord Banta.

Over in purgatorseas, Kavizious and Kyzer were discussing their plans..
"I take it we have our men set up waiting for us in the realm of Tolkien,
everything will be in place I hope Kavizious, if not then I will guarantee
you that Zantar will damn us to his lock box of hell and I for one do not
want that to be the case Kavizious, do you"?! (He asked). "No way that
is going to happen Kyzer, I can not allow this! Takine and Banta will not
let us down again, if they do, I will kill them both myself"! (Kavizious
demanded). Kavizious had prepared a black magic spell that could be
released and bring death to whoever was to make or receive contact too
or from Kavizious while using black magic.. That way if either Takine or
Banta disappointed him again, he could kill them while communicating
from realm to realm, and it also could be used if Cynthia pulls that trick
again and tries to make contact. She would be in for a very special surprise.
"This is bigger than just you and I Kyzer, ever since Master Elisabeth and
master Cyris brought me to that realm, and introduced me to the first
battle I have ever lost! There's something very powerful about this Mid
World, and it's black magic is very strong there! These insignificant sea
creatures don't deserve to keep that world, while we are stuck here for
eternity Kyzer! I have my men in place over in the new world and once
we make it to the elder and ask him to join us in our rightful eternity, we
will cross over into the waters of the Eighth Sea, and reign hell down upon
their miserably, doomed souls"! (Kavizious promised).

BACK IN MORDAINIA, KING KEY and Mateos were in the war room going over Mateoses recon mission when Burke entered. "I have been thinking about what you said Mateos"! (Burke said). As he cocked back and punched Mateos right in his mouth. "It's ok my lord, I deserved that"! (Mateos assured the King).. "Yes, you did.. But it doesn't mean it wasn't the truth! (Burke admitted). You were right Mateos, it's time I stop feeling sorry for myself and actually protect the kingdom that didn't turn their backs on me, like I have all of you for so long! I wouldn't be making my wife or son proud of me at all, and its time I change that! I apologize my King, to you and your family for not living up to my responsibility's. I can promise you from this day forth, the legend of Burke, has returned.. And General Mateos, I thank you for telling me what I needed to hear, I know that couldn't have been easy, I respect your courage! Friends"?! (Burke asked). Reaching his hand out, a sign of respect, as it was graciously excepted, and met with a firm arm lock, hand shake between Burke and Mateos, and then Burke and King Key. "So what's the plan"? (Burke asked Mateos and the King).. "We get in, take out Takine and get the sea hell out of there! It's past capturing him and bringing forth to the kingdoms courts. The King has sentenced Takine to death, for the crime against the kingdom, the crime of treason Burke! We were just going over the plans now. Me and you will sneak in while everyone's sleeping and we kill Takine and any sea monkey that tries to stop us. We can not let him continue to help Kavizious try and open the portal and get back to our realm. We must stop

him Burke"! (Mateos said). looked at King Key and said.. "Don't worry my King, me and Mateos will get this done, I owe the kingdom for my absence lately and need to make amends to you and your people, and it will be my honor to ride along side General Mateos"! (Burke admitted). The King wished his general luck, and welcomed back the kingdoms most deadly weapon, Burke thee Assassin! As the two snuck off, out of the kingdom, in route to the Triangle of Death, where they were to sneak into the sea monkeys domains and kill Takine the traitor, Burke thanked Mateos for opening his eyes, and vowed to not only carry out the mission, but to watch Mateoses back and protect him with his life.

After Mateos and Burke had left the kingdom, King Key wanted to go back to the palace and scold the ladies for what had transpired, but he knew just how worried his wife and her mother would be about the generals safe return. The king figured it best to let this one go for now, he knew just how sorry his mother Cynthia and Miss Aleina truly were. Besides, they did do it all out of love for him and Ky. So when Key made it back to the palace, he ended up explaining the plan. He told them how Mateos had got through to Burke and how they need not worry, Mateos will return safely, and Takine will no longer be a threat to the kingdom.. But what King Key didn't realize, was that Cynthia and Aleina were even more worried now, than they were! The two women felt so guilty, they couldn't help but feel responsible for Takine, and they knew that with Mateos and Burke On their way, he was all ready dead. King Key picked up his new daughter Rylee and spun the little princess up over his head around and around until her beautiful little smile, turned into the tiniest, cutest little giggle. The King kissed all the women in his life goodbye and swam off to strategize a defensive plan with the royal army, to protect the kingdom the best way they can, just incase Mateos and Burke don't complete the mission. "We need to be well prepared against an attack of great proportion, if Kavizious makes it back here, we must be ready and able to stop him! We must defeat this hell demon once and for all"! (Said the King)..

As Mateos and Burke had reached the very dangerously dark waters of thee abyss, in the Triangle of Death, they came upon the entrance of the cave. They would have to leave Zar and the other sea dragon while the two made it through the tunnel system in this cave maze. There was a very intricate tunnel system in the cave they had to go through just to get into the sea monkeys domains, while fighting through the very heavily guarded caves, quietly.. But these sea monkeys didn't stand a chance against General Mateos and Burke thee Assassin. These two would let nothing come in the way of their mission, nothing! As they made it through the tunnels and out of the cave, with very few casualties and even less noise, they still needed to locate Takine. Mateos went left and Burke went right, they figured it best to split up to find him and kill him. Mateos swam through some tall sea weed and on the other side was Banta, Mateos swam up on him from behind, fast and quietly. Mateos snatched up Lord Banta with such a quickness and before he even knew it, Burke had heard the scuffle and swam to the aid of his General, he put his knife to Banta's throat and said.. "You know why we're here, Where is he"?! (Burke demanded). Banta raised his arm and pointed, he couldn't answer due to Mateoses hand over his mouth. Mateos took the butt of his sword, and whacked Lord Banta in the back of head, knocking him out instantly. He didn't want to kill him, but he knew he had to do something before he called out for help. The sea monkeys make this noise deep from within their throats and in seconds, thousands of them would rush to the call. Once they knew that Takine was in the spell room, they made sure no one would find their Lord Banta before they got to their target.

Takine was in Lord Banta's private spell room, conjuring up a spell that would control King Key's mind and make him open the portal with the Trident of Tolkien. As he was in the middle of a chant, Mateos swam in quietly right up in front of Takine while Burke snuck up on him from behind and grabbed him. He had one hand over his mouth and one hand holding a knife to his jugular vein. "Hello Takine! (Mateos said). What do we have here"? (He asked). Holding up one of his black magic spells in front of his face. They needed to find out what Takine has done so far, and how close he was to bringing Kavizious back. "Whats your plan Takine, I want to know what your next move is. Tell us now before I gut you"! (Mateos said). Pulling out his sword and dragging it across his chest and stomach. Takine shook his head back and forth and mumbled.. "Nothing, I'm suppose to hear from Master in a few days, while working here on my spells, but that's the only one I have finished". (Said Takine). Mateos looked at Burke and nodded, Burke took his knife and slit Takine's throat from ear to ear, and as Takine's limp body slid down to thee abyss floor, Mateos said.. "Good, now lets get the sea hell out of here before any of these nasty sea mutants smell his blood".. "I" (Burke replied). As they left the spell room and fled to the tunnels of the cave they entered through. Except this time, their were a lot more sea monkey guards they were going to have to get passed in order to make it out of there. "I got this"! (Burke demanded). As he went through the tunnels first, killing anything and everything that got between them and thee open abyss waters.

They made it back to Zar, who had to eat and digest a few of the sea monkey minions, in their absence. "Good boy Zar"! (Mateos said). rubbing his snout, and just as quick as they got there, they were gone and heading back to their beloved kingdom, as fast as their sea serpents would take them.. But by now, the Sea monkeys had found Takines body and a bound and gagged Lord Banta. "Quick sound the alarm, I want them found and killed, NOW"! (He demanded). Lord Banta's men had sounded the alarm, and within minutes, he and thousands and thousands of his soldiers were through the tunnels and out the cave, giving chase to Mateos and Burke. "I want them captured, we can not let them make it back to the kingdom"! (Lord Banta ordered).. All you could see was a sea full of sea monkeys riding on their sea horses, as fast as they could, chasing down the trespassers.

CHAPTER

29

MEANWHILE WAY IN THE REALM of purgatorseas, Kavizious and Kyzer were approaching the last stretch of their journey. "We are almost their Kavizious, its not to much further now"! (Kyzer told him). That's when all of the sudden, it went completely pitch black, and then these lightning like bolts of light, lit up the waters of purgatorseas, and then these loud rumbles began. "What is going on Kyzer"?! (Kavizious demanded). "We are here my lord. (He replied). We have made it to thee elder. This is it Kavizious, get ready to either rule all the realms or be enslaved in the gate keepers, lock box of torture"! That's when he appeared, thee elder, the gate keeper, the most powerful sea creature from any realm, Master Zantar! "Who dares to enter the forbidden waters of lost souls, this is way outside the parameters of which you are allowed! Go, go back before you cant"! (Said thee elder).. Kyzer looked at Kavizious and nodded, gesturing for him to tell the gate keeper why they are here. Kavizious moved forward, approaching thee elder, and said.. "Forgive us my lord, but we have traveled a great distance to speak with thee all powerful gate keeper of purgatorseas, you are thee elder we seek, no"!?! "I am the one in which you speak of. Tell me why I shouldn't lock you and your men away in the box for the rest of eternity, tell me who you are and why you have risked each and every one of these sea demons souls to damned eternity, in the box"!? (Zantar thee elder asked).. "I have a proposition that I think you might like! (Kavizious said). Just hear me out my lord, you just might like, what we have to offer"! "I'm listening! (He said). As he took the box and chains off from around him, opening it up as if he was about to feed their demon souls to the box of torture, for the rest of eternity..

Kavizous told thee elder Zantar, all about his travels to the waters of Mid World's Ocean, the Tolkien Sea (thee Eighth Sea).. Kavizious explained how its not just them who are slaves to this realm. "No disrespect, but you deserve much more than being stuck ruling in purgatorseas! With me and Kyzer by your side, we can rule every single realm and you remain the gate keeper of realms, but you just do it in a world in which you are worthy of, not this pitiful existence of eternity Lord Zantar. You need to look and see around and see what they thought you were worthy of, we will go to every single realm and make them pay for their disrespect! You show them what you are truly worth Zantar, will me Kavizious and General Kyzer by your side, we will create an army of demons from every realm, we will crush our enemies with such force, it will be as if they never existed. We take their past, presence and future and wipe it out of the waters, forever"! He told him how he has been in thousands and thousands of wars, millions of battles and has won them all, except one! "This world is like nothing I have ever seen Zantar! There's so much black magic and mystical powers radiating through these waters, and its powered by this powerful Trident, the".. He was interrupted by thee elder Zantar. "The Trident of Tolkien"! (Zantar said). "Yes my lord, how do you know this"?! (Kavizious asked Zantar, the GateKeeper).. Zantar turned his back to Kavizious and Kyzer and said.. "Because that belongs to me"! (Zantar said). With such anger and bone crunching power, Zatar turned back around and said.. "If you take me to where my Trident is, I will melt him and his entire world in front of his eyes before I enslaved him in my lock box of torture for eternity"!?! (Zantar promised). As bad as Kavizious wanted the Trident of Tolkien for himself, he knew if he ever wanted to get back to the powerful and magical abyss in Mid World's Ocean, then he was going to have to let it go. It was Zantars Trident in the first place, so he was going to have to be ok with it, in-order to complete his mission! "I"! (Master Kavizious agreed).. "There's just one thing Kavizious"! (Zantar said). "Yeah, whats that my Lord"? (Kavizious asked). I cant chose the realm we go to, I can only open the gates and it chooses for us"! He told them. Kavizious and Kyzer both looked at each other, then back to Lord Zantar, and Kavizious said.. "Then we keep crushing ever world and taking over realm after realm, recruiting and growing our army until we get to our final destination of The Tolkien Sea (thee Eighth Sea).. But it shouldn't take us too long to make it there my lord. Like I said, my black magic is very powerful, I will work on a spell to control the destination of worlds, when you open the gate to the realms portal Zantar! (Kavizious told him).. You deserve better than this my lord, you, me and General Kyzer will control every realm and rule every single world in existence Zantar. Nothing can stop us"! Zantar thee Elder, took the chains and his lock box, and wrapped them back around himself and said.. "And so it shall be done"! (Said the gatekeeper). As he spun around faster and faster, creating a whirlpool of magical waters and smoke clouds, popping off specs of light, making it snap and crackle like big magical, water proof fire crackers and lightning bolts, sucking up Kavizious and General Kyzer, along with every other sea demon soldier that has pledged their loyalty, into the heart of the cyclone vortex as the gates to the portal to the other realms appeared and opened.. But where they would end up, is anyone's guess, but every world that the three of these sea demons end up traveling too is doomed. They have no idea, the hell that Kavizious has just unleashed.

Meanwhile, as Mateos and Burke were almost back to the Kingdom, Lord Banta and his sea monkey army were closing in fast. "Quick Mateos, we are almost there, I can see the kingdoms wall". (Burke said). Just as they came racing around the last bend, King Key and thee entire royal army came charging by them, going in the opposite direction. General Mateos and Burke the Assassin, pulled back on their sea serpents reins, stopping and changing directions, as the King and his men clashed right into lord Banta and his army of sea monkeys. "I knew they were close to catching up with us, but I didn't think they were this close"! (Burke said). To Mateos, as leaped from his sea dragon, as he pulled his sword and started carving into Banta's soldiers, one, by one, by one. General Mateos joined in the battle as well, as he grabbed one of the sea monkeys by the head and tossing him into another sea monkey and his sea horse, he sees his wife and daughter, fighting along side Cynthia as she was concentrating on her magic, sending a bolt of light and shocking all the surrounding sea monkey soldiers, to death instantly. King Key was in the midst of a sword battle with Lord Banta, when he said.. "Last chance to leave alive Banta, do not make me use my Trident, I will wipe out the entire lot of you"! (Promised the King).. Lord Banta nodded to his general Zokan, his second in command. Zokan made that loud throat call that only a sea monkey could. The call echoed through out the entire waters of battle, as it got louder and louder, as each one of the sea monkeys returned the call and started retreating back in which the way they came. Banta was not happy. Before he left, Lord Banta had let it be known that this wasn't over. He couldn't let the King and the kingdom, to come into their waters, and kill someone without consequences and repercussions for their actions of crimes against Lord Banta and his sea monkeys domains.

"Lord Kavizious will not be happy"! (Said Banta). Addressing his men, when they returned back to their home waters, under thee abyss in the triangle of death. "How did this happen, how do I tell him that Takine is dead, and we didn't capture the men responsible!? He is going to want answers and when we don't have any answers or the Trident of Tolkien, he will kill every last one of us"! (Lord Banta said).. As he swam up in front of his general and said.. "Give me your knife Zokan"! (He said). General Zokan took his knife out the holster and handed it to Banta. Lord Banta, then turned to the rest of his soldiers, and said.. "Lord Kavizious is going to want to know, who's fault this is, and to pay with his life. Who's fault is it Zokan"?! (He asked). Turning back to him, awaiting his answer. "It's mine sir. I'm your second in command and I let you down. I'm sorry my lord, it wont happen again. We will be ready next time, I assure you my Lord"! (General Zokan replied).. "NEXT TIME?! There wont be a next time"! (Lord Banta screamed).. Taking General Zokan's Knife and jammed it in to his neck, handle deep, and started to swim off. As the General gurgled blood and water, he grasped at the handle of the knife sticking out of the side of his neck but was too weak, and as General Zokan's limp body collapsed to thee abyss floor, dead, Lord Banta said.. "Chose a new General, and prepare for war. We attack the Kingdom of Mordainia at dawn. I want that Trident for a piece offering for lord Kavizious so he doesn't kill every last one of us, and I have a plan"!

CHAPTER

30

Back at the Kingdom of Mordainia, General Mateos and his partner in justice for the kingdom, Burke, were welcomed home with such cheer and appreciation. Once everyone was all reunited and has said their hello's, the King had to debrief General Mateos and Burke thee Assassin, on their mission, and discuss the level of threat, from Kavizious, that was caused by their target, Takine. "It is done my King! (General Mateos reported).. Takine is dead. Show him Burke, show King Key". Burke opened his satchel and threw the scalped top piece of Takine's head, on the war table, and it landed directly in front of the King. "Good work gentlemen, your kingdom thanks you both"! (Said the King). "I"! (Burke replied). Nodding in acknowledgment and respect to his King, As did Mateos. "Did Takine get any further in helping Kavizious open the portal In the triangle"? (Key asked). "No, we stopped him before he completed any spells of magic, but Lord Banta and the Sea monkeys wont just let this go my lord. We are going to have to protect the kingdom from another attack"! (General Mateos said).. "We can handle Banta and the Sea Monkey minions, it's Kavizious I'm worried about Mateos! (Admitted the King).. As long as I have the Trident of Tolkien, and Takine didn't succeed in opening the portal for Kavizious, than the kingdom is safe, for now. If Banta and his men are stupid enough to attack our kingdom without the leadership of Kavizious, than we will kill them all. Prepare your men to defend the kingdom and its perimeters, General Mateos". "Yes my lord"! (Mateos replied). And Burke, you come with me"! (Demanded the king).. "I, my lord"! (Burke thee Assassin replied).. Leading him to the palace, and as they entered, King Key turned to Burke, and said.. My people will show you to your new quarters, you are to reside here, amongst royalty, and to be treated as such, you deserve it". (Key told him). "For how long my lord"? (Burke asked his King).. "For as long as you wish Burke! (King Key replied).. For as long as you wish"!

Meanwhile, Kavizious and his demon crew, have gone through the portal and have arrived in there world, when Kavizious said.. This place looks familiar to me".. But it wasn't the waters of Mid World. "Yes, this place does look familiar"! (Kyzer also said).. "It should! (Replied Zantar the gatekeeper).. Well it is none other than Sea Hell, and you Kavizious, you might remember your time here, but do you remember who ruled this world when you first got here?! Why it seems that your friend Kyzer, your second in command, use to be your leader, the ruler of the Sea Hell realm. It seems that he has forgotten how he was over thrown and cast out, down to purgatorseas. You see my loyal demons, it was fate that we were brought together, and this is the first realm we were chosen to come to and seek our revenge"! (Zantar said). Kavizious turned to Kyzer and said.. 'You ruled this place once brother Kyzer, it's rightfully your's! So lets go take it back, let's make them pay for their betrayal. (Kavizious said). Let's go raise some sea hell"! Kyzer was thinking way back, once upon a time when he ruled sea hell, and how he was overthrown from his position as King of Sea Hell. All his memories had come flooding back to him. You could see the anger brewing inside of him. "Yes, and I know just where to begin"! (Kyzer said). As he swam off, leading a group of very magical, very dangerous group of killer sea demons who are about to destroy anyone who doesn't join their army and bow down before them, but first Kyzer was on his way, to make the new King of sea hell, suffer. There would be no fate suffered that the King of sea hell could hand down upon ones soul, as the fate he himself, was about to suffer, at the hands of Kyzer, Kavizious and Zantar! He will soon realize just what pain, truly is.

As the sea demons were heading to the castle to destroy the King of hell and lock his soul up for eternity, in Zantar's lock box, They stumbled upon a lost hell demon, and just when Kavizious was about to recruit the lost soul, when he realized who he was. "Takine, you failed me I see"! (Kavizious said). "I'm sorry my lord, I was almost done with a spell to make

King Key hand over the Trident, when Mateos, along with Burke thee Assassin, snuck into the minions domains and, well you see what happened my lord"! (Takine replied). "No worries Takine, you will come along with us, I'm sure Banta will preserve your body, while your soul is out of it. We will get you back to your body, back in the waters of the Eighth Sea Takine, we have a plan. We will be back soon, we just have some soldiers to recruit, and some realms to overthrow and take control of, on our way to our final destination of Mid World's ocean, the Tolkien Sea (thee Eighth Sea).". (Kavizious said). As the demon army approached the castle, and with great ease, they had captured the new King of hell and locked him in Zantars lock box of torture, for eternity, before Zantar whisked them all up into his cyclone, as they pushed through the gates and through the portal to the second realm. They had figured out that the only way the gates will open to the portal, is once they lock the ruler of that realm up in Zantar's lock box of torture, for eternity. Where the ended up this time, they did not know, but one thing they did know was that, they not only controlled purgatorseas now, but they also control sea hell, and soon they will take control of every sea hell realm, including the Tolkien Sea.

CHAPTER

31

OVER IN THE REALM OF Mid World's Ocean, the King was with his family, out in the royal coral reef garden, it was very early in the morning, and it was Princess Rylee's first time in the garden. She absolutely loved the bright colors of the sea flowers and little sea creatures that lived in the reef garden. You could hear her little giggles, anytime one swam across her skin, or a flower swayed up against her. Princess Rylee, was so happy as King Key spun her up over his head, then passing her to his wife, Queen Kylynn. The royal family couldn't look happier"! That's when The Alarm sounded. General Mateos entered the royal sea garden and said to the King.. "Quick my lord, we have to get your family safely to the palace. They will be safe there"! (General Mateos said).. As he led the Queen and Princess to the Palace. "I sent the first wave of soldiers out the gates my lord. I'm about to send the second wave, just waiting on your command my King"! "I"! (Ordered the King).. Mateos swam off to give the orders, and as soon as the King's wife and daughter were safely in the heavily guarded palace, Key's kissed them good bye, and he too swam off to join the fight in protecting not just his family, but thee entire kingdom.

Lord Banta had led an attack against the Kingdom of Mordainia. He and his sea monkey klan, had descended upon the kingdom borders, flocking by the thousands. Banta knew there was no way for him and his men to penetrate the kingdoms magically reinforced wall and heavily guarded perimeters, so he needed King Key to bring the Trident to them. They took out every single one of the kingdom's soldiers that were out patrolling the borders, Banta's men were too many. Every wave of soldiers that were sent out to defend the kingdom, were completely out manned, and out numbered. King Key was going to have to go outside the kingdom's wall and push them back with the Trident of Tolkien. "This is our chance to get the Trident for Master Kavizious. Don't give Key the chance to use the Trident, get to him and take it from him before he commands it to defend him and the kingdom, the Trident will kill us all. Get your men in position Enzio. (Lord Banta Commanded).. His new General, and second in command after Lord Banta had just killed General Zokan. "Do not let me down General, get it done, no excuses Enzio, we have one shot at this"! (Banta reminded him).. If they fail in retrieving the Trident, then no matter what they will die. They will die from King Key and the Trident, and if they survive some how, Lord Kavizious will kill them, either way, they die!

"We cant keep sending soldiers out there to die Mateos. (Said the King). I have to go out and move them back with the Trident. I just didn't want to destroy the entire sea monkey race, but Lord Banta is leaving me with no other choice! General Mateos, I'm going to need you and Master Burke to come with me when we send out the next wave of soldiers. Keep the sharp shooters and wizards continuing to fire upon the sea monkey's while the next wave of soldiers head out, you and Master Burke stay on my side's and watch my six, it will give me just enough time to wheel my Trident, and blow these Mother Fuckers out of our waters! (Said the King). You with me"!?! (Key asked). His two most valued warriors. "Let's go kill these leeches". (Mateos replied). As the King put out his hand, and Mateos placed his upon King Key's, and then so did Burke. As the three men approached the front gates with the next wave of soldiers that were about to swim out to the waters of battle, awaiting them was Queen Kylynn, along with her Mother Miss Aleina and King Key's Mother Miss Cynthia. We are helping, and we wont take no for an answer. Them men shrugged and gave in, they knew this was one battle, they couldn't win. "What's your plan ladies"? (Asked the King).. "Oh don't you worry my son, me and the girls will hit them with magic that they have never witnessed before. We been practicing, and lets just say.. We mastered our version of black magic" (Cynthia admitted). With a huge smile upon their faces, the girls let out and little giggle and Queen Cynthia said.. "May I do the honor's my

King"? The King nodded and Queen Kylynn ordered.. "Open the gates"!
As the front gate opened enough for the next wave of soldiers to attack
Banta and his men, Out came the King with Trident in hand, along side
his protectors, the three mystical and very magical sea witches and his two
top warriors, the general and thee assassin. "Here he comes Enzio, He is
outside the walls and he has the Trident, get me that Trident! CHARGE"!
(Lord Banta commanded).. As his army of sea monkey soldiers, charged
into battle, against the soldiers of Mordainia.

Lord Banta didn't really have too much of a plan to retrieve the
Trident of Tolkien from King Key. He just tried to out man him. For
ever one soldier the royal army had, there were a hundred sea monkey
soldiers. When the sea monkey's come, its like an infestation of sea monkey
minions. Which are usually a secluded species, until their whole race is
threatened to be exterminated. They are literally fighting for survival of
their species. As The King set himself to work his Trident, he raised the
Trident up over his head and as soon as it started to light up, Enzio's men,
popped up out from the ground of thee abyss. "Look out my lord"! (Burke
yelled). As he swam over to the sea monkey's that popped up out from the
sea ground, and before anyone could react, Burke thee Assassin carved
them up into pieces with his sword. The King nodded, thanking Burke
for the quickness in which he stabilized thee assault against him. As Lord
Banta realized that Enzio had failed, he raced forward towards the King,
and right before he made it to him, King Key wielded his Trident and with
great force, Key jammed the glowing Trident, down into thee abyss floor,
creating a sonic boom, that sent all the sea monkey's flying backwards
off their sea horses, by the thousands, making them disoriented and go
completely def, only hearing a faint ringing, but not the ones directly
within the base of the sonic boom, their eyes exploded out of their heads,
blood seeping from out their ears and mouth, as they fell to thee abyss floor,
as well as their sea horses. The poor sea horses were an unfortunate casualty
of war that just could not be avoided. General Enzio, gathered up the rest
of his men that were still alive, and he gave his throat call, letting the others
know it was time to retreat, the ones that could hear it, and the ones who
couldn't, followed behind anyways because, sea monkey see, sea monkey
do, and Enzio led the retreat back to their domains under the abyss floor of
the Triangle of Death, without Lord Banta who was killed back in battle.

General Mateos, along with the royal army and the rest of the kingdom were celebrating their win over Lord Banta and his army of sea monkey's, everyone except for the King. King Key couldn't help, but feel sorry for the sea monkeys, they were just scared of what Kavizious would do to their whole race. "This is unacceptable! (Said the King). We can not let this happen again, I just had to wipeout half of the sea monkey klan because of Kavizious. He isn't even in this realm and he causing complete anarchy, it's time we take the fight to him! (Declared the King).. I am getting more and more powerful each and every day, I have become one with the Trident of Tolkien, I am the chosen one! Kavizious is out there in purgatorseas building an army of sea demons like we have never witnessed before. He will be back and I cant just wait for him to find his way back to our world, he will not stop until he opens the portal in the Triangle of Death. I have to travel there and open the portal, I have the Trident of Tolkien for a reason, it has chosen me to save our world. I know how to work the Trident and not just banish Kavizious to sea hell or purgatorseas, I will take his soul and trap it. I will rip his pathetic soul into a hundred pieces and lock each piece away worlds apart from each other. I am going to the Triangle of Death and bringing the war to Kavizious, I not only need to save my family and kingdom, I need to protect the weaker species of our seas. Species such as the sea monkeys that resort to doing things they never would, because they are afraid. We shouldn't be celebrating this battle as a victory, because it wasn't, it's a tragedy! I am the King of not just Mordainia, but I am the chosen one, I am the King of the Eight Seas and I must protect every creature in these waters, by any means necessary! I must go, I understand if you chose not to go! This is one mission that I will not force any soldier in the royal army to make this journey, it is your call, but I will take volunteers. Any and all members of the kingdoms army only, I need my kingdoms Guards, my defense unit here with the people here, protecting the kingdom while I'm gone. All I ask is any soldier who does not come, stays back and works with the guards and people to protect our beloved kingdom. We leave at dusk"! (Demanded the King).. As he swam off to the war room. Queen Ky went to go swim after her husband King Key, when Mateos stopped her, and said.. "No my Queen, please let me, I'll go speak with him"! (He said). Queen Ky looked to Cynthia who nodded, Queen Kyleen agreed. General Mateos and Master Burke, swam off to the war room after their King, their friend, King Key.

As the two of them entered the war room, they didn't even get a word out, before the King said.. "Don't try and stop me Mateos, I've already made up my mind, I have to do this"! (Said King Key).. "Stop you? I'm not here to stop you! (General Mateos said).. I just want to know if I can ride Zar this journey"! (He said). With a big smile upon his face. "You know I'm in, let's go kill this demon leech"! (Said Burke thee Assassin).. Grabbing and gripping the Kings arm, as they shook hands. "I hope the ladies understand we need them here to protect Princess Rylee and the Kingdom, I need them here just incase, their magic will be better used here, watching over the Kingdom"! (said the King). "They'll get over it my King, trust me, they don't have a choice"! (Mateos replied).

A little later that day, after the King explained why he needed the ladies to stay behind, he left the palace to go grab his trusty sea dragon Zar and prepare for this long journey, the King was absolutely stunned when he seen his entire royal army all ready to go and join their King on this magical quest, to protect their way of life. King Key didn't say one word, he just looked at General Mateos and Master Burke and smiled. King Key nodded and turned towards the gates at the front of the kingdom, and as they reached the front gates, King Key turned to his men and said.. "I couldn't be more proud of you all. This is going to be a very tough journey and an even tougher battle. General Mateos, your men know what their going up against correct"?! (Asked the King). "Yes my lord, I have a select group of soldiers staying here, protecting our kingdom while we are gone, I have complete faith in my men sir, as should you"! (General Mateos answered).. "I! (Replied the King).. Ok let's move out".. And just like that, the King and his men, were out the kingdom's gates, and disappearing into the shadows of the caves in the bottom of thee abyss, one, by one, by one. On their way yet again, to battle once more, to protect their kingdom's survival. Even though Kaviziouses army is bigger and stronger than ever, so is the kingdom of Mordainia's royal army! King Key has mastered his roll as the chosen one. By now, he has become one with the Trident of Tolkien, Key has complete control of thee entire eight sea's and everyone and everything in it's waters, but not only has the King mastered the power of the Trident, they also have Burke thee Assassin back at full capacity, leading the royal army, right along side General Mateos. The three of them, King Key, General Mateos and Burke thee Assassin, are just as powerful and dangerous as their enemies top three sea hell demons, Master Kavizious, Master Kyser and the elder gatekeeper of pergatorseas, Master Zantar.

CHAPTER

32

MEANWHILE, IN THE NEXT WORLD that the three sea hell demons, and their sea demon army were at, about to destroy and take control of, Kavizious was growing impatient! "We have been to a hundred worlds already, and conquered them all. When are we going to go take what should already be mine Zantar"?! (Kavizious demanded answers).. "Soon my boy-o, soon"! (Master Zantar answered).. Master Zantar turned to Kyzer and Master Kyzer handed him over the ruler of the world they were in. Master Zantar took the sea demon and sentenced his soul to his lock box of torture for eternity, then turned to Kavizious and Master Kyzer and said.. "I like it when their souls are trapped in a shell, I like when I have to rip their souls from their bodies, before I carry out their sentence of eternal damnation in my lock box of tortured souls"! (Master Zantar said).. With a snicker, as he locked his box and chained it back up around his torso. Master Zantar looked at Master Kavizious and said.. "I want to get to this world in which you speak of just as much as you do Kavizious, I want what has been taken from me also, I want my Trident! I will keep opening the gates to the portal and where we go I can not control without my Trident, so until you can create a spell using your black magic to bypass and get us to thee abyss of Mid World's water's, then we must continue taking over every world in every realm, until it is the last realm in any world left and we have to go there. I don't care how long it takes us, and how many worlds we go through, I will get us there and I will get my Trident back! You asked me to join you Kavizious, you came to me, I'm doing my part, you need to do your's and conjure up that spell with your black magic potions and I'll keep getting us to the next realm". (Master Zantar said). As he created his whirl pool, of wind and waters, swallowing them all and sending them through the portal and into another realm.

I n the meantime, back in the Tolkien Sea, The King and his Trident had led his royal sea army through the deadly waters of thee abyss and straight into the heart of the Triangle of Death. Just as King Key had used his Trident to open the portal, and go find Kavizious in purgatorseas and crush him once and for all, thee elder gatekeeper, Master Zantar, was opening the portal at the same exact time from within a parallel universe. This had created some type of separation with the entrance of the vortex, and created a world inside the portal, and as Thee elder gatekeeper, Master Zantar along side Master Kavizious, Master Kyzer and Takine were with their entire demon army, stuck in this new vortex world face to face with the chosen one and his Trident, King Key, who was along side Burke thee Assassin, General Mateos and his men, the most fierce army in all of Mid World's Ocean. As the two armies sized each other up, realizing what had just happened, the Trident lit up and started vibrating, causing the vortex to spin faster and faster, sending each one of them swirling around and around as magical bolts of light sparked everywhere, that's when a big bright light appeared like a bomb just exploded, sucking each and every one of them through the gates of the bright shinny light, and spat them all out into a realm in which not one have them have ever seen or been to before, it was as neutral waters of battle, as it could possibly get, neither side had an advantage!

In this new world, in these mystical waters in which were about to be stained red with blood forever. This realm will come to be called, thee Blood Red Sea, forever and ever, because of this epic battle of good and evil, that was about to claim the lives and souls of more Sea creatures and sea demons at the same time, than ever before. The King turned to his men, knowing that they didn't have much time before the demons would attack, and he said.. "Mateos, Burke.. You and the royal army, buy me as much time to wheel the Trident as you possible can, and I'll do the rest"! "I"! (General Mateos replied).. As did Burke, and just like that, Kavizious and the rest of the demon army, began charging forward, in attack mode. "This is it me, stay strong and fight hard"! (Said the King). As he began wheeling his Trident, around and around, until it began to light up, glowing so bright, brighter than it ever has before. Just as the two armies collided, there was a loud sonic boom, an explosion so loud and fierce that it sent everyone flying backwards, causing severe chaos and confusion! Once all the magical smoke and murky waters settled, the battle began again.

CHAPTER

33

BACK IN THE KINGDOM OF Mordainia, Queen Kylynn was playing with her daughter, Princess Rylee and talking to her mother, Miss Aleina and mother in law, Miss Cynthia. "I cant raise this daughter alone, Daddy had better bring my husband and babies father back safe and sound, I cant go on without Key"! (Ky said). "Then lets go help them defeat Kavizious, once and for all. (Cynthia said). My black magic powers are strong my Queen! If we cross thee abyss and go to the Triangle of Death, I can use my magic to contact my sons Trident and use its power to activate the portal, I can get us to them and help your husband Kylynn, my son, and your father and her husband"! (She said). Stretching her arm out and grabbing a hold of Aleina, pulling her in closer to her and her daughter. "I'm in"! (Aleina said). "Me too! (Said the Queen). Aleina, come take Princess Rylee, me and her grandmother's have to go, the men need us"! "Yes my lord"! (Axina replied). Swimming over and taking little miss, Princess Rylee from the Queen. "Mother, you go round up as many soldiers as the guards can spare. Cynthia, you go and grab all your spells and potions. I'll go round up some weapons for us and we will all meet back at the sea stables". (Queen Kylynn said).. As they all kissed Princess Rylee and swam off in different directions.

Once at the stables, the girls had everything they needed for their little journey to save their men, or die trying. They each grabbed a sea horse and headed off towards the front gates, once they and all the soldiers were geared up and loaded up. Once the gates had opened and they started to exit, there was a strange sound. "Quiet, listen"! (Aleina said). All of the sudden, Zar, the kingdoms most loyal and trusted sea dragon, came charging out of the caves and from out of the shadows, he appeared. "Zar"! Both Cynthia and Queen Kylynn both screamed and jumped from their sea horses. "Whoa, calm down Zar! What's the matter boy-o, are you ok?! Wait are you alone, where is everyone Zar, are they ok"?! Cynthia was frantic, as she had Zar by his reins, trying to calm him down as she looked into his eyes, trying to use her magic to see what Zar has seen. Both Aleina and Kylynn had grabbed a hold of Zar, patting him and trying to get him to relax, and it worked. Zar calmed down, and Cynthia was able to use her magic to see into his eyes and see what the poor sea creature has just witnessed. "What is it Cynthia is it bad"?! (Kylynn asked). "They are trapped in between two worlds, there's a bubble in the vortex and it created this mirrored world that only exists when traveling through the portal to another realm. It's a world, inside of a world, in-between two worlds, and only one army can leave this vortex warp hole that they somehow created. We have to go NOW"! (Cynthia screamed). As she smacked her sea horse on his ass, making it swim off back towards the stables, she then grabbed a hold of Zar and said.. "Come on boy-o, show me the fastest way to my boy"! (Cynthia said). As they all disappeared one, by one, by one, into the shadows and then, POOF! Just like that.. They were gone into the caves, and on their way through the abyss, and straight to the Triangle of Death, to use Cynthia's black magic, and open the portal..

Cynthia had created a spell, that will melt the souls of any sea demons, from any realms or any world, but she has to see the sea hell demon in-order for it to work. She couldn't just give the spell to Key and let the boys handle it, no. She had to teach both Kylynn and Aleina the spell and the three of them need to be in a triangle pattern as they each do their part to activate the spell. Cynthia figured that while the demons are busy fighting their men, her and the girls can pull this off, they had to pull this off. If she can melt their sea demon souls down to a puddle, Key can use his Trident and banish each one, little drop from the puddle to a different realm, worlds away from each other, it's the perfect plan.

While on their quest to help save their kingdom, the ladies had stumbled upon waters that they had never seen before. Where are we Cynthia, I don't remember ever going through these waters before, do you"!? (Aleina asked). Moving up very close, next to her. "No, I don't! (She replied). Keep your eyes open, something's wrong"! No sooner did she finish saying that, when.. "Owe"! (Said one of the soldiers).. "Owe, owe, owe"! Then another and another. They were being attacked by these tiny little balls of light. "Quick, form a circle formation"! (Cynthia had commanded).. And as they fought off the little attackers, Cynthia was chanting a magical spell. At the end of her chant, she raised her arms and then dropped them down so fast, in a swooping motion, sending these bright shards of light pouncing through the waters and shocking every single one of those little nasty bright lights of hell, killing damn near every one of them. A couple got away, but not before Aleina had snatched one up, capturing it in a glass jar. "What are they"? (She asked). As she showed it to Cynthia and Kylynn. They both shook their heads, not knowing what they were, except they were very annoying. Aleina opened her satchel and threw the jar in it, and said.. "Welcome to your new home, you little sea slug. Don't get to comfortable though, I'll dissect you when we get back to the kingdom".. And off they went, again.

CHAPTER
34

OVER IN THE MIRRORED WORLD, (the vortex bubble world), in between two realms, the two armies were locked in battle. Takine was one of the first to suffer his fait by the hands of Burke thee Assassin, AGAIN, but this time, there was no coming back from his demise. Once you are killed in this realm, that's it, you may never leave. Both armies were completely wiped out, there was just nine sea demons left. Three of them were, Master Kavizious, Master Kyzer and Lord Zantar, behind them was a half dozen or so, sea demon soldiers. The Royal army wasn't much better off, other than their top three warriors, King Key, General Mateos and Master Burke, there was just about a dozen or two, royal soldiers still swimming. "You need to end this now Kavizious, you will never defeat us! You can never destroy our kingdom, we will never let you! (Said the King). Never"! "Hahaha! (Kavizious laughed). "You fool, it's not me you should be worried about! Meet Lord Zantar and the sea hell devil himself, Master Kyzer". (He replied). "I Believe you have something that belongs to me"! (Zantar said). Taking his lock box and chains off from around his torso. You see, what you failed to realize is that I don't need an army. They were mere pawns, sacrifices if you will, look at your army King Key.. You killed them all, their blood is on your hands. We will replace our army in no time, but you.. You don't even realize that this was the plan. Once we kill the last of your soldiers, it will just be the six of us"! (Lord Zantar said).. With a big smile forming upon his face.

As a swirling cloud of magic started forming under Zantar, growing bigger and faster, with little sparks of magic, popping off all throughout the foggy whirlwind. As the whirling waters of magic grew bigger around Zantar, so did he. Zantar began to grow bigger, and his voice got louder and deeper, "Give me my Trident back, NOW"! (He Screamed). Swimming forward with his sword raised, swinging his chains and lock box, up over his head, with Kavizious and Kyzer right behind him.. But the King was not to be backed down, King Key with General Mateos and Burke right by either side of him, he raised (HIS) Trident, up over his head, as it was glowing brighter and brighter, The King and his men began advancing forward, towards their demon enemies. Just as the two sides were about to crash into battle.. That's when, all of the sudden..

Thee entire waters in the realm they were in, grew black and started swirling around and around. Magical sparks of light started to appear all over the place. The top of the waters opened up with a very bright light, blinding everyone for a few moments. The portal opened up, and down came Cynthia, wheeling her magic. Right behind her came Queen Kylynn and Miss Aleina, with more royal soldiers. As mad as the King and Mateos were that they didn't listen, they knew they wouldn't have a chance without them! "Ok ladies, you know the plan, lets go! (Cynthia said). Make them suffer Key, get em"! Cynthia blew magic dust upon Key and his men, making them come out of the magical daze she created when entering the world in-between realms. King Key began chanting, gripping his Trident, while Mateos and Burke joined the royal soldiers, and began to attack Kavizious and thee other demons. King Key knew that it was going to take a lot more to take down lord Zantar. So while he was powering up his Trident, Cynthia and the girls had finished their spell. Kavizious ans Kyzer, began to shake violently. Kavizious and Kyzer started spinning around and around, glowing brighter and brighter, until they exploded. Two little beams of light that were left behind were Kavizious and Kyzer just were, moved through the waters and disappeared into the top of the Trident. Burke thee Assassin and General Mateos, had already taken out the very last of the Demon soldiers who were left, just before thee explosion.

Everyone turned their attention to King Key and Lord Zantar. "Quick, help the King"! (Aleina said). To his mother Cynthia. Key had a hold upon Zantar with his Trident, trapping him from moving, but he was beginning to struggle as Zantar was fighting harder and harder to brake free. Cynthia swam over and began chanting next o her son, shortly followed by Queen Kylynn and Miss Aleina. They were all chanting the same chant, as Lord Zantar fought to brake free, but the hold was getting stronger and stronger. Burke and Mateos swam over to Zantar, trying to get his lock box from him. King Key chanted louder and faster and slammed the Trident right into thee abyss floor, sending a very bright shock straight into Zantar, as he was sucked right into that same beam of light, and straight bake into the top of the trident, and disappeared. Burke and Mateos were holding Zantar's chains and lock box in their hands, when King Key pointed the Trident at them. A bright light shot out the Trident, grabbing a hold of the lock box and chains, sucking that too, back into the trident of Tolkien. The light on the Trident went out, and everything was quiet, too quiet.

They had defeated the sea demon army, but not only did they finally defeat Kavizious, they had defeated his entire army, along with Kyzer and Zantar, the lords of sea hell and purgatorseas. They defeated Takine, twice, living Takine, and then Demon Takine. "So how do we get back home now"?! (Master Burke asked).. With a smile on his face. "Would you like to do the honors my King"?! (General Mateos asked).. King Key swam forward, and as he raised his Trident up over his head, he said.. "We will discuss you ladies journeying through thee abyss without us later, but I'm glad you did, thank you"! The Trident lit up, and then so did the top of the waters.. As the salt waters swirled around, and around, the whirlwind grew darker and bigger, with the bright sparks of magic forming throughout it, the mirrored bubble realm burst, popping open, and they were all swallowed up, into the light. Through the portal, and spat out into the triangle of death, back into their own world of waters, back in thee abyss of Mid World's Ocean, the Tolkien Sea (the Eighth Sea).

To Be Continued …

-The Depths.. Vol.1-Kings Vs. Demons.. Is a magical journey, through the deep dark waters, in Mid World's Ocean, the Tolkien Sea (thee Eighth Sea). It is, a mystical quest, way deep down, through the dark caves, of thee abyss, into and beyond the kingdom of Mordainia.-

-By: M. Burke-

-Dedicated to … My fallen friends & family members, I love & miss you all..-